THE BLUE FLOWER
OF
FORGETFULNESS

THE BLUE FLOWER
OF
FORGETFULNESS

Cyrus Samii

URTEXT
San Francisco

Back cover photograph by Babak Dabestani
Rose fields of Lalehzar, Kerman

ISBN-13: 978-0-9790573-5-9
ISBN-10: 0-9790573-5-3

Published by Urtext 2010. Second edition 2010.
San Francisco
www.urtext.us

Printed in the United States of America

For my grandmothers,

Fairytale and Free.

One cast off the veil

and gave three generations

an education

While the other lifted it and showed

how gossamer-thin the line is

between the two worlds.

And when the man fleeing Death finally arrived at the most remote corner of the world, he took a deep breath, and sighed a sigh of relief. Looking around, he soon noticed he was dressed differently. So he proceeded to the bazaar, selected a simple robe, and came to pay ... when the shopkeeper extended a skeletal hand with a vice-like grip, "If you are doing this on my account, don't bother."

Hamoush

I knew of longing and of loss. Devious kings and chaste maidservants, misplaced betrothal rings and faithful parrots. Princes who sought blood-red roses in wintery streams. Captive princesses who bled carnations. I grew up with outwitted *jenns* and strands of never-to-be-straightened golden hair. Ladies-in-waiting who wore suits of swan feathers all but one night of the year. Chick pea children and huts with chickens' feet. The sole flower without dew.

I knew one had to wear out seven pairs of iron shoes, walk over seven mountaintops and through seven lost valleys to reclaim a love that had been betrayed, though I never did find out what to do for one that had been frittered away day by day. I knew to bathe in baths of scalding milk to recapture beauty, and to summon a lover by burning a strand of his hair. I knew not to follow the faun, to be kind to beggarwomen in black, and to be suspicious of the centaur.

I had looked into the eyes of blind beggars and known betrayed shahs and out-of-favour vazirs. I had met the porter, the tailor, and the one-eyed *ghalandar*. I was sure the dolls on my shelf were just waiting for me to fall firmly asleep before revealing secrets about magpies' nests and copper rings. I had heard their whispers as I dozed off, and though I had never rubbed salt into a self-inflicted wound, I had, once, with half-opened eyes, seen them dance. I knew the unfortunate answer to the question, "Who will trade new lamps for old, old lamps for new?"

Noting every nuance in my father's voice, correcting him when he failed to repeat the softly spoken words that punctuate the beginning of every tale, I knew all the stories. All except for the one where love fails to win the princess' hand. I learned that the hard way, watching ministers, generals and kitchen boys set off across oceans and continents; returning, arms laden, sacks bulging, only to be sent off to perform one last feat, to bring back one more bauble.

And I was there when she passed them all over to give herself to a wizened, white-bearded old man who never really loved her. Though my hair has turned grey and I have lived long enough to know better, at times I still catch myself wondering again how it all went wrong. When I do, I cannot help but think of Firouz. Not that it was his fault.

More than anything in his life Firouz loved Iran, and imagined her a sleeping beauty who could only be awakened with a kiss. So he spent his life wandering through forests and slaying monsters for a chance to bring her back to life. Having slain a dragon or two, having hacked his way through bramble-wood forests and found unseen doors, he proceeded to kiss her.

He kissed her with the passion that brings convent-bound women to revoke a life of communion with the divine, with the desire that brings extraordinary women to entertain the advances of the most unremarkable men, with the enthusiasm that brings adolescents to dismiss doubts of anatomies and abilities, with the longing of the reprobate who after twenty-two repentant years as a monk, revokes his vows for just one night with a woman—young, old, fat, thin, talkative or silent. One with whom he might share a cigarette or spend a lifetime.

He kissed his sleeping beauty to bring the colour back to her cheeks, to see the smile on her lips, the glint in her eyes, the lustre of her laughter. Having managed to extract a sigh or two, having detected a flutter in her eyelashes, a more fervent heartbeat, he pursued her with an even more ardent desire. And Iran gave him enough sideways glances and languorous looks, whispered his name coyly biting her lips. She struck enough seductive poses, tossed and turned enough in wrinkled sheets to have him spend the rest of his life kissing her. Had it not been for a strange turn of events, an encounter with the cracked lady and the mirror, that is precisely what he would have done.

I could not say when Firouz first began embracing Iran. If I were to answer other than, "He had always loved her," I would venture to say it was 1931, the year he arrived in Tehran to pursue an education at what was known as "the American College." It was really no more than a secondary school that taught discipline, fair play and meritocracy to a generation of boys brought up on privilege and favouritism.

From the school across the street, we looked on in our grey skirts, white shirts, and braided hair. Between English and Volleyball, Poetry and Penmanship, we exchanged notes about the tall one with wavy hair and the bright-eyed one who drew in his breath and exhaled "ooouuf," every time a woman walked by. The one who bit the filters of his cigarettes. The big-nosed one. The sunken-chested one who, it was whispered, had witnessed his father's death. The one we all agreed would miss his vocation if he did not spend his life in Parisian cafés smoking cigarettes, drinking endless cups of coffee, composing poetry.

Ardeshir, Arsen and Abdullah, Pirouz and Mozaffar, Gholamreza. We seldom had a chance to see them away from the watchful eyes of parents or guardians. Not that we needed to. Romances went on for years without a single word spoken. Love blossomed without even the remotest chance of reciprocation. We loved from a distance, invented impossible excuses to spend fifteen extra minutes on the sidewalk outside the school, preposterous pretences just to watch them play soccer.

They scarcely noticed. Never knew what lies we told, what punishments we suffered. Never saw us dying a thousand deaths as they walked away.

For months I walked past the gates of the American College in the hope that the boy with soft eyes would look my way. But he was interested in Leila, whose only advantage as far as I could tell was that she wore glasses. So I argued that my vision was blurred, that I suffered from headaches. Every two weeks I got my eyes tested until my father succumbed and bought me a pair of cat's-eye glasses with tortoise-shell frames. I wore them for months without so much as a glance in my direction. And then resolved to keep them forever.

Despite our longings, despite our desires, despite our acrobatics, we almost never met. When we did, we met in the street. Lingering on sidewalks when school let out, we communicated when Fatemeh or Nazanin plucked up enough courage to initiate a conversation, or when a boy addressed one of us with more than an *"Akh joon,"* literally "Ahhh life," but enunciated to convey lascivious desire.

And though we seldom spoke, we were intimately aware of our respective situations. We knew of the boys at the American College, of their Presbyterian professors and larger-than-life principal who treated the sons of generals and teachers equitably and spoke Persian with a funny, lilting accent.

"Stand straight, think straight," was his favourite saying. As if standing straight could correct these boys' defects. As if there were some innate connection between their posture and their moral integrity. And maybe there was, for boys for whom duplicity was a means of survival, honour a lamentable weakness, and truth a commodity so valuable it was to be used only sparingly.

One winter's day, Doctor Jordan summoned the students onto a field of freshly-fallen snow. Rather than embark on the high-minded lectures on Truth they had come to expect from him, he challenged them to walk a straight line. Each boy put one faltering foot in front of the other, producing meandering paths that, at best, approximated straight lines. All but one. For there was one student who set his sights on a distant tree and proceeded to place one determined foot in front of the next, producing a path remarkable for its directness and purpose.

I loved that story of the apocryphal student, and to this day believe it was Firouz. Every day of his life he followed a straight line in wooing the country he loved. In the schools and universities where he studied, in the ministries where he worked, in the projects he undertook to win her heart. That is, until the day he stood up in the middle of the cabinet meeting, recited a line of verse, muttered his apologies, and to the amazement of all at the table, including some who had created tortuous lines in freshly fallen snow, walked out. But that would not happen until much later.

First Firouz would have to learn to walk straight, though his parents' particular motivation was to have him study at a school famous for producing cabinet ministers and members of parliament. Lying about his age, they picked out an appropriately-priced gift and sent him off to an interview. The Presbyterians sent back the carpet and kept the boy. There was something in his keen intelligence and thirst for learning that must have caught their attention. Or perhaps it was the boldly-repeated phrase that led them to overlook the lie and the bribe.

With his unerring sense of giving the answers expected of him, when asked why he wanted to attend the American College, he responded with a phrase he had heard a British rector recite on the BBC:

Dear Lord don't make me like Porridge,
    Stodgy and hard to stir;
Make me like Cornflakes,
    Crispy and ready to serve.

At least that is the story I heard from my cousin, Ali Akbar, and he should have known. He fondly referred to Firouz as Cornflakes for years, or more accurately, for decades. Actually, that's not entirely true. At soggy times he was Shredded Wheat, at animated times, Snap, Crackle and Pop, and on at least one memorable occasion, Captain Crunch.

3

I still remember the first time I saw Firouz. He was twelve and I was almost thirteen. On the day my father stood by the gate long after I waved and turned the corner, he passed me in navy blue shorts and a white shirt, a satchel on his back and a lunchbox in his hand. During those years I often saw him walking on the other side of the street and sometimes turned around to see him rapidly approaching. Then I stopped and re-tied an awkward shoe lace or found a shop window in front of which to linger to avoid that clumsy moment when we might share the same sidewalk.

Though our paths often crossed later in life, though we walked in step up mountainsides, and arm in arm with the thousands, in those early days we seldom walked together. Firouz never found an excuse to let me catch up, and I did not have the boldness to strike up a conversation. Still, I took more than a passing interest in this strangely serious boy who walked with such a palpable sense of purpose to the American College.

Every schoolday Firouz walked out of the heavy oak door with two knockers, one massive and one delicately feminine. He then walked past the house where I lived. The balustrade punctuated by a princely soldier. The ringed hand holding a blackened ball. Proceeding past the local grocery store, he made sure to give the owner a firm "good morning," and hurried past the obese man whose folds of flesh forever defied Firouz's understanding of the male anatomy.

He then passed the barber. Every two weeks his uncle gave Firouz five rials and sent him through the beaded door. And every time, on his return, Hamed took him by the hand and dragged him back. There I personally witnessed Uncle Hamed demand his money's worth, insisting, "Dear sir, you have short-changed my nephew. You have only given him a three rial haircut. Please give him two more rials of haircut."

Just beyond the barber shop Firouz turned off Ghavam Saltaneh onto Naderi Avenue. He walked past the Bon Chic bakery with its cream-puff pastries, past Café Moustache named after the owner's prodigious handlebars that rivalled the postage stamp lion's and that he would, in fits of melancholy, curl and place behind his ears.

Firouz walked past Russian bookstores and Armenian photo studios named Vahé or Vartan. Toy stores showing off their bright BSA bicycles, which he proudly informed his classmates stood for Birmingham Small Arms. His father once bought him a top-of-the-line racing-green Hercules bicycle, insisting, "I am not rich enough to buy cheap things." It was one of the two lessons Firouz grudgingly learned from the man who never taught him that, when shaving, it is the blunt razor that cuts. That he would have to learn, as most of them did, from a woman.

Passing the stamp-shop arcade, Firouz drank in the images of statesmen, inventors and industrialists. He then turned right onto the tree-lined road that led to the American College and a store that sold a hodgepodge of articles from petit-beurre biscuits to Olivetti typewriters, from pastels to picture books on the Hermitage's Impressionist collections.

It was owned by a funny old man with Coca-Cola-bottle-bottom glasses. Impeccably clean-shaven and smelling of lilac water, he always wore one of two grey suits and a paisley blue tie. "Do you have any Kierkegaard?" the older boys asked him routinely, giving each other knowing looks. After rummaging around for a minute or two among protractors and compass sets, he replied without fail, "We used to, but we're out right now." Barely restraining their laughter, the scoundrels burst into great guffaws in the street. Firouz seldom joined them, opting to stay behind and ask solicitously, "I have been saving up for a Parker pen for months now. Do you think I should just buy a Schaeffer instead?" It was guaranteed to bring a smile to the funny old man's face. He loved to hold forth on the merits of Parker pens.

Firouz loved the walk to school. Years later, when that

rogue of a police officer held up traffic to dramatically and unnecessarily wave Firouz's shiny silver car through the red light, he insisted the chauffeur drop him off blocks away from the office so he could savour something of those early morning strolls.

He loved the walk and loved the school, these American missionaries who had forsaken home and family to fulfil vows of abstinence and poverty in a remote country. And a promise that they would teach these children right from wrong. It was a ludicrous proposition for a country that had survived for centuries confounding and confusing authority.

At the school across the street we knew of their ploys, and knew better than to try them. "I'll pretend to be sick and miss the exam. Just watch, the make-up is bound to be an oral and I'm sure to do well," Farhad said, to my cousin Ali Akbar's disbelief. The boys watched in anticipation as Farhad was asked three questions, all of which he stuttered and stammered through, all of which he failed to answer correctly. But when the exasperated teacher asked, "So young man, you tell me what grade you deserve. In good conscience tell me what grade I should give you," the scoundrel responded with a wink toward his audience, "Sir, you must give me a 97. After all I only got three wrong."

In another age, the professor would have laughed and relented, the king would have had the vazir's mouth filled with gold, but this wit was wasted on the Presbyterians. They had forsaken all rewards in this life for the single unlikely satisfaction of teaching these boys the basic discipline that any first-grader in Kansas already knew.

There was an often repeated story about the time the professor asked Firouz, in English, "Have you prepared your Arabic lesson, young man?" *"La,"* he responded in Arabic. "Give him an A," boomed his professor. To everyone's amazement Firouz, who had failed to do his assignment, was rewarded for actually responding "No" in the language he was supposed to be learning.

La, at the American College there was no need to pretend.

Nor was there any challenge in outwitting foreigners who were entirely oblivious of the game, who were ignorant of the rules. For they cared not whether their students passed examinations or handed in assignments successfully. They cared only that their wards should learn.

4

Under the circumstances Firouz forsook memorizing passages from *Leaves of Grass* and the Latin nomenclature of plants and animals. Where Ali, Asghar, and other classmates engaged in accented conversations using passages from *English Made Simple* ("Abraham Lincoln was a great man, was he not?") or adopted the new idiom to older pursuits ("Hello gorgeous."), Firouz achieved a command of the language that few could match. He learned to speak English like his mother tongue, and applied himself to reading Shakespeare.

Lear and Hamlet were his favourites. The remorse of blinded kings and the insanity of princes we all understood intuitively. While itinerant vendors sold second-hand suits and porters sang verses proclaiming the strength of their backs, I watched him pace up and down under arched and entwined trees, memorizing verses on life and death, love and its betrayal, madness and method. More than any other he was attached to an obscure line from *Hamlet* that he would declaim whenever anyone stated the obvious. For the longest time he would recite it as if he had the answer to any and all questions. Later, when pondering the dissolution of all he held dear, he would catch himself whispering, "There needs no ghost, my lord, come from the grave / To tell us this. There needs no ghost ..."

Firouz loved the books the Presbyterians assigned. His classmates seldom bothered to crack them open, relying instead on his good nature. He did not let them down, obligingly writing essays on Okies and dustbowls, guillotines and

men in iron masks, recrucified Christs and unfound doors—
worlds beyond their experience and their comprehension. He
loved those books where good prevailed, and when thirteen
he especially loved those by G. A. Henty. Set on St. Bar-
tholomew's Eve or at the Battle of Agincourt, Henty's stories
were of courageous young boys who walked in the footsteps
of legendary heroes and saved the day through supreme acts
of bravery or sacrifice.

At his insistence, Maryam's brother Salman read *Sturdy
and Strong, How George Andrews Made His Way.* "There really is
no place for this high-minded idealism in our world," Salman
asserted precociously. And then, putting words to action, he
presented Firouz an illustrated edition of the *Shahnameh,* insisting, "Firouz *jan* you really would be much better off reading our native authors."

We too had heroes who slew dragons and a humble Persian blacksmith who defied a bloodsucking, snake-sprouting
tyrant. But, as Salman was quick to point out, the one who
slew the dragon was the same hero, Rostam, who killed his
own son. Bested in battle by Sohrab, he denied three times
that he was the mighty warrior, claiming instead to be the
weakest of Rostam's servants. Only after he had dealt the
death blow and to his horror found the jewelled amulet he
had given the Turanian princess during their one night together, did he understand that the dying warrior was his son.
It was then Rostam realized that Sohrab's single wish had
been to find his father. A simple filial goal Rostam had forever averted by his treachery.

We too had romantic heroes. Farhad carved tunnels
through mountains of stone to prove his love, and win the
hand of the princess. But no one really believed he could perform that impossible feat, and when it was apparent that he
would suceed, a weeping old woman was sent to convince him
that Shirin was dead. Swayed by her crocodile tears, he slew
himself with the mallet that carved mountains, and Shirin,
after numerous twists and turns, married the king.

We too had ill-fated, star-crossed lovers who wandered

the world in pursuit of the beloved. But after twenty years of searching, Majnun no longer sought Leily's face, and looked only for her footprint.

Certainly there was a king who fell in love with a servant girl. But she was love-sick for the goldsmith and would not return the king's advances. He conspired to find out her secret. When he did, he lured the goldsmith to his court and slowly poisoned him, letting him waste away before the servant girl's eyes. The goldsmith lost his sparkle, and after he died, she forgot him. For, after all, love of the dead is not enduring. Somehow Firouz was meant to learn only to love what is everlasting and divine.

Firouz did not love the everlasting and divine. He loved, instead, the stories of Thomas Paine fighting English cannons and rifles with words and passion. Roman legionnaires making a last ditch effort to hold the bridge, knowing full well that it would be their final act in life. Firouz lived for the return of the rightful king and was particularly taken with the tale of a dragon tattoo that established a simple soldier's royal heritage. How, when unjustly whipped for a crime he did not commit, it shifted from his back to his chest. I'm sure he imagined himself valiantly holding off the barbarians at the pass, leading the charge into the valley of death, in that cart being taken off to do that far, far better thing.

Salman should have kept that copy of the *Shahnameh*. It was a nice edition.

5

At the American College, Firouz grew up with the ones he later encountered at cocktail parties and at seated dinners, on Friday morning mountain hikes. Board members who poked fun about the time he blurted out "Themistocles!" when Demosthenes was the correct answer. Government officials whose English essays on Heathcliff or Havisham he composed.

The ones who remembered the day he shaved the peach fuzz on his lip (slightly later than the rest of them). The ones he took for a surreptitious spin in his uncle's Citroen and managed not to stall even once. The ones who nicknamed him Perry Como, for his striking resemblance to the singer who crooned *It's Impossible*. The ones who joked with the time-worn lines "You're too young to be smoking, your breath still smells of your mother's milk," when he had his first cigarette. They were all trying to cover that sweet scent with the bitter taste of nicotine. They grew up together.

On the sidewalk in front of Anoushirvan Dadgar Girls' School, he first encountered the women he and his classmates fantasized over, the ones they married and the ones they never got over. We grew up together. Firouz grew up, from a distance, with the girls who unbuttoned extra buttons on their blouses when he was near, the ones he would awkwardly pass on his way to school, and the one who felt compelled to keep herself at arm's length for fear he would hear the sound of her trembling heart.

We knew each other, and when we did not, we knew of each other. There was always someone to give a particularly poignant insight. "I know Mahmoud, of course I know him. In fact, I know all there is to know about Mahmoud. Rather than wash the blender in the sink like you or I, he poured soap and water into it, and pressed the button, fructify. Forget everything else. If you ever have any questions about Mahmoud, just remember the blender."

We knew, more than any stranger should, of other strangers' lives. And those of us at Anoushirvan Dadgar were acutely aware of the lives and the trajectories of the boys across the street. Though I found Firouz's self-confidence exasperating, I kept track of him from those first days at the American College. Maybe we all did. Though there were any number of schoolchildren who would follow shining paths, there was something about Firouz that made us sit up and pay attention.

Something astounding about his devotion to his straight-line path. A star in the ascendant, there were those of us who believed he was the awaited one, the pure-of-heart-one who would awaken a sleeping princess and reanimate a slumbering empire. And then there were those, Salman among them, who were convinced that there really was no place in Iran for his high-minded idealism. That we needed a pure-of-heart thief who would steal the flying carpet and save the day. A pure-of-heart scoundrel who would steal the princess' hand and the nation's heart.

6

We grew up together and we grew old together. We went to school together, worked together, played together. We all knew him and he knew all of us. But he only ever had one best friend.

They met under less than auspicious circumstances. Playing soccer in the school's rock-strewn field, Firouz found himself facing off against a newly-arrived boy who went flying down the field at breakneck speed, frantically dribbling the ball, winding and weaving his way to the goal, oblivious to his opponents as well as his teammates, so consumed was he with caressing and coaxing the ball across the field. Not bearing to part with it until after he had gently and expertly enticed it past the goalie and into the net.

The only time he seemed to recognize an opponent was when he bothered to dribble the ball through the defender's legs, continuing to weave his way down the field while the defender suffered the single greatest embarrassment one ever could on the soccer field.

And Firouz had stood in the way. He couldn't even keep the ball in the air for more than three or four kicks before it hit the ground with a resounding thud, but he plucked up his courage and attempted a tackle against the boy who was running circles around everyone. He went sprawling on the rock-strewn dirt, injured his knee, limped off to the sidelines, and watched the boy dribble excitedly toward the goal line, while everyone laughed.

Later that day Firouz was ridiculed for his performance by a diminutive bully with a wispy moustache who helped himself unceremoniously to Firouz's lunch. Firouz felt a sinking feeling as he considered his choices. As he rose to take his beating, the boy who dribbled the ball madly down the field walked up, quietly took the lunch box from the bully's hand and handed it back to Firouz. There was an unspoken strength in his action that could not be overlooked. It was enough to dissuade the bully, who scoffed, laughed, and walked off.

From that day on Firouz and Nur ed Din became friends. In seventh grade they sat in the back of the classroom scribbling notes, whispering conspiratorially. They sat together, studied together, played together. Their favourite time was when the entire French class recited rhythmically, "Bon jour Mon sieur La za ri an, com ment all ez vous." Followed by "Après la pluie vient le beau temps," "La vie est belle," or some such phrase. Firouz and Nur ed Din would time it so they would always finish two syllables after the rest of the class, to the great chagrin of Monsieur La za ri an.

As freshmen they laughed together, studied together, sat together. As upperclassmen they looked forward to the ringing of the bell when they could fly through the city on Firouz's motorcycle. It was an old, Russian model left over from the First World War and weighed a ton. But it ran and it took them where they wanted. Fatemeh almost rode it once, and Nazanin maintained that she actually did ride it—twice.

When school let out the young friends would rush over to Firouz's house, hop on the motorbike and go for a spin. If they felt like it, they would head up Pahlavi Avenue just in case there was a Marlon Brando movie playing. Or maybe they would drive by Leila's house on the off chance they might see her. Sometimes they rubbed charcoal on their cheeks only to be turned away by brusque cabaret-owners who feigned anger and chuckled as soon as they thought Firouz and Nur ed Din were out of range. At other times the young heroes woke up long before sunrise and hopped on the bike to have a breakfast of goat's head soup in Custom's Square.

Nur ed Din looked forward to the early morning truck driver breakfasts but had a particular weakness for the ride toward the mountains. He especially loved it late at night when they breezed down empty roads, the wind in their faces, trees and light posts rushing by. Firouz went out of his way to drive through Pol-e-Rumi for the delicious coolness they felt every time they went around the bend and dipped down to the river.

On those nights they felt giddy with speed, with the power of a Russian two-stroke engine, with the freedom of a full tank of gas. Firouz would turn his head and say something and Nur ed Din would just laugh, not understanding a single word. Firouz would repeat himself, turn his head even further, articulate even more articulately, and Nur ed Din would laugh even louder.

Once while riding faster than ever before, Nur ed Din felt a splash against his cheek. He looked up to see if it were raining, but it was a starlit night and not a cloud in the sky. He felt another drop, and yet another. He couldn't imagine where the raindrops were coming from. And then it dawned on him. Firouz's tears were hitting his face. There was an intimacy in that moment that Nur ed Din never forgot and that Firouz never knew. An intimacy in Firouz's tears he always cherished. Even if they were caused only by the wind and the speed of a two-stroke Russian engine in the downhill.

7

I always felt they were an unlikely pair. From tenth grade on Firouz wore a coat and a tie, even in the sweltering heat. He often sported a silver tie-pin and his wavy hair glistened with the brilliantine that struggled to keep it flat and in place. But Nur ed Din showed up to school his collar unbuttoned, a striped school tie hanging loosely around his neck, his shoes scuffed from a game of street soccer.

Firouz was the son of a reputable merchant who bought tea from Ceylon, ginger from Zanzibar, coffee from Yemen, and cardamom from the hills of Mongolia. A man who risked his capital on wooden ships accosted by typhoons and gales, dinghies that hugged the shore from Bombay to Bandar Abbas, caravans that fended off attacks by Silk Route marauders. A man who took unimaginable risks from his four-by-six storefront in the dusty, dimly lit bazaar.

But Nur ed Din was an orphan and his uncle, Mustafa, the leader of an obscure sect. Not like the Ismailis who pay their leader his weight in gold, emeralds and pearls, and have made the Aga Khan a byword for opulence, wealth and glamour. Not like the Ali-allahis who believe in the divinity of Ali and have such an acute sense of fatality that they are thought to be devil-worshippers. Nur ed Din's uncle was the leader of no such sect. He was simply handed down a responsibility from his father, who had it from his father before him, to provide guidance through the trials and tribulations of life to a handful of followers.

Nur ed Din's story, repeated by giggling grey-skirted girls, was that his grandfather had been a holy man with a voice that moved women to ecstasy and men to tears. He had come into this world on the birthday of Ali Ibn Abi Talib, the Prophet's son-in-law, an auspicious though not unusual beginning. What was truly miraculous about his birth, prompting the giggles, was that he came into the world circumcised. There was no need to wait until the eighth day and dress him in a white robe. He came into this world less than complete, and as Allah intended him to be.

His parents immediately sent for a mullah who only served to confirm their fears. "He is the Dear Lord's son and one day he will be summoned back to his Father," said the holy man. "He is on loan to you. Make sure you return him in good working order." Acquiescing, they named him Abdul Latif, Slave to the Gentle One, after the most prized of God's attributes.

On that day his brother took a piece of charcoal and inscribed blackly on the white plaster wall: "The thirteenth of *Rajab*. Today Abdul Latif came into this world. It is partly sunny, partly cloudy."

As he grew older, Abdul Latif came to understand the circumstance of his birth and took to asking the Lord for a sign that he was truly blessed. "Are you there, Lord?" he asked on a number of occasions when there was not a cloud in the sky. "I can feel you looking after me but, God, I need to know. So if you really love me, please make it rain. I'm not asking you to move mountains Lord, just for a few drops of rain." The Dear Lord had not failed him. The rain fell out of nowhere, confirming what everyone else had known all along.

One day while the rainbow still lingered, he revoked all material possessions and installed himself in the deserts of Kerman, living a simple and frugal existence. Soon infertile women and perplexed men found their way to his hut. The story of his birth, along with some minor miracle, cemented his reputation. A sect was formed that recited his teachings, committed his lessons to memory, and sought his advice on matters ranging from matrimony to diet. This was the legacy handed down from father to son until it came to rest with Nur ed Din's uncle, Mustafa. As Uncle Mustafa had no children, when the time would come for him to depart this vale of tears, the responsibility would be Nur ed Din's.

While students made plans to become mathematicians or generals, poets or farmers, and I resolved to pursue a career in architecture, Nur ed Din devoted himself to engineering, a discipline he knew he would never practice. But still he persevered, graduating with honours from the American College. Like so many of us who believed our educations could only be pursued outside Iran, Nur ed Din enrolled at the American University of Beirut, as did his friend, Firouz.

One sunny day, they took the train across the Great Salt Desert, crossed the Persian Gulf, landed at Basra, and proceeded to Baghdad where they acquired a weakness for the cardamom-flavoured coffee they would always associate with the bittersweet taste of delay. They both travelled light. We all did. After all, what we wanted to take with us, we could hardly carry all the way to Beirut.

8

In Beirut we formed a loose-knit group, the sons and occasional daughters of forward-looking Iranian families who believed, presciently, that though land, jewels, and bank accounts could be confiscated, no one could ever take away what we knew.

There was a portly young man we fondly referred to as Elephant, who had a somewhat smaller, slightly less portly friend we playfully called Little Elephant. Little Elephant's particular talent, for which he was remembered more than anything else he ever did in his life, was turning around to converse with back-seat passengers while negotiating vertiginous mountain-road curves at high speeds.

I looked forward to those days when we drove through mountains and strolled through olive groves and wheat fields, climbed desolate peaks and ambled through lush valleys, singing strains of songs, reciting fragments of poetry. Giddy with the fresh mountain air, we sought out springs and drank deep. There was one I loved above all the others. It gushed from the mountain like a waterfall, and in the pool that formed below I placed cherries, apricots or plums. Within minutes the fruits were so deliciously cold, I could scarcely bite into them.

In the spray of the waterfall we picnicked on sandwiches of bread, cheese and walnuts, or honey and butter mingled into a delicious ambrosia in our knapsacks. We lounged, relaxed, and for a moment realized how truly blessed we were. And then Houshang would intone, as if on cue, "I have found the meaning of life, I don't give a damn what Immanuel Kant has to say." It was a refrain recited throughout the course of the day, the only variation being the name inserted. Descartes or de Beauvoir, Spinoza, Truman, or Mao Tse Tung.

On those days we were truly happy. All except one. For there was one among us who, no matter how beautiful, no matter how dramatic, how overwhelming the site, insisted on proclaiming, "It really is very beautiful. It is wonderfully beautiful. It is incredibly beautiful. But it is not quite as beautiful as Tangaloo."

Tangaloo must have been a truly fantastic place. I made a point of looking, but failed to find it in the barren, Zagros mountains. Sorour described it as a spring, a weeping willow, a pomegranate tree, and a shady, grassy spot. Throughout her life Sorour travelled the world and saw the most amazing sights. And when she did she would sigh again and say, "It really is very, very beautiful. But not quite as beautiful as Tangaloo."

Nor was it clear that Firouz enjoyed the beauty that surrounded him. While the rest of us were reciting poetry or picking flowers, and Parviz was stopping in memory of departed friends, Firouz was intent on making it up the mountain in record-breaking time. Houshang, who had found the meaning of life, teased him, "Are you going to enter your name and time in the book on the summit?" as Firouz single-mindedly pursued the trail. Firouz could take the jokes, he was pretty thick-skinned. In any case he wasn't as bad as Touraj who, when his friends twisted his arm, would say optimistically, "Of course I'll come. I like hiking and I enjoy your company. But if it rains, I'll have to come back and study."

Sometimes we went for walks, and at other times we pooled our resources and selected one of us to see a film. That lucky individual was under the obligation of giving a full account of how ravishing Anna Magnani was in the love scene, how Robert Mitchum let his cigarette dangle from the side of his mouth, how the criminals almost got away with it, but for a basic flaw—falling for a woman, putting one more coin in the jukebox, wanting too much.

At first we took turns, but soon realized Firouz had no particular talent for reliving the film. "They rented the upstairs room, drilled a hole, climbed down the rope and stole the money," he matter-of-factly recounted, failing to act out the parts. Houshang, on the other hand, would put on an entire production, turning up his collar, changing the tilt of his hat, re-enacting robberies and cocktail parties, lovers' quarrels and getaways with a flair and enthusiasm that was infectious. Soon he was the only one selected. We looked forward to his performances, counted the days until a new blockbuster hit the screens, eagerly contributed our allowances, and speculated on how Houshang, who bore a striking resemblance to Mickey Rooney, would capture Tyrone Power's pathos, Sidney Greenstreet's calculating deviousness, or the power of Orson Welles' oratory.

Despite his stiffness in these matters, Firouz still managed to impress us all when, after a Hitchcock film, he declaimed from Shakespeare, "I am but mad north by northwest." We all thought we got the reference when Cary Grant got on the plane. It cemented Firouz's reputation and elevated him a notch or two in everyone's esteem, but not in mine. I already knew.

At times we convened to celebrate some particularly Persian holiday. On those days our group expanded to include the classmates preoccupied in enjoying the decadent pleasures Beirut and anonymity afforded them—the ones who were not to be found in the mornings, and from three o'clock on were sure to be encountered at a table or two at the Kit Kat Bar (rooms attached).

At these celebrations we felt loneliest. On days like these, all the camaraderie couldn't make up for the distance from our homes. I missed my father, and wished he would come visit again, like the time when we had walked down the streets arm in arm, and passers-by shook their heads. Detecting the looks that needed no translation, we just laughed and continued strolling up the boulevard, arm in arm.

Firouz missed the people he grew up with, the ones who knew him and loved him to a fault. There was an ancient gardener he had known ever since he had set foot in his uncle's house. Every year, on the First Day of Spring, Firouz looked forward to the moment when he would inquire of the wizened old man, "Another year has passed, Mashdi. Do tell me, how many years is it now that you have been with our family?" To which the ancient gardener, would reply, to Firouz's great delight, "When I was seventeen, your grandfather offered me one week's work. To the best of my calculations, that week is not up yet."

No amount of camaraderie could replace the poetry in that reply. Not for Firouz, and not for me. I had often seen the antiquated Mashdi pushing a wheelbarrow in his knee-high black plastic boots, engaged in his one week of work. No gathering of friends could make up for the absence of a family that extended beyond blood to the people who knew us better than anyone else. I missed the Bulgarian engineer who maintained he owed his prosperity to my family and dropped by every year with a new chess set and another variation on the Napoleonic opening. He always brought me a doll or a scarf, and once a toy gondola I loved so much, it never left its plastic case.

We all missed Firouz's cousin who, after asking after his health at great length would inquire in a provincial accent Firouz imitated impeccably, "Firouz *jan,* do you need anything, anything at all? Is there anything I can do for you? Tell me what it is. I am your uncle's son, after all. Tell me what it is, and if it is within my power, I will take care of it."

It was a line of inquiry that always led to, "Do you have enough money?" Firouz would reply, quite correctly, "My father has provided sufficient funds for my needs. When I require any money I just go to the bank." To which the crest-fallen "uncle's son" would reply, "If one day, you don't want to go to the bank. If, for whatever reason, you don't feel like going to the bank, please come to me." At first Firouz found the cousin ridiculous, but in Beirut he missed him terribly. There were days when he could not bear going to the bank. There were days when none of us could.

9

Though I knew for a fact they aspired only to be gentlemen from the waist up, I was never once approached. Nor was Leily, who was quite striking, or Fatemeh, who smoked cigarettes and cursed like a sailor. Instead they extended us small kindnesses, treated us as they would younger sisters.

They dealt with us as they might have dealt with their sisters, except they sought our advice, asked, "How would a woman want to be treated?" It was all right, I was not really interested in any of them. And though I often saw Firouz in gatherings, we never discussed such matters. For the most part, we engaged in conversations about books, courses, or mutual friends and acquaintances.

And then one day he showed up at my doorstep unannounced to ask, "Yassaman, it's a beautiful morning. I was wondering if you might want to join me for a walk." "Perhaps he is making up for all those times he walked right past me without as much as a hello, the times he did not linger in front of a shop window or invent some other pretext to walk down the street with me," I thought to myself as I hurried to find my favourite coat.

Strolling along familiar streets, we exchanged pleasantries until, turning a corner, we passed Malabar House. "What an ugly building," Firouz remarked innocuously. And it was true, it was an ugly building. But it was, nevertheless, one to which I was attached. "Firouz, there is a story behind each one of these buildings," I responded, "even the ugly ones. The bare facts are inscribed in art nouveau letters by the door front. It was built in 1916. The architect was Marcel LeGrand and the contractor, Zaim Abu Razzagh. Look at the balconies and the detailing, do you see that minaret? A rather ordinary feature, but it bears a striking similarity to the one in Lucknow. Do you know that during the famine, the Nizam of Lucknow paid thousands of labourers to build Bhulbhulaiya during the day and half their number to take it down at night? He fed a starving city with bottomless clay pots and ended up with a structure with one hundred and forty nine identical doors and a name that most people believe means "labyrinth." But it doesn't. Bhulbhulaiya actually means 'the journey that leads to forgetfulness,'" I said, turning to face him.

"Thank you for the lecture, professor," Firouz responded with a smile. "I had never realized how much could be read into a building that did not deserve a second look."

In the silence that ensued, he continued, "Have you read any Steinbeck? I think you would appreciate *The Grapes of Wrath*. I'm moved every time by those poor Okies who just want to live honourable lives from the sweat of their brows. Do you realize that half of our classmates' families still own villages in Iran? They might as well own the villagers as well, what with the way they tax them. Most of them don't even bother to visit the lands that provide them with their wealth."

I needed no ghost to tell me that. So I hastened to point out, "There are exceptions, Firouz. I have heard of one *khan* who never leaves his land. In his youth he read a verse by Hafez and swore never to set foot on land he didn't own. His vow has resulted in a string of villages named after each of his children. They are conveniently established one day's ride from the other."

Firouz could not help but laugh. He knew the story and was friends with two of the one-day-apart-village children. But he still insisted on saying, "There is an expression in the English language for that. I believe they call it 'the exception that proves the rule.'"

Not much had changed since his school days. Only stories of decency and compassion, honest labour, and just reward resounded with Firouz. He loved Steinbeck and developed the odd habit of reading every book by the authors he liked. He took pride in being able to say that he had read every book Hemingway had written, that he was intimately acquainted with all of Zola's work, even though it meant carrying *Nana* around for an inordinate period of time. "Still reading *Nana?*"

schoolmates asked months afterwards, making a running joke that continued through Beirut, back to Tehran, to cocktail parties and seated dinners. "Still reading *Nana?*" I asked on walks through London parks in exile.

But he could say he had read all the works by the great French writers, all the turbid Russian masterpieces. He acquired the Modern Library editions with the winged, torch-bearing logo, and inscribed them with his name and the date of acquisition. Years later in Los Angeles, I discovered a copy of Dostoyevsky's *The Idiot* in my bookcase, signed in a flowing hand and dated April 14, 1948. Firouz was insatiable in his pursuit of knowledge. He was also insatiable in his desire for completeness. All of Dickens, all of Twain, all of Melville, all of Hugo. All the Modern Library.

10

I came to expect Firouz to drop by on Saturday mornings, and he seldom disappointed. "You have now been here for two years, has your Arabic expanded past the one word that got you an A?" I asked on one of those walks, revealing a familiarity that spoke of days spent in front of the American College waiting for school to let out and boys to grow up.

"Which one word? What are you talking about?" he feigned ignorance. "I consistently got A's in all my classes," he replied, knowing full well the episode to which I was referring.

And then Firouz, who so expertly dodged such questions, conceded, *"La.* I really haven't learned much other than how to order a decent meal at the Sheikh's." Pausing for a moment he added, "But the one phrase I have learned is *Tavakkolto al-Allah.* It is an abbreviated version of the *sureh* in the Quran that says: 'Put your trust in Allah and devote yourself to your goal. You will succeed.'" His response surprised me. I had never known him to be particularly devout. In any case, *Tavakkolto al-Allah* was most commonly inscribed with a flourish on the back of lorries, and jokingly interpreted to mean "Place your trust in Allah, I'm behind the wheel."

It was only later when I saw the words framed and placed on the blank white wall above his desk that I understood. And it was not until much later, on another of our Saturday walks, that Firouz finally told the story, as good as any tale of cindergirls and glass slippers, that put things into perspective. "One day my grandmother went to pick up my father and my uncle Hamed from school," he started, "and one of the two, and there is considerable debate that continues to this day, walked out without his galoshes. She immediately sent the young criminal back to retrieve the lost items, but to no avail. My grandmother had only recently bought the galoshes over the objections of an unreasonable and stingy husband, and could not conceive of going home without them.

"She looked everywhere without success, and finally resolved to buy another pair from her meagre savings. Taking the children by the hand, she proceeded to the bazaar. But try as she might, she failed to find a pair of galoshes in anything resembling the right size. In any case, she could ill afford to buy them. As night fell and she made her way back past the schoolyard, she implored a good and gracious God to save her from the impending disaster she would encounter at her husband's hand. As the sun set, she found, on the school steps, an urchin selling precisely two pairs of galoshes, one of which miraculously fit her son's feet. From that moment on, she never once doubted God's existence."

While his grandmother's belief prompted her to pray toward Mecca five times a day, the galoshes inspired in Firouz a conviction that if you were a good person and diligently pursued your desire, you would be rewarded in this world. There was not much *Allah* in his *Tavakkolto al-Allah*. In fact, there wasn't much other than a belief that good people who work hard will live happily ever after. Still, Firouz would approach Nur ed Din with questions about God. But he never really listened to the answers. He was too busy formulating the standard and unassailable arguments against religion. Too busy demanding the same scientific proofs of God's existence.

In any case, Nur ed Din was not inclined to engage in these discussions. More than anything else in life, his heart longed for the *mo'azzen*'s call. It was the moment he yearned for with a desire so deep that he physically felt the absence. As the setting sun began to usher in the first coolness of the evening, he knew the moment he waited for was at hand. Soon he would hear the soft strains of the mullah calling the faithful to prayer. Then he would perform his ablutions, scent his hands and face with rose water, wipe the tears from the corners of his eyes and softly chant the familiar words, *"Besmellahe rahmane raheem ... Sobhana rabbi al a'zeem ..."* He had never needed to justify it to anyone.

II

Years later, when Firouz looked back on the tender days in Beirut, he would wonder out loud if he had anything other than the most perfunctory of memories. Of course he remembered the American University. He had some recollection of the campus, of the often-photographed view of the Mediterranean, of our Saturday walks, weekends on the beach. He remembered the Saint Georges, the Phoenician, the Metropole and the Kit Kat Bar (rooms attached). He remembered having dutifully visited Pigeon Rocks and the Ottoman citadel.

But his memories stopped there. They never captured the veiled woman carrying a bowl of steaming soup, her teeth clenching a corner of her *chador* to keep her modesty intact. And reveal the most exquisite curve of her alabaster neck. Though when I pointed it out, he was inspired to say, "Let me remember this moment long after I have forgotten the names and faces of professors I never cared about. After I have forgotten the examinations I agonized over." He never did remember the gait of the girl who, in walking down the

street, turned every head. The dance in her step, the bright-
ness that shone from her eyes, that glittered in her hennaed
feet. The exuberance that stood out in such contrast to the
dusty restraint of the streets. He forgot that moment and so
many of the moments that made up our years in Beirut.

Where his memories failed, mine extended to vignettes I
did not live, episodes I never experienced. Slices of life heard
second-hand from indiscreet friends and acquaintances that
I included in weekly letters to my father, attempting to bottle
and distill the essence of my existence in Beirut. I desperately
wanted him to know the people who populated my days and
nights and imagined a time when I would introduce a friend,
and my father would politely shake hands and exchange
pleasantries before making a cryptic remark and giving me
a knowing smile. Every week I wrote him the stories I loved,
and later learned to recount them in cafés, on Saturday morning walks, and on mountain hikes. There were stories I told
and retold so many times that years later people would ask
me for the details, as if I had been there.

As if Davoud had pulled me aside and confided his love for
Ayman, the lithe Lebanese wrestler. As if he told me that for
four years he devoted himself exclusively and wholeheartedly
to his seduction. How he enrolled in the courses the young
Arab was taking. How he changed his major when Ayman
experienced doubts about becoming an engineer and decided to pursue a degree in diplomacy. How he also changed
his dormitory, his eating and sleeping habits to be close to
the lithe Ayman. As if he sought me out to say, "Yassaman,
during those four years, I never once missed a day of school.
Not one single day. I could not bear the thought of not looking into my chosen lover's eyes, however lame the pretext.
Do you know that on graduation day I was finally rewarded,
not by Ayman but by the damn Provost. I don't know if you
remember, but I was presented with a certificate recognizing
what he called 'the improbable feat of my perfect attendance.'"

12

I wrote these stories in letters to my father, and learned to tell them in gatherings. But there was at least one story I did not repeat. And though I restrained myself, Firouz could not refrain from telling of the time he and Nur ed Din went to see *Blood and Sand* on a double date. During the scene where the matador falls for the temptress and toward his inevitable dissolution, Firouz managed to extricate himself to see what kind of progress Nur ed Din was making. And there was Nur ed Din, as dashing as Tyrone Power and certainly far more handsome than Perry Como ever was, seated next to a striking young woman. His hair glistened. His eyes shone.

But he was not engaged in an endless embrace, she was not even resting her head on his shoulder. He was sitting with his hands on his knees, next to an awfully perplexed young woman.

It was a scene that Firouz never could forget. Or quite understand. Though I assured him, "There is nothing particularly remarkable about that episode, it really is quite mundane," he would marvel time and again, "Nur ed Din was a handsome man. When he walked down the street, women followed him with their eyes. My God, he was a handsome man. But he hadn't even managed to put his arm around her shoulder. A man like that, can you imagine?"

Years later, while reclining on his sofa, balancing a teaglass of vodka on his head, he would tell the story of Nur ed Din and the statuesque date one more time. It was invariably accompanied by the story of the New York snow.

"I was on an official mission and checked into the Waldorf late at night. I remember because I had to walk some distance to find a twenty-four-hour drugstore where I could buy razors at a reasonable price. I returned to the hotel, went to sleep and requested a wake-up call to make it to my meeting bright and early. I got the call, but was advised by the bellhop to go back to sleep. At his urging I looked out the window. I could not believe my eyes. The entire city was blanketed in snow. I had walked down those same streets less than seven hours ago. I had bought a pack of super-speed Gillette razors less than seven hours ago. Seven hours ago. But there were at least three feet of immaculate white snow covering the city, softening the lines of the skyscrapers, deadening the din of midtown Manhattan. In less than seven hours the entire city had been blanketed in snow."

He was baffled and amazed. It was with this same sense of wonder, this same sense of recounting something that defies the laws of nature, something entirely beyond comprehension, that he told the story of Nur ed Din and his date. It was the one memory from his years in Beirut. The only real memory he retained of those tender years.

13

From the American College Firouz went to the American University. And from the American University Firouz went to America. Chicago, to be precise. Nur ed Din returned to Iran. "My elephant has a longing for Hindustan," he said, quoting the expression most often used when a woman leaves the man she is with for her one true love. We said our good-byes and sincerely promised to write. Nur ed Din set off for Tehran, Firouz left for Chicago, and I ended up in Southern California. It was 1953.

Firouz had always yearned for America. It was the place he had first learned to love through the eyes of John Steinbeck, Walt Whitman and Howard Fast. But it was more than that. It was a place that churned out trans-Atlantic ocean liners the size of cities and aeroplanes dubbed flying fortresses. A nation that produced tractors and steam rollers, harvesters and oil derricks, highways and wrecking cranes, grain reapers, silos and skyscrapers. It was a "Go west young man" land where you were limited only by ambition, determination and desire. A place where you could write your own J. Paul Getty destiny.

"I will understand America's magnificent success. I will find the institutions that give it strength, creativity and resilience. And when I understand what it is that makes America great, I will reproduce it in Iran," he told himself and anyone else who was willing to listen. He said he came to the Windy City to learn what made the greatest nation in the world tick. I believe he came because as a child, he had seen "Chicago" emblazoned on a postage stamp commemorating the World's Fair. He could imagine no more enchanting name. More than New York, Dodge or Detroit, more than Charleston or Chattanooga, more than Hollywood or Houston, Osh Kosh or Kansas City, Chicago evoked Firouz's vision of America.

It was Burnham's "make no little plans" city, Sandburg's "bareheaded, shovelling, wrecking, planning, building, breaking, rebuilding" city. The city that took the vast produce of America's even vaster heartland, the grain and the beef and the pork, the wheat and the iron ore, and processed, packaged and distributed it across the globe. Its freight yards were a sight that boggled the imagination, covering acre after acre in a maze of lines, tracks and switching yards.

He was fascinated with the sound Chicago made as it rolled off the tongue, the softness of that first syllable that lured you in, followed by a jab and an uppercut. He was even more pleased when he learned that it meant "the place of the rotten smell." It smelled, it sweated and it made no bones about it. It was the city that had the audacity to adopt a motto proclaiming, "I will." For Firouz it represented everything about America he admired. So when the time came to choose, he chose the University of Chicago. When it chose him, he ended up in Chicago, Illinois.

I often paused to remember Firouz while walking down LA's palm-tree lined streets, past Alhambra-esque buildings with honeycomb minarets, through subdivisions with at least one hundred and forty-nine identical doors. I pictured him taking the "Elevated" into town, catching second-storey glimpses into bedrooms with unmade Murphy beds, offices where secretaries sat filing their nails and dreamy-eyed accountants pored over balance sheets in their shirt sleeves, never once making eye contact with the travellers just outside the window. After that all-too-brief glimpse through a door forever half-opened, I imagined him wandering the streets of Chicago looking for the answers to his questions.

They were in the buildings. In the flying buttresses at the top of the Chicago Tribune building, declaring their gothic pedigree and their superfluity. His answers were in the stones inlaid at eye level. Stones from the Houses of Parliament, the Pyramid at Giza, and the cave of the nativity, the Taj Mahal, and the Light House at Alexandria, Chartres and Stonehenge. Stones that kept him wondering, until the day he turned the corner and, to my infinite delight, encountered a stone from Injun Joe's cave.

His answers were in Masonic skyscrapers adorned with Assyrian bas-reliefs three stories high and in the neon sign on the Allerton Hotel that proclaimed "Tip Top Tap." His answers were in the plaque at The Drake hotel that proudly read "The site where the second drink was served after the end of the Prohibition." It begged the question about the first drink, but he never needed to have that particular question answered. Our friend, Asghar, made it a policy to be the second man on every woman's list. "That way I don't have the headaches of a relationship, and sooner or later they all run to me for a shoulder to cry on," the rascal explained with a smile. The coat of arms in the same hotel, decorated with winged dragon and battle axe, declared in Latin, *Aquila Non Capit Muscas,* "An eagle does not catch flies." A policy Asghar would have been well served to adopt.

Firouz's answers were in the buildings obscured blackly by the El, that dark demi-monde populated with doughnut shops, truckers and hookers. Where fried chicken and, on Fridays, fried fish sat under glowing orange lamps at five-thirty in the morning. His answers were in the names: Wrigleyville, Streeterville, and Forestville; Ducktown and Packingtown; Gold Coast and Back of the Yards; Bohemian California, Whiskey Point, Sleepy Hollow, and Ravenswood. In a street named Motor Ave and another named Innovation Way. His answers were in the Old Man Time clock complete with beard, scythe, hourglass and people scurrying by in the foreground, only occasionally stopping long enough to glance up and adjust their wristwatches.

His answers were in the buildings that bore testimony to that urge to make no little plans: a fountain double the size of the one in Versailles, an aquarium dressed up as a Greek temple, a radial street bearing testimony to its Beaux Arts ancestry. All that remained of the brilliant vision.

His answers were in the Chicago Trade Building, pork belly futures capital of the world. In Pilgrims bearing wheat and Indians bearing corn, and in Ceres, Goddess of the crop, who makes harvests bountiful. Ceres, proud mother of Persephone of the pomegranate seeds. Ceres, the determined, who managed to extract her daughter from the clutches of Hades—at least for half the year, and who for the other half leaves the earth barren, abandoned, and frozen. Ceres who remained faceless in Chicago because she stood on top of a skyscraper so tall no one could ever see her features.

14

But Firouz wanted answers other than those. So he would find his way to Bronzeville, order two fingers of whiskey at the Checkerboard Lounge, and wait for Ole Joe Coles to show up. The old-timer had taken it upon himself to educate Firouz on the basic principles of life. "A man don't need but two suits." "Never own nothin' that eats while you sleep." "It's not how much money passes through your hands, it's how much of it's yours." And, "You can't tell how long a snake is until after it's dead." This last pronouncement having been uttered as others were eulogizing a recently departed colleague of indeterminate if not dubious merit.

Firouz always listened dutifully to "You-don't-get-ole

bein'-no-fool" Joe Coles and his unassailable logic. There was a glitter in his eyes, a radiance in his sly smile, that made Firouz want to believe the stories told by this man who had risen through the ranks to become the single most powerful organizer in a town where union leaders ended their lives under not-so-mysterious circumstances. Firouz even took to repeating the lessons he learned, particularly the one about jobs being like women. "You don't leave one 'til you've got another," he would say, though throughout his life he would leave many jobs but never his one true love. He looked forward to the Checkerboard Lounge, the unsolicited words of advice, and those he solicited in a roundabout way. He learned to love Joe like a father, and cried like a baby on the day he died.

Firouz came to Chicago for the city, but it was the countryside that captivated him. There was something about the expanse of rolling plains, a power in the endless fields of wheat that resonated with him. He loved the city but longed for the countryside. The fields of grain dancing in the wind. The corn stalks bent over with the weight of abundance. The sky that went on sky-blue forever. The rain clouds that lackadaisically rolled in from over the horizon as their shadows sped across the land. He once saw a tree struck by lightning, crack, and catch fire. He once came across a town hit by a tornado, witnessed the path of destruction it had cut until it arrived at a two storey, red-roofed home where it took a left and headed straight out through the fields.

But it was not just the landscape that spoke to him. He believed that somehow this vast and bountiful land engendered in its inhabitants the honesty of the soil after the rain, the strength of the hills, the simplicity of the seasons. He spent his time observing their comings and goings in Romeoville or Plainfield, but his favourite was Medinah for its reference to Muhammad's fateful flight from Mecca. Or perhaps to a Shriner's fez-wearing, third-degree, scimitar-and-pyramid understanding of the Orient. He would sit in the diner on successive Sundays and watch overalled farmers walk in on cue, open the door as the clock struck eight, walk past the counter with the pickled turkey gizzards at nine, sit down at ten, wink at the waitress on eleven, and order a Schlitz at the precise moment the clock struck twelve noon. He would eavesdrop as the preacher repeated his sermon over pineapple-upside-down-cake, retelling the story of the boy who wanted to know what it was that made fireflies glow. His father couldn't rightly tell him. Neither could his uncle. But the child desperately wanted to know. And when after some investigation, he accidentally found out, he ran through the house yelling "Papa, papa, it's on the inside, it's on the inside."

Of course it was on the inside. For these people it had always been on the inside. There was a beauty in their smiles that came from within. For them, inside and outside, appearance and essence, were one and the same. Once, on being introduced to Trevor, exchanging a few sentences and subsequently inquiring, "Who is that guy?" Firouz was told only half-jokingly, "That's Trevor. There isn't anything else to know. You met Trevor. You talked to him. You know him as well as his mother does."

And perhaps he did. He loved these people who wore their hearts on their sleeves and their emotions on their brows. And so he would spend his time listening to Uncle Mike's stories of how he would hoot and holler and shoot the old year out and the New Year in. How on the day Florence passed he had taken out the shotgun and kept on firing until the sheriff had stepped up and said, "It's okay Mike, it'll be okay. Let me take that gun, you're liable to hurt someone," though no one else was around.

He loved the directness in their words, their humour in stating the obvious. He learned to expect the Greyhound bus driver to intone, "If it's too cold for you, just let us know, we'll turn the air-conditioning down. And if it's too warm, well, it just don't get any cooler than it is right now." He learned to appreciate "four-sixty" air-conditioning: four windows down and sixty miles an hour. He learned that "if you don't change your path, you're gonna end up where you're goin'," and that "wherever you go, you leave a great future behind you," both of which pleased him immensely. From the man with two fast-food franchises he learned that "a man of my position simply can't afford *not* to read the Wall Street Journal." And from the man who sold him retread tires, that "you're jus' buyin' someone else's misery." All of which he could understand. But it still did not prepare him for the day in the pool hall when the retired switchman was asked why he was looking so glum, and responded matter-of-factly, "I can't get it up."

15

He came to Chicago because once, in his youth, he had seen a postage stamp with a name that held all the magic, the power and the romance in the world. He loved the city and learned to long for the countryside. But his thoughts were preoccupied with the writings of a European theoretician. In Chicago Firouz discovered Max Weber, a man who, on his deathbed, declared in capital letters: "The Truth is the Truth." Not some character in a G. A. Henty book, but a man who fought anti-Semitism in 1920's Germany, inviting Jewish students to his house, testifying in a military court for the poet Ernst Toller. A man who fought for years to defend the maternal rights of Frieda Gross, a friend who had had the most torrid love affair with a ridiculous Swiss anarchist.

Weber could dissect the history of commercial partnerships in the Middle Ages just as well as the religion of China. He could describe Roman agrarian history and had made the most brilliant connection between Capitalism and the Calvinist doctrines. He had charted the evolution of Western Civilization and could convincingly describe every current and counter-current, every shift in the tide. A man who understood the lunar attractions inside each one of us, what motivates each of us to action or inaction, to bid or forbid, to allow or disallow.

"The first time I encountered Weber was in Politics 301,"

Firouz wrote on cream-colored stationery long-since faded. "I was lost in the language, in the barrage of ideas—methodologies, goal-oriented rational actions, ideal types and cognitive aims, Kultur and Geist. The terms overwhelmed me, Yassaman, the flurry of ideas left me reading and re-reading passages without any greater comprehension than when I had first started out. I found my eyes growing tired, my will sagging before the task of understanding what it was this purportedly brilliant mind had to say on politics, economics, and society.

"And then I encountered the sentence that gave me pause: 'In the place of the old-type ruler who is moved by sympathy, grace, and gratitude, modern culture requires for its sustaining external apparatus the emotionally detached, and hence rigorously *professional expert.*' I read the sentence once and I read it again. I could not contain myself. I stood up and walked out of my carrel, repeating the words over and over. It explained everything that was wrong with Iran. How Shah after Shah could assume the grandiose and absurd title of 'the pivot of the universe' and how his emotions, his whims and his royal frailties could result in mouths filled with gold or, more often, dirt.

"But more than an illustration of a bankrupt system, Weber provided a solution—the emotionally detached professional expert. That is what our country needs. Emotional detachment, professionalism and expertise are the road to our advancement. I will create a system where tribalism and paternalism no longer prevail. A system that espouses order and predictability over the vagaries of whim and sentiment. By adhering to the principles of objectivity and rationality I will create the foundations for a modern bureaucracy in Iran."

I can see Firouz walking out of the library and into the sunshine in great strides, breathing deep. Walking past Hieronymus Bosch and William Carlos Williams, past Thomas Wolfe and Lionel Trilling, past Jorge Luis Borges and René Magritte, past Marcel Duchamp and Lao Tzu, none of whom he would ever learn to appreciate.

"When I returned to my cubicle," his letter continued, "I

saw Weber with fresh eyes. I had the desire and the patience to understand the distinctions between purposeful rationality, value-oriented rationality, affective or traditional action. I wanted to understand what was meant by the sociology of religion, economic rationality, interpretive understanding, or value relevance."

He knew these things when he took his comprehensives. On that day he even established a convincing command of the German language that he promptly relinquished. More importantly, he had found a mission, a goal and a purpose that would continue long after his brief command of German and his demonstrated understanding of Weber would be reduced to a few key phrases and a couple of undecipherable platitudes. He walked out of that library with a burning desire to implement the most amazing bureaucracy.

"The kind of bureaucracy that is the foundation and the benchmark of every modern society. A bureaucracy based on professionalism and merit, the bureaucracy that Max Weber envisioned. A bureaucracy that 'depersonalizes itself,' that achieves 'calculability of results.' This is the road to Iran's advancement." He asserted in a flowing hand.

It was a rather unlikely flying carpet, an odd bronze ring, a peculiar tinderbox that Firouz latched onto to free the Persian princess. But I had seen more fantastic talismans. Blue beasts, brightly coloured beans and dark mirrors, walk-through wardrobes, invisible cloaks, feathered caps and seven league boots. Bulldogs with eyes the size of saucers, pumpkins, cabbages and golden apples, wounded rabbits and star children, blind beggarwomen and leprous beggarmen. Why not an academic treatise?

In his enthusiasm Firouz strode out of the library and straight to professor Grava, the closest thing he had to a mentor. There was something about his walrus-moustache-gruffness that Firouz admired immensely in the effete setting of ivy-clad gothic towers. That and his deadpan delivery of the most iconoclastic statements. "There has been no significant scholarship on that particular subject for the past twenty years," Grava was fond of saying. "Given that, I prefer to stick to my own ignorance rather than subscribe to someone else's."

Firouz admired him from a distance and attended every course this mountain of a professor offered. But he never received more than a brusque reply to the theories he propounded. In response, Grava would wipe the chalk off his Slavic fingers, adjust his polka-dotted bow tie, dismiss Firouz's high minded idealism with, "Be that as it may," and proceed to reiterate some eminently banal and cynical statement—"As you peel away the layers of our existence, you never arrive at the heart of the matter: We are onions, not avocados."

On this particular Tuesday afternoon between two and four Firouz walked excitedly into Grava's office to share his discovery with the man who had given him the keys to a brilliant future grounded in a social-historical context, the path of which could not be denied. Professor Grava heard him breathlessly explain his position, agreed with him on the soundness of his argument, the logic in what he said, and asked, "So what do you want to do this for? Why are you on this crusade to create a bureaucracy made on efficient discernible principles with 'predictability of results' like your friend Max Weber wanted? You know Weber never founded a bureaucracy. He wrote books."

Without a moment's hesitation Firouz responded, "To help my people, the Iranian people."

"If you want truly to help your people," the gruff Slav replied with a line he must have used on more than one occasion, "go and sell them shoes." And then, by means of explanation, "Public policy is most often misguided, misdirected, misspelt, and misapplied. People always need shoes."

Somewhat deflated, Firouz walked out of the office, shook his head, and muttered *"ablah,"* which can be most accurately translated as "idiot." He dismissed his professor for a cynical old fool, and resolved to pursue the path that could only take him and his country to glory.

16

Drinking deeply of the land and the people, he immersed himself in America. If you asked him why, he would have said, "In order to understand a great nation's success." But Firouz was no sociologist, nor was this a controlled experiment to distill the active ingredients of a great society. It was just that in America he felt at home.

He was at home. Nowhere else in the world would he ever encounter the feeling that this was where he belonged. Not if the wall he was leaning against gave way to reveal a lost kingdom with his likeness imprinted on golden coins. Not if he plucked up his courage and followed the bluebird through the waterfall. Not even if he "sailed back over a year, and in and out of weeks, and through a day, and into the night of his very own room."

Nowhere else would he encounter the Frank-Capra-man-on-the-street-respect-for-humanity he loved. Every time professors and presidents were called by their first names, he smiled to himself. Every time politicians were asked to account for their actions by the common man, Firouz revelled in the beauty of the system. Every time the downtrodden raised their heads, clamoured for justice, and obtained it, Firouz rejoiced. Even after the day he walked into the Uneeda restaurant to be met with stony cold glances, an uncomfortable and sudden silence, and a waitress who never actually made it to his table, America was a place where he could have lived for the rest of his life.

Even the Iranians who married women named Mary Jane, Susan and Gwendolyn, the ones who lived out their lives in Ann Arbor, Bethesda, and Boulder never loved America as Firouz did. They never really appreciated her for more than the two-car-garage quality of life she afforded them. But he loved her, and devoted himself to her, if only for that summer when he wasn't taking courses to graduate early. The summer he worked at the factory installing one of the forty-seven pieces that make up a Chevy car door. Taking the elevated out at five a.m. to arrive just as the graveyard shift was getting out, bleary-eyed.

He loved the walk to the factory at the first break of dawn. Striding through the street with the swelling masses of workers from all over the world, all wearing the same work-blue blue work uniform.

"You gotta get the money," Joe Coles had told him, and that is exactly what he did. He worked the early shift, willingly went in on weekends and holidays, and in an act of superhuman effort, sold encyclopaedias door to door after he got off. At the end of the summer of '55 he had saved the unimaginable fortune of five thousand three hundred twenty-two dollars. At a time when you could buy a new two-tone red and white Bel Air with a V8 engine, loads of chrome, and whitewall tires for thirty-five hundred dollars. He could have walked onto the lot and driven off with the Bel Air. But he didn't. He saved his money during the week, and on the weekends he scrubbed off the smell of the factory, and, while shaving, recited Sandburg's lines to the mirror:

Of my city the worst that men will say is this:
You took little children away from the sun and the dew,
And the glimmers that played in the grass under the great
    sky,
And the reckless rain; you put them between walls
To work, broken and smothered, for bread and wages,
To eat dust in their throats and die empty-hearted
For a little handful of pay on a few Saturday nights.

On more than a few Saturday nights he shed his work-blue uniform, brilliantined his hair, put on a jacket and tie, took a date out to dinner and resolved not to die empty hearted "at least not tonight." After dessert, he would lean back and repeat an expression he had heard Joe Coles use while puffing on a cigar, "I wonder what the poor folks in Brooklyn is doin' now."

At other times he would borrow a car and take his date for a ride in the country to watch the harvesters cut swaths through grain fields. He never ceased to be amazed at the neatly bundled packages they left in their wake. He would turn on the radio, hoping to sing along with "Darling je vous aime beacoup, je ne sais pas what to do," or "Goodnight Irene." But his favourite was "Every time we say goodbye I die ... a little." He would sing along with such sincerity that it never failed to endear him to the woman in the passenger's seat, as he blatantly overextended the pregnant pause between "die" and "a little," and put his arm around her shoulder.

Sometimes he would go out of his way to drive through apple orchards to see line after line after line of trees whizzing past in rapid succession, and then that wonderful moment when time stopped as the diagonals ran their way to infinity.

"Don't you love it when that happens," he would say to the woman by his side. And then he might mumble, "It's kind of like imposing order on the chaos of the universe." He had heard the theory that this was our role in the world in a Shakespeare class. He had taken it to heart, and had made the mistake of sharing his conviction with Shahriar whose response was to blow smoke rings and intone, "I am imposing order on the chaos of the universe."

At times, Firouz would share that story with the woman in the passenger's seat, fumbling through Beirut and the classmates so alien to his Illinois existence. More often, he kept it to himself.

17

He was quite popular on campus and had a string of admirers. There was Irena the violinist who wept at the sight of beauty, and Martha the librarian who sent him love letters on the jacket covers of recently arrived books like *The Battle of Britain,* or *Psychology Made Simple,* and Mary Helen the French major who tried, without luck, to make him appreciate the New Wave. Confident in his popularity and his chances for success he applied himself to perfecting the art of seduction.

He could always find a date for a movie, a dinner, a play, or a drive in the country. Like many men he was content with the physical evidence. Asking no further questions, he never understood that the art of seduction is more than an arm around a shoulder, a kiss on a doorstep, an autumn afternoon spent under a chestnut tree. He never quite understood that in seduction the object of one's affections is caressed, coaxed, enticed to reveal their innermost, secret beauty, the very essence of their being. And in the act of being seduced, blossoms. He never quite understood that one can seduce, that one can draw out and hold the most dazzling beauty without a roll in the hay. That at times a sideways look, a tremor in the voice, the manner of drawing deep on a cigarette, were all one could ever desire.

To the very end he never understood, and so he preoccupied himself instead with the physical evidence. And when things got out of hand, as they sometimes did, he engaged in what can only be called a "unilateral withdrawal." "It's the only noble thing to do," he explained to Joe Coles. "I can't lead them on, no matter how much they think they love me, no matter what they think they can put up with for love. They can never live in Iran. I know that. They couldn't survive for a minute without the comforts they're used to, the basic luxuries they take for granted, now could they? No, seriously, do you think they could survive in Iran? I know what it means to live like that. It's out of the question." He was convinced that there was not one of them who could live with him in Iran. So when things went a little too far, he was better off nipping the relationship in the bud rather than letting it proceed to its ultimate, logical and painful conclusion. "You can see that, Joe, can't you?"

"Opera ain't nothin' but the blues, excep' in Italian," Joe responded, shrugging his shoulders. And I've always loved him for that reply.

Firouz was going back. No matter how corrupt, no matter how difficult, no matter how hopeless. No matter how comfortable he felt in America. Not automatic garage door and In-Sink-Erator comfort, but the comfort of being with decent, civic-minded people. He was going back, even after that summer when he tasted his dreams and became the American he had always aspired to be, the citizen that in so many ways he had always been.

In preparation for his return, he took to voraciously reading the Western accounts of Iran that he would collect for the rest of his life. I must admit, I was at least partly to blame. After all, I did send him that copy of *Queer Things About Persia* by Eustache de Lorey and Douglas Sladen. I'm really not sure why. Perhaps it was in repayment for his Modern Library version of *The Idiot* that continued to grace my bookshelves.

The travelogue had been given me by a much older cousin who started his education at a military school in Vienna at the ripe age of six, and who maintained that all he ever needed to know of the Oriental mind came from repeated readings of Sir H.A.R. Gibb. No H.A.R. Gibb, de Lorey had been stationed in Iran with the French Consulate, while Sladen's previous "literary contribution" had been to author a book on *Queer Things About Japan*.

But the book had come from my cousin for whom the world was divided into two primary exigencies that best found expression in the system he devised for summoning servants to his bedroom on the fourth floor of the chancery in Belgrade. He contrived to have a buzzer installed at his bedside and had developed a kind of abbreviated Morse code. One ring for a whiskey-soda, two rings for everything else.

That copy of *Queer Things About Persia* initiated a search that led Firouz through *The Land of the Lion and the Sun, Toward the Peacock Throne, Across Coveted Lands* and countless others. In each and every one, no matter how poorly written, no matter how inaccurate, no matter how clichéd, he always found a line, a phrase, a fragment of poetry, a story, an image that he dutifully transcribed in a little black book.

Of the hundreds of thousands of sentences he read in any given book, he would choose a handful he preserved for posterity, commending everything else to oblivion. "I have not made one complaint against fortune since I know she acts under compulsion. The one thing which from time to time troubles me is my longing for Lahore," he wrote in a flowing hand, just as he transcribed Field Marshal Van der Goetz Pasha's then famous line, "Anarchy in Persia: nothing to be done: dust, cupidity and cowardice."

He meticulously entered sentences that confirmed what he had sensed long ago, or that provided him with a particularly lucid insight. In a casual perusal it was difficult to discern which of these guiding principles might be at play in any given passage. To understand whether he truly believed the words or if they were accompanied by a rolling of his eyes, a knowing glance to an invisible co-conspirator. All the reader had to work with was the passage itself: "A Russian puts on a hat, a tight coat and tight breeches, shaves his beard, and then calls himself a European. You might as well tie the wings of a goose to your back and call yourself an angel." Or "Despite all their concern for carefully preserving things, Iranians throw away with the profligacy of kings what other people consider valuable: time, energy, and so many, many human lives."

Without marginal notes, the reader was at a loss in trying to understand what prompted him to write, "Once more I try, and my imagination droops before the task of discovering how any human being could find in this refuse of the world's creation the peace for which his soul longs."

Sometimes he would make notes of simple facts, dates and numbers. To my surprise, at other times he would transcribe stories that only found value when re-told by foreigners. Like the thirty small and ordinary birds that went off in search of the terrifying bird the *Seemorgh* to rescue them from some untenable situation. And how, having failed in their quest, they finally realized that the legendary bird was no more than *see* (thirty) *morgh* (birds), that together they formed the magical and powerful beast.

When I asked him, "Firouz, how is it that you decided now to transcribe a story you wouldn't read as a child," he surprised my by saying, "It reminds me of the only story I ever remember my father telling me, the story of the princes and the breaking of the faggots. 'Here, try this,' my father instructed me. 'Try to break this one, and now this one. See how easy it is. Now try to break all four together. You can't, can you? We've got to stick together. They can never break us if we stick together.'" It was the other lesson he grudgingly learned from his father.

In his little black book he entered that story and the story of a king who was such an excellent marksman that he could tie a deer's foot to its ear. With the first arrow Bahram ever so faintly tickled the deer's ear, and when the deer extended a hind leg to scratch it, his second arrow sewed them together. But when Golandam failed to marvel at her lover's abilities and remarked that anyone who applied herself could do the same, he lost his temper and sent her away.

Years later, Bahram came upon a woman climbing a staircase with a full-grown cow on her shoulders. Astonished, he inquired how such a thing was possible, to which she replied, "I have climbed these stairs every day since this cow was a calf, and with practice and perseverance I can now carry the cow you see before you." The king clapped his hands, and offered her any reward she wanted, which Golandam declined, saying, "In my beauty and youth you spurned my love. You were too proud to hear me. I do not need your gold or silver, this moment is reward enough."

It was only by following Firouz's own life story that one could discern whether Bahram and Golandam were there for him to recognize and cherish love over his own damn pride, or to daily and minutely increase his load to finally carry the cow.

19

From a simple reading of the entries it never was quite clear what any of it meant to him. Obviously they were important because even when he was collecting editions across four continents, even when books overflowed from his reading rooms and bookcases into bedrooms and boudoirs, out of shelves and onto desks and tables, he never ceased to transcribe the words he somehow found significant. Yet there were no tear-stained passages, no well-thumbed pages, no rose petals embellishing favourite spots.

There was only one key to deciphering the words in the little black books seldom opened after they were filled. And that was the story of Firouz's life. The words and the parts, the plot and the play. The dénouement of fulfilled and unfulfilled promise.

It was as if his life and the words in the little black books were inextricably interwoven. As if the passages he transcribed from random books culled from random libraries, bookstores and auction houses somehow not only reflected his desire, but propelled it, propelled him on the trajectory to his fulfilment and to the dissolution that would inevitably follow.

It was as if the words themselves held power, like in the days when palliative prescriptions were dissolved in water and drunk by ailing patients to effect a cure. As Firouz drank in the words, the only remedy he sought was to obtain some understanding of why in the world he loved this country to the point where he would leave a land of opportunity for a land with so little hope.

He was a logical man, and the arguments of nationality and birth were simply fallacious. He needed more than that. He had lived almost half his life outside the country, family was practically non-existent, his classmates scattered, and however much he liked the poetic gardener and the occasional provincial cousin, they simply weren't enough to justify his misguided mission. There must have been something more than the accident of birth to justify a lifetime of devotion to a country that could only defeat, break, and promptly forget him as it had every other person who had attempted to bring it progress. History was littered with the names of those who had tried and failed in the process. Or those who simply diverted their energies to the mundane pursuit of amassing money.

But like so many of us, he did return, leaving the very day he handed in his last paper and took his last exam. He never moved the tassel from one side to the other, shook no hands, received no awards, made no speeches. In the course of an hour or two he packed his bag and walked to the station, careful not to break a sweat on the incline. He took the bus to the airport, and left the most magical world imaginable to return to Iran.

Toward the end, he had been distracted, impatient, pacing his room, anxious to leave. "What is it that makes you look through people as if they don't exist," a lover once asked, and he never quite understood how it was that she had known. He had tried his best to be present, polite, and engaging. He mumbled some denial and resolved to improve on the dissimulation of his feelings. But it was true, he had his sights set on Iran, and as the date of his departure approached, there was little else he allowed himself to see.

20

While Firouz prepared himself in Chicago for his brilliant career and I learned to design drive-through banks and diners, Nur ed Din returned to Tehran to sit at his uncle's proverbial feet, preparing himself for the day he would assume the mantle of the messenger. Uncle Mustafa prescribed a course-load that consisted of a good dose of herbal medicine, a smattering of Descartes, and extensive readings from the Quran. In addition to these, he shared with Nur ed Din the lessons culled from more than fifty poignant years as spiritual leader and confidant.

"The ailments of the human body are not difficult to diagnose," he would say, "for those they can go to any doctor. Those disorders can be addressed by drinking eight glasses of water a day, consuming a clove of garlic every morning, or a glass of whiskey before retiring. That is not why people come to us. They come for ailments of the spirit. But do not be misled. Often sickness of the spirit is mistaken for an ailment of the body. It is at times like these you must first prescribe cardamom for shortness of breath, violet flowers and pears as a laxative, or ginger to increase the appetite." Uncle Mustafa would list the herbs and their effects on various illnesses at some length before coming to the point. "But if the sickness of the body is an ailment of the heart, it will make no difference how much laudanum, opium or baba au rhum you prescribe. Nur ed Din, listen carefully because you must be able to distinguish the ailments of the heart, and above all, you will need to be able to tell when your patients suffer from love-sickness."

Uncle Mustafa would then proceed to tell the story of the Great Hakim and the melancholy king, prefacing his remarks, "I know you have heard this story before, but believe me, before I am finished with you, you will hear it again. The Hakim, who had established a reputation as a learned physician though he was a man who above all else loved wine and women, was summoned one day to the court of a king who suffered from melancholia. Physicians and soothsayers had tried everything to cure the king, prescribing all that one prescribes for melancholy—lavender, lilac water and infusion of chamomile—to no effect. At their wits' end, they finally resigned themselves to summoning the Hakim.

"Noting the listless eyes, the white tongue, the Hakim engaged the king in casual conversation. He spoke of the weather, of the war in Bukhara, of the crops and of the great poets. At the mention of poetry, he noticed, or was he mistaken, a quickening of the king's pulse. He made some other observation, maybe recited a verse or two from the poet of choice for forlorn lovers, and confirmed his suspicions." At this point in the story, Uncle Mustafa would quote poetry. Oddly, he would never recite the same verses.

Uncle Mustafa would then continue, "He knew he was on the right track when the king's pulse quickened at the mention of the beloved. Having deduced the king's ailment, over the course of the next few days the Hakim casually recited the names of flowers, Laleh, Maryam, Narges, Niloofar, Banaf-sheh, interspersing them with the names of the Prophet's wives and daughters, Khadijeh, Massoumeh, Zahra, Ayesheh, and Ameneh. Finally he hit upon the beloved's name. Similarly, he established the city in which she lived. Having found the cause for the king's malady, he contrived to cure the king by uniting the sufferer with the beloved."

It was a story I had heard before and Nur ed Din would hear again punctuated by prodigal sons and principled pros-titutes—the stories drawn from Uncle Mustafa's own experi-ences. It was a story Uncle Mustafa professed to love because of the Hakim's powers of deduction. But there was more to it than that. He loved it because it was the story of a wonder-ful success.

Though Mustafa had relieved many sufferings, though he had shown compassion and understanding, though he had provided insights into innumerable ailments, he had never cured the melancholy king. He was plagued, instead, by his one great failure. It was a failure he carried with him day in and day out and that sometimes surfaced in the most unlikely places.

As it turns out, Uncle Mustafa once had an older brother, a brother he looked up to, a brother taller and more handsome than he. A brother who was to have inherited the spiritual leadership of the flock. It just so happened that one day the brother left on a voyage with his wife. People leave every day. Trains, planes, and buses depart every day, there is nothing extraordinary about that. But on the day of the departure the brothers had a falling out. Mustafa never said what it was about, maintained it had been over a trifling matter. In retrospect it probably was. But neither one had been willing to concede, to kiss and make up.

Mustafa had let his brother walk out the door without swallowing his pride, without for a moment forgetting who was right, whose arguments were more convincing, or why anyone should care. Mustafa's last memory of his brother was not an embrace, a smile or a wave as the train pulled out of the station and slowly picked up speed, but a formal and strained goodbye.

They were brothers. They loved each other. But on that day they had a falling out. Trains, planes and buses depart every day, and every day they return. But Mustafa's brother never returned. The last memory Mustafa had of his brother alive was of that cold and painful goodbye.

It was the single greatest failure of his life. He taught numerous lessons with varying degrees of eloquence, but the lesson of the goodbyes was one that resounded each and every time he told it, every time he imprecated a brother, sister, wife, husband, lover, son, or daughter not to let their loved one leave angry, not to let them walk away like that, not to suffer a lifetime of remorse.

21

Throughout the week, Nur ed Din pursued his studies, dutifully did his readings, and looked forward to Tuesday afternoons. For on Tuesdays, those of Mustafa's congregation with questions to ask or petitions to present to the Divine knew they would find him at home. They would be sure to share a cup of tea or a glass of *sharbat,* and if they had a question not to be discussed in a larger group, were assured that at one point he would rise, don his mantle, beckon, and take them on a stroll through the garden.

The questions discussed in Uncle Mustafa's sitting room

were mundane—arranged marriages and love marriages, debts owed and how to pay, debts owed and how to collect, how to make ends meet, and the question from a persistent young man with fair hair who would ask sincerely, "And at the end of it all, then what?" Nur ed Din loved the erudition of his Uncle Mustafa's answers, the lines quoted from the Quran and from Hafez. But more than the debates in the sitting room, Nur ed Din looked forward to those times when he was invited to join his uncle in the garden.

Sometimes Uncle Mustafa would signal Nur ed Din with a wink. Then Nur ed Din would walk tiled pathways two steps behind petitioners as they unburdened their hearts, telling of desires, betrayals, needs they could never tell their loved ones. He listened to the stories he longed to repeat, and the ones he wished he had never heard. And he never ceased to be amazed at his uncle's amazing facility in consoling the broken-hearted.

Nur ed Din looked forward to Tuesdays when his uncle dealt with quotidian problems in the sitting room and perennial problems in the courtyard. He looked forward to Tuesdays, but even more so to feast days when they would sprinkle water and sweep the yard, scatter rose petals and put out chairs as the congregation gathered to pay their respects. Then Nur ed Din would finally see the faces of love and its reversals. And try his best to discern the traits attributed by husbands, wives and lovers.

He loved the feast days, but he lived for that day when he and a whole city forgot the ebb and flow of money made, money spent and money owed, and for a day, an afternoon, an evening, lost themselves in the rhythm of an endless sea of black. He lived for *Ashoura* when the city of Tehran lost itself in remorse, perhaps for the blood of a prophet's grandson shed in the harsh plains of Karbala. Or perhaps for the loves lost, the graces forsaken, the exuberance slowly dissipated or chiselled away day after day in their own lives.

He lived for *Ashoura* when the entire city dressed from head to toe in black and walked the streets beating chests and backs with chains, chanting time-worn verses, lamenting the death of Ali Ibn Abi Talib's son, the Prophet Muhammad's grandson Hussein who had been trapped in the desert with his family and followers to die of thirst or be slaughtered by the vast forces of the bloodthirsty Yazid. Yazid who had rejoiced when they brought him Hussein's severed head, until one of the elders admonished him, "I have often seen that face kissed by the Prophet's lips."

Ashoura meant sharing in the trampling of the beheaded body, in the severed head and the lips that continued to recite the Quran even after death. In the unquenched thirst. In the agony of nephews, nieces and children killed off one by one. In a moment of ecstasy for a pain that transcended anything he would ever feel, Nur ed Din might even take a dagger and let the blood flow down his face.

"Neither generals nor governors came to his aid. No one came to his aid," Nur ed Din found himself chanting over and over again. Forgetting time and place. Aware only of the sound of hands striking hollow chests, and that pregnant silence before thousands of hands descended on thousands of chests. No, the powerful did not come to his rescue. They never did. Hussein and his family had died in the plains of Karbala thirsty and within sight of the oasis, picked off one by one by Yazid's army until they finally sallied forth to be slaughtered.

To this day devotees of Hussein have pity on any creature facing death, making sure that at least it does not die thirsty.

"Abbas my uncle I don't want any water," Nur ed Din found himself chanting on this particular *Ashoura*, reiterating the entreaties of Hussein's poor parched children. As thousands of chains struck thousands of shoulders. As thousands of hands beat thousands of chests. No, they did not want any water. Not if it meant Uncle Abbas going forth to have a hand cut off, an arm severed, to die pierced with arrows, clenching the flask with his teeth as precious water spilled pathetically onto the sand. No, of course I do not want any water, Uncle Abbas.

As Nur ed Din walked in this sea of black, this sea of heavy hands falling with resounding thuds on hollow chests, this sea of dull sobbing and wailing pierced every so often by a shrill cry, he thought of how distant the affairs of the world were. How this sorrow was greater than all the sorrows in our lives, how the mourners for the death of Hussein did not mourn this way for the deaths of their own husbands, wives, mothers and fathers.

But as he looked around, Nur ed Din surprised himself in observing that even in this moment the vendor on the corner was still preoccupied with short-changing his customers on the liver and kidney kababs. The man walking by his side was still concerned with the part in his hair and his position in society. And the eligible young women on second storey balconies were still making eyes at the devoted men so fervently pounding their chests.

Right there on the second and third floor balconies as they wailed, beat their chests, and rent their garments, they were picking out their men. There was even one, dark complected, with a beauty mark (he had seen her somewhere before, but where), looking straight at him. In between blows to her head, face, and chest, she was gesturing with her hands. But they weren't gestures. They were numbers … six … thud … four … thud … nine … thud … four … thud … nine … thud thud thud. Six four nine four nine she signed one more time as the crowd implored Abbas not to go. Six four nine four nine as the children denied their thirst. Nur ed Din was dumbfounded. On the most sacred day of the year, he had just been singled out from a second storey balcony and given a telephone number by the young woman with the beauty mark. Six four nine four nine. He looked around to see if anyone else had noticed, and turned to catch her eye one more time. A crow flew off a telephone pole. "Abdullah," a woman's voice called in the distance, "Abdullah." Six four nine four nine her eyes said, as he was swept away.

22

"Who would be so forward as to sign me her telephone number on the most sacred day of the year?" Nur ed Din asked himself the following day as he walked the streets, appalled. Wondering if he should call. "But I don't even know her name," he thought to himself. "Well, there is only one way to find out," he resolved as he crossed and recrossed streets, turned around, retraced his steps.

But his wanderings only seemed aimless. He always set out with a particular destination in mind, faithfully pursued it until something he saw, something he remembered, something he had forgotten pulled him in a new direction. Of course he faithfully pursued the new destination until the next urge pulled him some other way or found him retracing his footsteps. As he did, he thought of the woman with the beauty mark, and where he had seen her before.

It perplexed him that he couldn't quite figure out who she was. Passing the American College he remarked that the field where he used to dance his way to the goal, that patch of dust in the middle of a rock-strewn wasteland, had been paved over to make way for houses and apartments. The school buildings were still there, as were the bull and griffin columns of Anoushirvan Dadgar Girls' School. Maybe she was one of those who showed up when school let out. Like that girl he would see at his soccer matches. At first he had been surprised to spot her among the spectators, but soon learned to look for her in the stands.

He turned right and walked up Pahlavi Avenue, under the arch of entangled and entwined branches. He stopped at Bamdad's and reflected that he had never had anything other than blackberry ice cream there. He had liked it so much that he really saw no reason to try any other.

Ice cream in hand he took the left on Bozorgmehr Street, and passed a window at which he used to throw stones late at night, after almost everyone had fallen asleep. What had become of the excitement he used to feel while walking down that street? In the beginning he used to pass by at odd hours of the day and night just on the chance that he might see her. He would go out of his way to walk by her room, or stop by the juice seller's across the street, hoping she might look out the window and see him casually sipping carrot juice. The juice-seller, who had caught on, used to joke, "Young man, I am running out of carrots, should I double my regular order, or do you think you might propose to her in the next couple of weeks?"

Later, he would anxiously anticipate the pre-arranged meetings when he would throw pebbles at her window and listen for the sound of her footsteps on the stairs. But one day she told him it would be better if he would not drop by so often, and a month or two later she married that forty-year old engineer with the black Mercedes 180. Nur ed Din still thought of her from time to time.

With determined strides he made his way past her house, and lingered under the king's permanently benevolent gaze at the café on the square. As he looked down the street that ran straight and wide, he reflected that at the turn of the century Nasser ed Din Shah had intended to build a boulevard in imitation of the ones he had seen in Paris, but there had been a public outcry so severe that the Pivot of the Universe, was dissuaded from pursuing his ambition. Straight streets, it seems, would have removed one of the signs of the Mahdi's final coming.

"Now people have forgotten that this world is only temporary," he remarked to himself, "that it is only in keeping for the One who disappeared down that well and will return when the signs are in place. In the old days kings kept stallions saddled in silver and gold, day and night for the Mahdi, for his imminent and welcome return. In the not-so-distant past kings paid rent on their palaces to the twelfth Imam through his intermediaries on earth. And now people are preoccupied only with the affairs of this world. They have forgotten every single sign of his return."

"Like the girl with the beauty mark. Where have I seen her?" He racked his memory but couldn't quite remember. But it really didn't matter. Because right there, sitting on the park bench, having her fortune told by an itinerant gypsy, was the woman with the beauty mark. She was smiling most charmingly and laughing at whatever it was the fortune teller was inventing. He hesitated for a moment, debating whether or not to approach her. At precisely that moment she looked up and their eyes met.

"She may have seen the hesitation in my step," he thought as he took a more resolute stride in her direction. As she paid off the gypsy. As he walked over to her, making sure not to change his gait. "I'm sorry to disturb you," he said, "but I believe I saw you on the balcony overlooking the square the other day. You were gesturing something with your hands. I think it was six four nine four nine. I'm sorry to be so forward, but I do believe it was you. It was you, wasn't it?" The girl could not help but to laugh at the earnestness in his voice and the directness of his question. Shaking her head, she responded, "Is this the way you are these days Nur ed Din? Not so much as a 'hello' or 'how do you do.' No inquiries after health or family, no 'how are you doing?' no 'where have you been?' Straight to the exchange of telephone numbers. Is that a way to address an old friend?"

Visibly taken aback, Nur ed Din racked his brain but could not come up with anything more than a feeling that he had seen her before. And what was she saying anyway? She was the one who had spelled out her telephone number between blows to her breast on the holiest day of the year. "She should have been flattered that I knew the number by heart," he assured himself. At a loss for words, he registered a playful frown that he would grow to love, a pouting of her lips that he would learn to evoke, as she continued, "You don't remember me, do you?"

A drowning man desperately hoping his life would flash before his eyes, Nur ed Din fumbled again through memory to find that one vital piece of information that could save him. Giving himself up to the ultramarine tranquillity that continued as far as the eye could see, he heard her say, "We met when we were both young. Before you went to Beirut. I lived at the house on the corner of Villa Avenue and was named after the white plaster angel under the awning. We spent the summers together. Don't you remember? You almost died when that branch broke."

Nur ed Din remembered hitting the ground hard, remembered lying on his back gasping for breath, remembered the odd sensation of not being able to breathe, of wondering if this was the way it would all end. But it wasn't on Villa Avenue, it was in the village of Damavand. He racked his brain once again, and failed to come up with anything that might save his life.

Oblivious to it all, Fereshteh said finally, "But I really do have to go, I'm already late. At least you have managed to remember my phone number. Please give me a call. I'm going to the Caspian for a couple of weeks." And then with a laugh, "I'll be back soon, and my house on Villa Avenue is now a restaurant. If you like, you can take me to dinner on the fourteenth of next month."

Nur ed Din collected himself, said goodbye to Fereshteh, and began to count the days to the fourteenth.

23

Later, when Nur ed Din and Fereshteh walked the streets together, she would be taken for a foreigner. She bore the raven black hair, almond eyes and olive complexion of the ideal Iranian "type," but was invariably taken for Italian, French or even American. No one could believe that an Iranian woman would laugh with so little restraint, with such apparent enjoyment in a public place. And especially not in the street.

"But my, how she has managed to learn our language; not even the hint of an accent," shopkeepers, itinerant vendors, and beggars would remark to Firouz as she bought steaming hot beets on the side of the road, or stopped to put more than a few coins in the begging bowls of the blind, crippled, and destitute. She, in turn, would respond with peals of sparkling laughter.

On the night of the fourteenth she could not restrain herself. She kept on smiling, laughing her effervescent laugh as she asked him the question he couldn't answer. "Nur ed Din, do you remember me? Tell me the truth. Do you remember me Nur ed Din?"

He responded with the lines he had prepared, "Do you know that when I set eyes on you the other day, I thought to myself, I know this woman. There's something about her smile and the beauty mark on her cheek. I must have seen her before somewhere, perhaps in a dream. And then you signed your telephone number from the balcony."

"Of course I gave you my number, but we met long before," Fereshteh responded, disregarding the compliment, and failing to hide the disappointment in her voice. "Don't you remember the horse chestnut tree you played in when you were a boy? You said you could see all the way to the Caspian and reported on storms, shipwrecks, and, correct me if I'm wrong, a dead man who washed up with a string of pearls around his neck and nothing in his pockets but a black diamond, a blue sea-emerald, and a rose ruby.

"We didn't believe you for a minute, but we loved your stories. If you don't remember me, you must remember my brother Farhad. His favourite game was to cross the stream without getting wet. Except he was much too small to ever jump across it, so he threw the rocks that fit in his fist into the water, hoping to make a bridge. And you tossed in the boulders he could never budge, with a huge splash. Do you remember the look in his eyes? It was as if you were the warrior Rostam when you lifted those rocks over your head."

Nur ed Din remembered. Of course Nur ed Din

remembered. Those summer days spent in the village in the shadow of the volcano were the most cherished moments of his childhood. Days spent wandering through apple and sour cherry orchards, horse pastures, wild flower and honey fields. Watching palanquins and gold-earringed slaves, unsuspecting merchants and Andalusian castles move lazily across the sky.

Of course he remembered her. "My God, Feri, it's you. How could I not remember you? You made me kneel down on one knee and recite: 'I am but a humble fisherman, but the gift I bring, no king could give.' I don't think I ever quite recovered."

"So you do remember me after all," she replied, "I was worried you might have forgotten." "Yes, yes, of course I remember you. How could I forget? All through the school year I looked forward to seeing you and Farhad back in Damavand. But you weren't there the following summer. And then I went off to Beirut to study."

"I know, I know. I've kept up with you from a distance. When Narges told me she was seeing a Nur ed Din, I knew it must have been you. There aren't many Nur ed Dins around." And flicking her hair, "So you're still playing the romantic, throwing stones and breaking hearts." "Oh go on," he said with strained nonchalance, "I'm sure your friend had no difficulty moving right along without me." And then trying to interject humour, "In any case, I may have broken a window or two, but no hearts." "I guess you didn't, at least not that time. Narges was always looking to marry a man who would give her a wedding ring and two trips a year to Paris, with or without him."

Over dinner, Fereshteh pointed out where her room had once been, and with some urging, revealed the hiding place where no one had ever managed to find her. She showed him the smiling plaster angel she had been named after, the quince tree in the garden, the pool in the back where she used to keep Speedy and Spotty, her pet goldfish, and the fireplace mantel from which she had fallen to acquire the scar over her left eye. "But you can hardly see it," he assured her clumsily.

It was wonderful just sitting with her, listening to her stories, sharing the sparkle in her laugh. Recalling the Damavand summers and the luxury of watching time pass as the dung beetle pushed its prize across a patch of dirt. To lie in meadows that must have existed when the world was still young. It was wonderful to be with someone who understood the beauty of leaves that curled up with your touch, flowers that opened in the morning and closed as the sun went down, who understood that the brilliant red of the cardinal's fluttering wings was a divine blessing that exceeded any artifice man could ever achieve in rose-stained windows or blue-coloured tiles. To be with someone who might actually appreciate a blank piece of paper by way of explanation.

24

Within weeks Fereshteh and Nur ed Din grew so fond of one another they began to save their stories, as if it would be a betrayal to tell someone else. They looked forward to the moment when they could share the events of the day, an anecdote remembered from childhood, or some particularly poignant passage or poem.

On weekends they attended exhibits of lion goblets wrought in the softest gold, iridescent ceramics embellished with slant-eyed Mongols, silver Sassanian archers with curlicue beards, miniatures where lovers embraced and mountains hid the faces of men and beasts. Scenes that spilled over meticulously drawn borders. If there was a travelling show, they might see sculptures of fallen warriors, reclining nudes, and seated mothers.

On these excursions Fereshteh invariably gave the first beggar she encountered all the coins in her purse. "Be reasonable," Nur ed Din pleaded with her. "You can't give all your money to the first vagrant you come across." As a concession to reason, and against her instincts, she learned to exercise

just enough discipline to give every successive beggar a few
coins until her purse was empty. Then he would watch her
search her pockets for the coins she knew were not in her
purse. Moved by the moment, he would ask her to stay still
for a second as he wiped an imaginary eyelash off her cheek.

One day they went to a show of Japanese prints. In each
was a representation, a reflection, or a lunar reference, though
the prints were of blind warriors and blind poets, cherry blossoms and white-faced, mat-carrying street walkers, rotund
sons of dissolute Ronin. Honourable deaths more desirable
than life. Fereshteh found herself captivated by the image
of a woman gone mad with grief for a Samurai lover who
would never return. She wandered the streets with loosened
hair and bare feet, holding a parchment that spiralled toward
the crescent moon. The letter was tattered, the words torn,
smeared with tears, but some were still decipherable: "nature
conspired … lightning … moonrise … clouds … birthmark."
And Fereshteh thought to herself, "If I die tomorrow, he would
not even have a single letter to hold in his hands, to place in
his shirt pocket as he walked through the streets, reciting the
words by memory, occasionally taking it out to confirm that
he had got it exactly right, or just to see the words written
in my hand. To fold along well-worn creases and put back in
the pocket closest to his heart."

That night she slept restlessly, woke up long before morning and wrote him a letter. She thought to herself, "Some
things pulled out of sleeplessness shouldn't perhaps be sent."
But knowing she would not have the strength to send it in
the light of day, she put on the appropriate denomination of
lion and sun stamps and placed it in the mailbox.

It was a letter that captured the essence of the moments
they spent together. More than anything else, it captured the
fact that they were in love. Everyone else had known for weeks.
Strangers could walk into a cocktail party, onto a platform,
past a ticket line, and pick them out immediately. They were
the couple in love. But here she was giving expression to "the
warmth that wells up as I watch you come up the walk, the

restlessness with which I await your calls and comings, unable to do anything, to stay in one place for over a minute or two, without going to the window to see if you're there, even though I know you're halfway across town. Or the sudden need to see you and hear your voice that makes me jump up and leave the house after pushing it down as long as possible, furious because I fumbled the keys while locking the door, or because the taxi driver didn't speed through the yellow light."

She sent it off, "wishing you were here or we were both somewhere else," and waited for a reply.

25

Nur ed Din was puzzled to open the mailbox and find a letter written in her hand. Having just spent the afternoon with Fereshteh, his first response was anxiety, a natural response from getting one-too-many late night telephone calls, one-too-many summons to accidents outlined in chalk. It was with some understandable trepidation that he opened the letter. She had never written him before. But as he pored over the words "going to the window to see if you are there, even when I know you're half-way across town ... seeing you in every crowd, sure that it must be you from your build, the way you walk, until I get close enough to realize what I knew all along, that is not the way you hold your head, the hands are not quite right ..." he was swept away.

He wanted to rush into the street, to kiss the first person he met, to waltz the street-sweeper's broom through the streets, to take Fereshteh in his arms and spin her round and round until they both fell to the ground, breathless. To cover her with kisses. To kiss her cheeks, her lips, her eyelids. To kiss that beauty mark, the hands that had spelled out six four nine four nine. To kiss that charming smile, that quizzical look she sometimes had, the tilt of her head, the laughter that made them take her for a foreigner. To kiss the look of love in her eyes. He read the words, and read them again. Repeating to himself "the need to see you and hear your voice ..." he ran out into the street, to find Fereshteh and confirm what strangers had known all along.

When he finally did knock on her door clutching the letter in his hand, he took her in his arms and spun her round over the sound of her laughter and her coy questions, "What is it Nur ed Din, what is it?" knowing full well what it was. Spinning round and round, drunk with her laughter, he showered her with kisses until she took his face in her hands, looked him in the eyes, and kissed him. There was a perfection in that kiss that explains why carpet weavers alter one insignificant detail in their swirling paisleys and trees of heaven. They include a flaw from the fear of precisely such a perfection.

Later, when reflecting on that first kiss she would tease him, "I was the one who seduced you." To which he replied, "I had been kissing you for years." And while his sense of time was not entirely accurate, it was true that, in his manner, he had been making love to her since that first dinner. Recounting stories he was sure only she could understand. In his playful imitation of the way she moved her fingers when impatient, as if praying a rosary. Watching her as she walked so seriously, with such an overstated sense of purpose, while navigating crowds or crossing the street, in stark contrast to her playful nature.

He had, in his way, been kissing her for months if not years. But here he was engaged in an exquisite kiss from which he could barely disengage himself to explore her body, to revel in the warmth of her touch, in the softness of her skin. And then, slowly, suddenly, layers of clothing were shed, and he found himself making love. And still he was unable to take his eyes off her. "How come you keep looking at me? Don't you ever close your eyes when you make love?" she asked.

But he could not bear to look away from her even for a moment. Could not bear to tear himself away from the look in her eyes. From the exquisite line of her neck, the hollow that formed where the lines met. He loved the way that, when he stopped kissing her for a moment, she would continue to seek out the kiss that had been there moments before. And when he did not return to her soon enough, how she would open her eyes with a languid look of surprise, find him spying on her again, smile, and engage him in the kiss that had been so cruelly interrupted. And he would shower her lips, her eyes, her nose, her eyebrows, her cheeks, her laugh with kisses.

Lying in bed, running fingers through tussled hair, her head on his chest, he found himself asking, "What took you so long to write that letter?" She told him of the day they had gone to see the Japanese prints. Told him of the distraught face of the moon, the bare feet, the torn kimono and the spiralling letter. Her laughter sparkled as he responded, "But, darling, that exhibit arrived last winter. We could have gone months ago."

26

It was precisely as the epic of Nur ed Din and Fereshteh's romance was being played out in taxis and trains that Firouz reappeared. At his suggestion, Nur ed Din agreed to meet him at Moustache, the café they had longed to frequent as children. The melancholy proprietor with the prodigious moustache had long since passed away, "But if he isn't here," the present clean-shaven owner endearingly pointed out, "at least there is a picture or two of him." Scattered across the walls were studio photographs, several sketches and an oil of the man with the moustache in various stages of youth and age, dress and undress. And a snapshot of Monsieur Moustache, collarless and strangely formal, next to a blonde woman in a flower-print dress.

Nur ed Din arrived early and took a seat at a corner table. He smiled as young couples found eagles and camels in overturned cups. He watched as waiters greeted favoured customers by name and steered them to particularly well-placed tables.

He chuckled as favoured customers graciously responded to waiters' solicitous inquiries after health and family while meticulously wiping down the silverware. He wondered if Firouz had changed, if America had made a different man of him, and then assured himself that very little could ever change Firouz.

From his corner table he watched Firouz stride into the room, quietly saw him scan the restaurant, looking first this way and then that until his eyes finally set on Nur ed Din. Only then did Nur ed Din stand up and, arms extended, walk toward Firouz. They embraced. "You have not budged an inch, you haven't changed a hair since the day I saw you last," Firouz remarked, to which Nur ed Din responded with a laugh, "Don't believe it for a minute, a lot of water has passed under this bridge."

"How is your dear uncle Mustafa doing?" "And the famous gardener, is his one week of work up yet?" they bantered, until Firouz brought a quick end to the small talk and led the conversation to all that was wrong with Iran. Soon he began to gesticulate, "I am going to create a truly efficient bureaucracy, Nur ed Din, something that is based on a system, on reason." He expounded excitedly, neglecting to include his mentor's cautionary words about the shoe trade. "I am going to build a system that owes no allegiance to clan, that is egalitarian, that is predictable in its outcome. After all, a smoothly functioning bureaucracy is the hallmark of every great society. Look at what the British created in India. I know it's not an easy thing to do, but if we are ever to progress, we are going to have to look to the advanced nations of the world and learn to adopt those things that made them great. It's the only way. Have you ever read Max Weber?"

"No, Firouz, I haven't read Max Weber, but do you remember our friend Abolfazl, the one who wanted to become a doctor? Yes, yes, the one who fell madly in love with the Arab girl who refused every one of his advances. Don't look at me that way, just bear with me for a moment. You're right, she made a fool of him, bestowed her charms on everyone else, even Massoud Karim. Well, Abolfazl did become a doctor. Graduated with top honours from the University of Heidelberg. He came back and started a practice in some remote village. He could have made buckets of money in the city, but he wanted to help where it really counted.

"I went to visit him. As we were dining, there was a knock on the door. 'Please doctor, can you come right away, my little boy is burning up with fever.' 'I'm having dinner with a guest, can't you see that?' Abolfazl dismissed the poor villager. The man persisted, but Abolfazl would hear nothing of it. He sent him away again. 'Don't bother me with your problems, leave now and don't come back tonight if you know what's good for you.' When the villager finally left, I expressed my embarrassment and astonishment, 'Abolfazl, how could you send that poor man away, can't you see he is suffering, his child is in pain. Go help him, you can catch up with him if you leave now.' 'You're naïve,' he replied, serving himself another helping of rice. 'I have worked in this village now for six months. When I started I thought like you, but now I know better.

"'They are all suspicious, they don't listen to me, don't follow my prescriptions. At first I would see patients at any time of the day or night. Then I was pulled out of bed in the middle of the night to treat a young boy dying of pneumonia. The poor child could have been cured with a simple dose of penicillin if only they would have come to me sooner. I have a fridge full of penicillin,' he said, pointing to the refrigerator in the corner, visibly distraught. 'Look, there it is, nothing in it but penicillin. As it was, I couldn't bear to see the child suffer, so I gave him something to ease the pain. The following morning the boy was dead. They didn't say it to my face, but their looks, their glances accused me of killing the boy. They never come to me unless there is truly no hope left.

"'So I have learned not to go to the patient's deathbed when summoned. Instead I wait until the following morning. If the patient makes it through the night, then I figure there is a chance of recovery.' This is what Abolfazl, honours student from Heidelberg, has taken to doing. It is what you are going to have to deal with, Firouz, it is what we are all up against."

"But that was Abolfazl, what else could you expect?" Firouz observed, dismissing Nur ed Din's cautionary tale.

They both laughed. "All right, but don't let me find you with a fridge full of penicillin," Nur ed Din persisted. "Enough about Abolfazl, tell me about yourself," Firouz changed the subject. "What are your plans? Are you still intent on becoming spiritual leader when your dear uncle Mustafa, may his shadow never decrease, passes on?"

"Uncle Mustafa, bless his soul, is getting old and he has already told his followers that I will succeed him. I have learned so much from him. I'm constantly amazed at the insights he has into people's lives. I guess it's something you learn after fifty years of dealing with husbands and wives, widows and widowers. In any case, it's a responsibility that has been passed down in my family for generations, and when it comes to be my turn I will try to walk in Uncle Mustafa's footsteps. But Firouz, I'm really not sure if I'm cut out for this kind of work. I've asked my uncle to help me, to tell me what to do. Do you know what he said? He told me, 'Trust in Allah, He will give you a sign.' So I suppose when the time comes God will give me a sign. He has done so for every other member of the family; I don't see why he wouldn't do the same for me.

"But there is something I wanted to tell you," Nur ed Din continued, taking the letter out of his pocket. He had considered how to tell Firouz about Fereshteh, and had resolved that his own words would fail him. He might be interrupted by an ill-timed question from a waiter, get distracted as someone walked into the room or someone else walked out. He had given it some thought, and had finally resolved to show Firouz the letter. He handed Firouz the creased and folded piece of paper, and said, "There's something I want to tell you, but you've got to read this first."

"What have you been up to, you scoundrel," Firouz responded, "what is all this about?"

"Just read the letter," came the answer.

Firouz read the letter, and after he finished, he read it

again. "Who is she, where did you find her," he asked, and then remarked, "Actually, from the looks of it, I think she found you. And here I was thinking you were wasting your time in Iran."

Nur ed Din told Firouz of the telephone number and the balcony, the encounter at the park bench, how Fereshteh was always mistaken for a foreigner. Firouz interrupted him, shook his head to add a sense of drama, and repeated, "And here I was thinking you were wasting your time. As it turns out, you spent your time was much more productively than I thought." They looked at each other and laughed. In fact they could not stop laughing. Not after the couple at the next table asked for the check. Not after the waiter came by to inquire if there was anything else they might need.

27

Nur ed Din's stories of Heidelberg doctors notwithstanding, Firouz pursued his ambition. For Firouz there was one institution in all of Iran and that was the Plan Organization. To plan was rational, forward thinking, and logical. To organize, according to the dictionary of etymology, was to provide with organs, to systematize and form into a coordinated whole. Each of these words was wonderful; together they produced the Five Year Plans that determined which hospitals, stadia, rail lines, prisons and palaces would be built, which dams, super-highways, schools and museums designed, which factories financed, which tanks, hovercrafts, gunboats and jet planes purchased. It determined budgets for the Ministries and even for the Palace.

Firouz naturally set his sights on the Plan Organization, filled out his application, and attached his c.v. Confident in his abilities, he felt assured he would soon be offered a position of consequence. When he didn't hear back after almost a week, he returned to be told by a bureaucrat, "You are well-qualified, but everyone who applies here has an advanced degree from abroad. We are looking for a certain background and experience that I do not immediately see in your curriculum vitae. Have you considered a career in academia? I happen to know they are hiring at the University."

"However noble the concept of meritocracy, and it is a concept I firmly believe in, it is obvious that it has not quite made it to Iran," his father pontificated when, after some delay, he heard the news. "Firouz *jan,* I have very good contacts in high positions of government, people who would be glad to do whatever they can in launching your career. And," he hastened to add, "I also have some excellent contacts at Tehran University."

Though he seldom left his six by eight *hojreh* in the bazaar, his father did in fact have a great number of contacts. Among them was the assistant to the Assistant Minister of Agriculture. This individual, when asked his position, would invariably reply, "I serve, at his Majesty's discretion, as the assistant to ahem, ahem, assistant to the Minister of Agriculture," the well-timed cough removing one degree of separation from the illustrious Minister himself. Even this individual Firouz dutifully visited.

But when the assistant to the ahem ahem assistant Minister of Agriculture kept Firouz waiting for half an hour just to show how busy he ahem ahem was, and proceeded to turn his back on Firouz while delivering a soliloquy on the value of initiative, Firouz took him at his word and left the room. While the man who claimed he could launch Firouz's brilliant career paced up and down his less than significant office, Firouz, without so much as a by-your-leave, exited, smiled knowingly at the secretary on his way out and kept on walking.

Like a bored lover lackadaisically following up on any expressions of pleasure, Firouz feigned interest in the leads his father gave him, lazily pursued those he felt might be even remotely fruitful, and in between took long walks. Sometimes by himself, and sometimes with me.

28

I loved walking the streets of Tehran and looked forward to those days when I would walk them with Firouz. Having walked the same streets separately for years, having walked the streets of foreign cities together, it seemed appropriate that we should finally be walking the streets of Tehran together. I loved telling him the mud-and-brick stories of a city that once existed within adobe walls. The baroque stories of crenelated walls built to satisfy a Qajar king's fascination with things European. The stories of the streets that replaced those walls. And the bottomless well that petitioners threw letters into in the morning, waiting impatiently until dusk to see if they were answered in the evening paper.

On our walks I pointed out apartment buildings topped with miniature replicas of the Eiffel tower, and railway stations adorned with swastikas. Palladian Singer sewing machine showrooms. Museums built in imitation of Sassanian palaces, banks and gendarmeries that mimicked Achamenian ones. Putt-putt golf courses and Hot Shoppes. The streamlined stories of averted futures.

"Firouz," I said as we passed Cinema Niagara, "have you noticed that there seems to be a convention for naming cinemas. They are almost all named after popular resorts. There's the Riviera, the Capri and the Rivoli." Firouz shrugged his shoulders, seemingly preoccupied with crossing the street. "Wouldn't it be fun to tour the places that have cinemas named after them in Tehran? Perhaps we could start with Astara," I offered. "Sure," said Firouz. But we never did.

We did, however, happen to walk together past the plane tree under which the obese man used to sit. The one whose infinite folds of flesh forever defied my sense of anatomy and, I learned, confounded Firouz's understanding of the male physique as well.

Though some things remained inexplicably the same,

Tehran was changing. Wide, straight streets were being built, squares and circles embellished with muscular, hard-hatted dragon-slaying men. Gold, silver and bronze statues of his majesty in military uniform. There were boulevards, and avenues, circles and squares named after the king (Shah Avenue), the king's father (Shah Reza Avenue), the king's son (Vali-ahd Square), the king's family (Pahlavi Avenue), the king's title (Aryamehr Avenue), the king's past and current wives (Fawzia Square, Soraya Street and Farah Avenue), the occasional princess (Shahnaz Square) and loyal general (Sepah-bod Zahedi Avenue). Stalwart world leaders also graced the signposts: Roosevelt, Gandhi, Eisenhower, Churchill, Stalin and Queen Elizabeth II (Boulevard).

In the land of roses and nightingales, streets were also dedicated to poets. Saadi, Hafez, Ferdowsi and Khayyam all featured prominently. Some streets were named after significant dates known only to school children. And then there was the street name I loved best. "The thirty meter one," *sime-tri,* they called it, after its at that time unprecedented width. Though I found the idiocies and idiosyncrasies amusing, Firouz returned from these trips tired and spent. It pained him immensely to see banks and insurance companies being built, bus systems started, cooperatives developed, all without him. He felt a pang of remorse as ministries established headquarters and winced when television networks erected towers. He was especially distraught whenever a particularly brilliant decision was made without him. To torment himself further he would recall Macbeth's lines:

> I have no spur
> To prick the sides of my intent, but only
> Vaulting ambition, which o'erleaps itself
> And falls on the other.

Though he joked about it, he prided himself on his o'erleaping ambition, believed it would propel him to unheard of heights. Unfortunately, he had not yet managed to begin his glorious ascent. "I keep scheduling meetings and interviews. But the people who could give me a project, a job, a chance to make a difference, are always suggesting I contact some other branch of government. The other day, after arguing passionately for the development of the national economy, I was told I should really follow up with the Ministry of Foreign Affairs because of my command of English. Can you imagine?"

Still Firouz proceeded to make the rounds from one questionable lead to another, tolerating (up to a point) the (definitely) misdirected and (conceivably) well-meaning suggestions of family friends in positions of dubious authority. Months later, he was no closer to his goal. Then one day the telephone rang to bring news of a pair of galoshes that fit his shoes perfectly. "Firouz, Davoud here. Do you remember me? We were at school together in Beirut." Of course Firouz remembered Davoud, though they had never been very friendly. He was the one who had set his sights on the seduction of the lithe Arab and had ended up with a degree in diplomacy.

Making the appropriate sounds of recognition and somewhat puzzled at the cause for the call, Firouz listened to him continue, "I heard that you had returned to Tehran, but have not had the pleasure of renewing our acquaintance. I also understand that you have been looking to start your career. I came straight back after Beirut and have been working in the Foreign Ministry for a number of years." Actually Davoud had made quite a meteoric rise through the Ministry based on his "friendship" with a rather influential member of Court. "I know a number of well-placed people, including several at the Plan Organization," he continued. "I don't know much about systems and organizations. But I do happen to know about passion and, coincidentally, about perseverance. Here's the Deputy Director's telephone number. I took the liberty of telling him about you. Please call, he's waiting to hear from you."

Firouz stumbled through his thanks for this unexpected kindness and thought how much better this was than the prospect of meeting with despondent university professors, air force colonels, and civil engineers who, his father was convinced, were the right people. Straightening himself out, he picked up the phone and was put directly through to the Deputy Director. Standing to attention, he was informed of the time and date for his interview, and that "the Plan Organization needs young, educated and committed men like you."

A week later, Firouz found himself interviewed by a slight Deputy Director with a David Niven moustache and a suit that matched the colour of his eyes. Firouz attentively listened to the Deputy Director hold forth on the need for planning and development at some length before inquiring, "So, when can you start?" That same day Firouz found himself heading up the Long Range Planning section of the Plan Organization and calling Davoud to thank him for his kindness. To which Davoud responded, "Congratulations on your appointment. You deserve it. I have always believed in your abilities. Best of luck."

That was all he said. Nor did he ever mention it again in their chance encounters over the years that followed. There was something in that uncalculating kindness that touched Firouz, that left him baffled and amazed. And yet it was a kindness that he found time and time again in chance encounters with shepherds and truck-drivers, musicians and dancing girls. A kindness he himself extended to casual acquaintances, random people encountered in the street.

29

Firouz was beside himself with excitement and anticipation. In his brief visits to the green marble building with the floating staircase, he had sensed the contagious enthusiasm of those who were already crafting Iran's future. He desperately wanted to roll up his sleeves and work with them through the night, smoking cigarette after Winston cigarette to produce the analyses, plans and budgets the country craved.

He was not mistaken in diagnosing the prevailing sentiment. He was wrong about one thing only. It was not just among the clean-cut young professionals at the Plan Organization that this sentiment prevailed. It was a feeling shared by all of us, no matter where we worked. It was a time when the flower of a nation's youth devoted itself to building orphanages and refineries, founding law firms and charities, building bridges and banks, establishing publishing houses and technical schools, textile factories and pistachio farms, power plants and museums, hotel chains, schools for the deaf, and the occasional political party. And I devoted myself to designing the concrete and curtain-walled buildings that housed their dreams.

The streets were full of stories of deserts turned into verdant valleys, factories producing shoes as good as the ones from Czechoslovakia, stone quarries supplying London offices with green and pink lobbies, philanthropists importing entire hospitals down to the cotton swabs from Cincinnati. The cream of a generation believed the land was a generous and giving land, that with a halfway decent and not necessarily original idea, sweat and a little bit of luck, we could accomplish whatever we set our sights on.

There was, it is true, a young, brash, and exceptionally good American-educated group at the Plan Organization. "The three-vented ones," they were called by colleagues schooled in Switzerland, France, or Great Britain, exaggerating by at least one the number of vents in their Hickey Freeman suits.

It captured so much of who they were. Their desires and appetites heroically exceeded (by at least one) the desires and appetites of others. Their epic energies exceeded (by at least one) those of ordinary people. They were consumed with a need to achieve more, to produce more, to do more and to do it now. In this sense, at least, they were larger than life.

Though they worked for the Plan Organization, they had little patience for planning, but skipped instead to implementing the solutions vital to Iran's advancement. It was as if they knew their time was limited, that they had but one shot, one arrow to aim at Ignorance, Poverty and Injustice. But that wasn't it, really. They were not prescient, just young and impatient. And they wanted so much.

Firouz soon demonstrated a prodigious talent for finding funding for projects to transform the face of the nation. Dams and power plants, highways and rail lines, ports and universities. He could persuade World Bank officials, German industrialists, and British bankers to invest in Iran's future, to build the infrastructure vitally needed for the long run economic health and success of the nation. Swayed by the power of his arguments, the elegance of his logic, the truth and sincerity in his requests, or by their own desire to believe in a nation that produced men like Firouz, they took out the Mont Blanc pens specially engraved for the occasion, and signed the loans and multilateral agreements that funded Iran's development.

The first time it happened was on a mission to the World Bank. The Plan Organization had sent an entire delegation, including the grey-eyed Deputy Director. Firouz had been included for his language skills, and in the hope that his University of Chicago degree would be looked upon favourably. They were trying to fund a dam in Lorestan that would generate electric power and provide the water needed to extricate the Lors from poverty, disease, and destitution.

At one point the World Bankers expressed scepticism about the institutional underpinnings of the endeavour, questioned the staff's ability to carry out a project this bold, the government's ability to devote the necessary resources. They questioned whether this was the right time, questioned the Lors' preparedness for this kind of a project. They asked the cautious questions old men ask.

Though it was not his place to do so, Firouz spoke up, looking the Deputy Director directly in the eye. "When we first built the railway between Tehran and Mashhad," he began, "it passed through Torkaman territory. One of the Torkaman elders heard about the train, and decided to buy a ticket.

He was informed that the price was thirty-seven tomans. He offered fifteen, and was refused. He offered twenty and was refused again. Thinking that they would have to come down from their price sooner or later, the Torkaman chief walked away. Through the summer he watched the train travel by half-empty and returned in the autumn to buy a ticket. Again he was told that the price was thirty-seven tomans. He offered twenty and was refused. He offered twenty-two and was refused. After watching the train travel by half-empty for the better part of a year, he returned in the winter, offered thirty tomans, and finally bought a ticket on a half-empty train for thirty-seven.

"The Torkaman had never encountered an item where the price was not negotiable, where the seasons, the seller's needs or the buyer's stature, charm or wit did not make a difference. But he learned that, at least with trains, the price was thirty-seven tomans no matter the circumstance." Firouz turned to address the entire table, "With our proposal it is no different. At first there will be indifference—even resistance. But over time, as people understand what is being offered and the terms of the contract, they will come around. Just like the Torkaman and the train."

It was a story he had encountered in a travelogue, a story he had dutifully transcribed with a flowing hand in one of his little black books. And it worked. It prompted the serious men in tortoise-shell glasses to examine their own lives and to examine their own all-too-brief experiences with Torkamans, Lors or Bakhtiaris. To suspend their scepticism and to believe one more time in the investments necessary for the long-term success of countries like Iran. It finally led to the signing of a multi-million dollar loan under favourable terms.

For Firouz it was the first of many successful requests to underwrite the development of his country, the first of many missions across the globe. On one of those he would wake up at the Waldorf Astoria in utter amazement to find the streets of Manhattan blanketed with three feet of pristine white snow. It was just a few scarce hours after he had walked those very streets, following the advice of the Gillette lady with the blonde hair and dazzling smile in purchasing razors that would not nick or cut.

"For the world's easiest shaves use the world's sharpest blades."

30

Over the course of his career Firouz found funding for dams and roads, power plants, seaports and airports. His employees marvelled at his extraordinary aptitude, unmatched track record and incredible powers of persuasion, his ability to convince foreigners of what he believed so strongly to be true. But they never quite understood that more than building highways, he wanted to build a professional cadre at the Plan Organization. A cadre based on a system and reason, that owed no allegiance to tribe. A group of professionals as good as those in any modern organization. Though at every opportunity he sent his team off to the best universities and institutes in America, in Europe and in Japan, they never understood how much he cared.

And when they strayed, like a child stepping away from a parent, a child on a rooftop stepping from and towards the edge, after he calmly yet firmly urged them to "come back right now," and failed, after he pleaded for them to "come back for your own good, please," and failed, the child inching away, closer and closer to the precipice, he would have the presence of mind to pretend to falter, and implore, "my hands are full, it's all about to fall, please help me," and they would rush to him, saving themselves in acts of compassion.

In those halcyon days when anything could happen and often did, before the Carnival and the subsequent dissolution, it worked. For a day, a year, a decade Firouz managed to quietly and unassumingly create a professional cadre in the long range planning section of the Plan Organization, though he was not remembered for it.

But he never sought recognition. Like Gary Cooper in *High Noon*, he was a man who two-fistedly stands up for what is good and decent. A man who walks alone as lesser men desert city streets in fear. A man with a star on his chest and a determined jaw who takes on the outlaws. A man who says very little, and on one of the occasions when he does manage to put a few sentences together, mutters while squinting, "It's a great life. You risk your skin catching killers, and juries turn 'em loose so they can come back and shoot ya again. If you're honest, you're poor your whole life. And in the end, you wind up dying alone on some dirty street. For what? For nothing. For a tin star." Just a solitary man who single-handedly stands up for what is right. A man who in the final scene, wins the shoot-out, saves the town, throws his badge into the dirt in disgust, and rides off into the sunset with Grace Kelly.

Which is roughly the trajectory Firouz followed. Except he didn't throw his badge down in disgust, but in resignation. He didn't have a big shoot-out, but a lifetime of small ones. He didn't fight his fight alone, but alongside those of us who believed in his High Noon principles. And he never rode off with Grace Kelly.

31

Playing Gary Cooper was one of two things Firouz did naturally, though not without effort. Nothing had value unless he could taste the sweat, know the persistence and the perseverance, the discipline exercised in its achievement. Ali Akbar once remarked that when running, Firouz spent more energy pushing himself upward than propelling himself forward, as if his first objective were to fight gravity. It was an accurate description of how he attacked life in everything that he did.

It was particularly evident in the way he swam. Not with

the elegance of a porpoise leaping and diving through the waves, but with the determination of a man trying hard to stay afloat. A man who knows he is bound to sink unless he propels himself forward, trying hard to look like the pictures in the instructional manual. Emulating the strokes in the time lapse photographs, he believed he swam properly. Except he had a stray left foot that did not exactly replicate the carefully prescribed trajectory described in diagrams one through seven of *Learning to Swim*. Despite his own conviction in the excellence of his textbook technique, he never quite got it right.

Still he believed in effort. And believing in the value of effort, he never called the Minister of Finance to help him obtain necessary approvals, never bent an influential ear at a dinner or cocktail party, never hired an influence peddler. He insisted on handling his own affairs.

One day he found himself walking up the stairs to his appointment with an official of the Tax and Revenue Department he had visited at least four or five times before to present documents that were summarily rejected because they weren't duly notarized, didn't have the requisite indecipherable signatures, or simply didn't quite meet the shabby official's amazingly elevated and exacting standards. As he walked up the tired stairs to room 513, Firouz scarcely noticed two young girls sitting by the elevator.

"My thoughts were elsewhere," he told me at his first opportunity. "I was thinking of how ridiculous the whole process was. To have to go from one office to another to get the approvals they should have wanted to give me so I could pay their damn taxes. Instead of helping me, the man behind the desk was raising objections. I did not hear the girls, but their voices followed me as I walked up the stairs. I opened the door to his office when their words finally registered: 'Rock, paper, scissors ... rock, paper, scissors ... rock ...' And it came to me that I had been playing rock, paper, scissors with an official of the Tax and Revenue Department for months."

Of all the realizations he had come to in his short life, this was the most painful, a slap in the face of everything he ever stood for. He had not yet learned to care and not to care, only the first half of the equation. And despite repeated remonstrations to the contrary, it is questionable if Firouz ever learned the other half.

32

As for Nur ed Din and Fereshteh, their love affair continued through the seasons and settings until one day as they lay, languorous limbs entangled, the phone rang. Not in the still of the night, not at the arsenic hour of dusk, but just after lunch. The afternoon phone rang to inform Nur ed Din that Uncle Mustafa had died.

"He was sitting under the cherry tree, sipping a glass of tea, when it happened," the Swiss housekeeper, Lucienne, explained when they arrived on the scene. "He was in the garden, and I was doing the dishes. He often took lunch by himself. Just a salad, and some fish when it was in season. Trout was his favourite, and he was also fond of whitefish. But they were all sold out of trout, and the whitefish didn't look too fresh. So I made him an endive salad. He liked endives."

Sensing impatience, Lucienne tried to come to the point. "Anyway, after lunch, while I was cleaning up, I heard the sound of breaking glass. I didn't think much of it at the time and continued washing the dishes. And when I thought of it again, I promptly forgot about it. But when I went back to the veranda, I found the tea glass shattered on the floor." At this point she could no longer contain herself and broke down. "I had heard the sound of Mustafa dying, I had heard the sound of his death, and I just kept on with the dishes. Maybe if I had come out when I heard it, he would still be alive." "Lucienne, don't torment yourself. How could you have known? We hear sounds all the time and think nothing more of them. There, there now, it will be all right. Here, have a sip of water, you'll feel better," Nur ed Din consoled, wiping the tears from her eyes.

Sufficiently recovered, she continued. "I found him sitting in his favourite chair underneath the cherry tree. I asked if he needed anything else, but he didn't answer. I asked again, thinking he may not have heard. When I came closer, I realized he was not breathing. He had a serene smile on his face. The smile he has when he's sleeping, worn out and exhausted."

Nur ed Din found his uncle just as Lucienne had described, sitting in his favourite armchair under the cherry tree, a peaceful look on his face and a broken tea-glass at his feet. Though Nur ed Din had been expecting the call for some time, nothing quite prepared him for this moment. So he immersed himself in the arrangements—washing the body, clothing it in white, and entrusting it to its permanent resting place.

Uncle Mustafa had also been anticipating this day, and in his characteristically selfless fashion had bought a gravesite in the foothills so those who came to pay their respects might enjoy the view. Recently, he had spent more and more time at his gravesite, passing mornings, afternoons and moonlit nights there. When asked why, he would respond, "I am old and tired and this will be my final resting place. I want to get a feel for it while I'm still alive." He also commissioned a gravestone. It was a simple affair: his name, his birth date, and a date that would be filled later. Having done so, he told his God, "I'm ready. Take me away any time you want. But don't make me wait too long. Whatever you do, please don't make me wait."

So there wasn't a lot for Nur ed Din to do. Except have the body washed, clothed in a white shroud, and buried. We paid our respects and stood beside him as he received condolences from his following. In that brief moment when he greeted them on their arrival or embraced them on their departure, I watched as one pulled him aside conspiratorially to tell him how she had been rescued from bouts of depression by Mustafa's amazing insight into her character. "He was the only person who ever really understood me," she revealed. Another got all choked up, looked deeply into Nur ed Din's eyes, and confessed, "Your uncle introduced me to my wife forty years ago. I married her based on your uncle's introduction and we've been together ever since, can you imagine that?"

Having shared these intimacies, they paid their respects to their new spiritual leader. In response Nur ed Din smiled and mumbled something polite. The truth was that despite the fact that he had reconciled himself to the eventuality, he was still unprepared for this day.

He had often asked his uncle how to deal with his one-day-to-be-inherited responsibilities. He invariably got the same answer. "Ask God for a sign," he was patiently and knowingly told by the uncle who at some distant and almost forgotten point had experienced the same doubts. Now that the expected moment had arrived, Nur ed Din did the only thing that he knew to do—he asked God for a sign.

He had heard the story of his great-grandfather and of the confirming rain. He had heard how a white dove had alit on the head of one successor, how a horse had neighed at precisely the right moment for another. So he put his trust in God and asked for some indication that leading these people through the trials and tribulations of this world was his role in life.

He was not very specific in his instructions. He did not implore his God, "If you truly love me, let me give sight to the blind with a wave of my hand. Let me make lepers whole with my breath, let me give speech to the dumb with a kiss." Nor did he imprecate his God, "Let me walk on water, just this once hold my hand as I walk across the lake." He did not ask his God for the gift of second sight or the ability to speak in tongues, the types of things that Madame Rosa and the most common evangelists exercise on a daily basis. He did not say, "Dear lord, if you love me make it snow on exams day," as any schoolboy might. He left all of that up to a knowing and charitable God who had ostensibly been through this process at least three or four times with other members of the family. He left it all up to his God and he waited. He waited for God to give him a sign. Every waking day for the rest of his life he waited for a sign from God. And on his deathbed he had still not received a sign.

But at the time he had not even guessed at the possibility of such a turn of events. He was confident of God's expedient response by return mail. So he devoted himself to the task at hand. It was the first time he had been called upon to speak in front of his following. As the congregation settled in, as we nodded at acquaintances across the room and scented ourselves with rose-water, he spoke.

"My uncle used to tell stories. I'm sure any one of you could tell a tale that touched your lives. I would like to tell you my favourite, and the one that did in fact change my life. Many of you could tell it better, but I trust that you will humour me as I repeat it one more time. It is the story of the accident." Taking a deep breath as the congregation exchanged knowing looks and expectant glances, Nur ed Din continued with a story that I had heard often and even repeated on occasion.

"Once my uncle was driving home from a late night event and had the misfortune of colliding with a motorcyclist. Distraught, he immediately took the young man to the hospital that was luckily nearby. Waiting his turn at the emergency room, he anxiously paced up and down the courtyard until the physician did a number of rudimentary tests, examined the arm clutched in pain, and concluded with the diagnosis, 'It is nothing really, just a touch of tenderness.'

"As the verdict was rendered, my uncle felt a huge sense of relief. And when he had a moment, he reflected on the doctor's terminology. The young motorcyclist was not suffering from soreness, inflammation, a bruise or laceration. The young man suffered from a case of tenderness." Nur ed Din paused to allow the full impact of his words to sink in. "I have often felt that throughout his life Uncle Mustafa suffered from a particularly acute case of tenderness," Nur ed Din said, bringing a smile to Fereshteh's face and to the faces of the congregation.

"There was a poetry in the diagnosis," he continued, "but that is not the end of the story. Filing the accident report at the police station, Mustafa was to witness a scene that he never tired of describing. A distraught woman of a certain age was sobbing as she told the officer, 'They emptied the safe, they took it all. Everything. Deeds, passports and identity cards. They took my children's gold coins, the ones they got every New Year and that had been in my safekeeping for the past twenty-seven years. They took the cash. Fifty-one thousand tomans. The emerald ring my father gave me on the day I was married.' Overcome by emotion, she burst into sobs. When she regained her composure sufficiently, she continued, 'They took the diamond necklace and the ring my husband gave me when our first son was born. They took …'

"At this point she was interrupted by the portly officer, 'Madame, why do you deplore the loss of material things. Devote yourself to the spiritual.' Uncle Mustafa could not believe what he had just heard. The police officer with the operatic face of a minor villain had just told the sobbing lady with the ransacked safe to forget about the possessions of this world. 'Stick to the spiritual,' he told her again. 'There is no permanence in things.' But she could not hear him. The words did not register. She just kept on crying and listing the possessions she no longer had.

"You have all heard the story before, it was one of Uncle Mustafa's favourites. It was also one of his favourite themes. 'Ants gather grain every day,' he used to say. 'All day long they gather grain, dragging loads fifteen point seven times their weight across dirt floors and up sheer walls. Every day of the week, ants accumulate wheat, barley and rice. At the end of the day they will have amassed huge amounts of grain, an entire treasury of grain. They devote their entire lives to storing grain in underground caverns. Surely we are more than ants,' he would say. 'There must be more to our lives than amassing possessions the way ants collect grain.' He believed that there was something more than houses, cash and cars; more houses, more cash and more cars. He has left behind his life as an example, and some stories to help us to remember him."

It was an emotional speech, but not so much so that it would bring tears to eyes. And yet, Nur ed Din found Firouz quietly sobbing in the back of the room. Firouz had never been one to show his emotions, and when he did it was almost always under the most private circumstances. When Nur ed Din got a second, he took a visibly shaken Firouz by the arm, pulled him aside and said, "Firouz, it's all right, my uncle lived a long and healthy life and died serenely with all his faculties intact. You couldn't wish for a better death. As for me, I will get along just fine. I have Fereshteh, I have my friends, and I have this congregation. What more could I want?"

Firouz wiped the tears from his eyes. "I know, Nur ed Din, I know. I was not crying for your uncle. I scarcely knew the man. He lived a good life and died a quiet death. Sometimes you cannot hope for more." He took a breath, hesitating, wavering for a moment. "I wasn't crying for your uncle. I was crying for myself."

Looking away, he confided, "I was crying for the day when I will lose a wife or a lover, when I lose a friend. I really don't know how I would be able to deal with it. For a moment I imagined myself a father losing a son, a husband losing a wife, a friend losing a best friend." He broke down again. The thought of it made Firouz, who had never cried on his pillow, sob uncontrollably.

Though I was taken aback on that afternoon, I am thankful that at least Firouz cried at Uncle Mustafa's funeral. Because when the day came that he lost the one he loved, he could not cry. On that day, his tears were all dried up. He could not even cry for himself.

But it is also true that at this stage in his life he had not yet lost anyone dear to him. He was still intently pursuing his one true love.

33

Having hacked through bramblewood forests, having slain demons and dragons and proven himself a gallant and worthy suitor, Firouz was firmly engaged in embracing a listless Iran. His kiss, he was certain, would bring colour to her features, make her sigh, blink, meet his gaze and awaken from a slumber that only resembled death.

Though I have always believed in turnip princesses, fairy dust and winged horses, I knew that Firouz's embraces were misplaced. If Iran was a fairy tale, it was not the story of a sleeping beauty waiting to be animated by the kiss of true love. Iran had never given herself to any of her suitors, no matter how earnest. The last to have possessed her was the castrated king who improbably escaped captivity to unite the country under the force of his understandable but unforgivable cruelty. No, there is no doubt in my mind that Firouz's kisses were misplaced.

There are those who maintained that Firouz had his Brothers Grimm confused with his Goethe. It was clear that if Iran was a fairy tale at all, it was the Sorcerer's Apprentice—in Walt Disney colours, soundtracks and proportions. A nineteen-seventies, Technicolor, Dolby-sounded Mickey Mouse in a red gown and blue star-covered hat, watching in despair as axes split more and more wood. As brooms and buckets spiralled out of control, as more and more 1967 Hillman Hunter automobiles renamed *Peykans* plugged more and more of Tehran's arterials. And still more factories were imported to produce Pepsi Colas, B. F. Goodrich tires, cheese puffs and those winter ice creams called Negrokisses.

Using half understood spells from the West, they maintained, Iran had succeeded in endlessly replicating populations, transforming Tehran from a town of one hundred thousand to a city of three million in fifty scant years. But this was not *Fantasia,* and there was no sorcerer to return angrily, reprimand a repentant apprentice with the words every child knows—"There is no shortcut to greatness, you must slosh your way to the top one bucket at a time"—and with the wave of a wand restore the old order. Just an old man in a white beard full of empty incantations. And even after his return, after the revolution and ideological war, Tehran continued to split in two, consuming all the land, villages, towns and cities in its path.

Others, my cousin Ali Akbar among them, offered that if Iran was a fairy tale at all, it was a Persian tale Firouz had never bothered to read, the story of the cold-hearted princess who would only be seduced by one who bested her. One who ran faster, threw farther, jumped higher. Her father had issued an edict offering both his kingdom and her hand in marriage to anyone who could beat her in competition. Bright-eyed, broad-shouldered young men immediately presented themselves, hoarse-voiced young women with drawn-on moustaches came forward, only to be beaten perfunctorily by the princess, even more perfunctorily put to death by the king.

The less athletic thought it ridiculous to accept such harsh terms. They could not fathom that anyone would actually engage in such a competition. And then, setting eyes on the princess, they would engage in the contests that could only lead to their deaths. Abundantly aware of their own deficiencies in running around tracks and throwing javelins, once they set eyes on her the youth of the nation could not help but risk their lives. In this perverse fashion, her father put to death the flower of his nation's youth. Still handsome young challengers came forward. In this version, Firouz was one of them. But only one. There were countless others who, despite the stories, despite repeated warnings, persisted in challenging the princess.

They knew she could jump higher, throw farther, wrestle the strongest of her challengers to the ground. But each of them believed she would be so smitten that she would want to be beaten. Like all youths, they were confident the princess would want to lose to the one who had won her heart.

So they spent their days devising ways to cross her path, their nights in serenades beneath her windows. Concocting excuses to appear in her dreams, they believed that if they could but kiss her once, that if they were given a chance, just one chance, the princess would stumble and fall. That she would stop to fasten the straps to her Greek-looking sandals, lose the race and regain her heart.

It is a fairytale that might explain Firouz's actions and the actions of an entire generation. It begins to explain how each of us devoted our lives to the seduction of a nation, how each of us ran the race and how each of us lost. The Prime Ministers who died in the process, Mansour and Hoveyda, Davar and Razmara, Bakhtiar and Teymourtash. Assassinated on the street, stabbed to death in Paris, poisoned in the Shah's prison, or executed by a military tribunal—of the fifteen Prime Ministers who accepted the challenge and courted the princess during those years, eight were murdered. And that does not count the unsuccessful attempts on Ala's life.

There were more than Prime Ministers. There were scientists and accountants, colonels and headmasters, lawyers, carpenters and mathematicians. There were bankers, statisticians and poets. Professors and doctors, teachers of the deaf and of the blind, people who devoted their lives to founding orphanages, clothing the naked or feeding the hungry. There were archaeologists and soccer players. There were men and there were women who sought to seduce her.

The cold-hearted princess did not succumb to our charms. She may have let us speed on ahead believing we could win, she may have stumbled and fallen once or twice, but when she did give herself, against all expectations, she gave herself to a wizened Ayatollah who had been exiled for years.

34

B ut what if you do not choose to believe in fairy tales? Then you might protest that that was not it, that was not it at all. You might say those dashing young men and women had never loved Iran. You might go even further and say that they were incapable of loving her, that they had merely loved what they thought they could change about her.

You might say that they lived in some Rex Harrison *My Fair Lady* fantasy, believing that with the proper Henry Higgins elocution, they could transform her into the belle of the ball, the Switzerland of the Middle East. You might say they never had any real appreciation for Iran, that they had never understood or loved her, except when she was on exhibit at the Metropolitan or the Louvre. And if they did have some questionable understanding of her essence, they had a much greater appreciation for things British, French, German or American.

You might say, "They were not propelled by love, but by the force of their own desire to turn Iran into some Balanciaga or Halston-inspired vision of who they thought she should be." Of how they could give her the right accent, the appropriate ballroom gown, the right nose, the right coiffure or smile to make her shine that evening in the ballroom, or later on that night in the bedroom.

You might say, "It had nothing to do with Iran. They were propelled by their own egos and their own versions of 'how things should be.'" And that would be all right too. Because in Iran there are an infinite number of interpretations for the same event. I have often asked the most trusted, the most insightful of friends, and have always been given entirely different and equally convincing interpretations of the same set of facts. In Iran there was never any one correct answer.

35

Though I have often neglected the counsel of trusted advisors, I have always believed in fairy tales. Moon-faced children and pumpkin escapes. Tinderbox soldiers and shoeless shortstops. Log-splitting presidents and landslide victories. Keys to the kingdom. Thunder roads and tin men. Secret gardens and redemption in a word. Working class heroes. Doors, bottles and boxes meant to have remained unopened. Red beards, black beards and blue beards. Young kings and Cinderella teams. Seabiscuit stallions and Munchausen Barons. I knew them all, believed in them all.

Listening to my father's stories of the prince who galloped softly up seven mountains (ta tagh ta tagh ta tagh) and softly down seven mountains (ta tagh ta tagh ta tagh) to find the pool where the three goldfish swam, I believed. As I ran my fingers through my father's greying hair, and the prince pierced with his last remaining arrow the one speckled fish that held in its mouth the sorcerer's cruel quail-egg soul, I understood. When he crushed the egg, and, *pouf,* killed the sorcerer in a puff of smoke, I knew he would save the enchanting princess whose drops of blood turned into red roses in a winter stream.

As I struggled to keep my eyes open, he would tell the stories I loved. And then he might say, "Don't you think there is more to this life than hungry ogres and suits of swan feathers? Don't you think we should explore some of the world's great authors?" This he would intone in the same voice he used when pretending to strain while picking me up, "Yassi joon, do me a favour and check your pockets. All your pockets. Are you sure you haven't any heavy objects, any rocks or stones? Are there any bricks?" After I laughed and turned my pockets inside out, engaging in the charade, assuring him, "No, *baba jan,* there are no bricks, look my pockets are empty," he would persist, "It simply is not possible. My little girl can't be this heavy. Are you sure there's nothing in your pockets? Do look again," before slowly lifting me up with a pretend groan. And tossing me ever so high.

With that same do-you-have-any-rocks-in-your-pockets tone of voice he would sometimes suggest, "Maybe we should read literature for a change, princess. Something momentous like Oscar Wilde." And then he would produce, as if out of thin air, Wilde's stories of happy princes and selfish giants. He was the kind of man who, on autumn days when first fires are being lit and leaves beginning to change colour, would point to a tree with a blush of red and say, "Look, Yassaman, she's put on her lipstick. I daresay she's waiting for her lover." At the rustling of the wind, he would cock his head, "Listen, little one, do you hear that? I do believe it is the music of her anklets as she dances for him."

So I knew of fairy tales. I had been to the palace of the three sisters, and had surreptitiously placed a dollop of honey on the yardstick. And there may have been times when I believed Iran was the silent, the pumpkin, or the princess bride. But thinking back now I know for sure there is only one story that ever captured Iran's essence. It was not a story my father ever recited, nor was it one he ever read. It was a story I encountered one dusty afternoon in the dark respite of a cinema.

"Let's see what Hollywood does with our palaces, bazaars and harems, genies and vazirs," my father had suggested. I agreed to go see *The Thief of Baghdad* though I really went to see Sabu. I had just turned nine and I wanted to see the sparkle in his coal-black eyes, the way the smile broke out across his face. How his café-au-lait body danced and glistened.

So enraptured was I that I scarcely noticed the part where the genie held the city in the palm of his hand, or the way the carpet flew through star-filled skies. I devoted my attention to Sabu and found myself wondering if I could wear those Haroun Al Rashid harem outfits when I grew up. And then, all of a sudden, my reveries were interrupted by a troubling scene. It was not from *The Thief of Baghdad*. It was not borrowed from the *Seven Voyages of Sinbad the Sailor*. I knew the stories recounted by Shahrzad, even the ones I shouldn't have. And I knew full well that the disinherited prince finds the treasure and marries the Caliph's daughter in a wedding that lasts seven days and seven nights. There is no blue flower of forgetfulness. There never was a blue flower of forgetfulness. That was never part of the story.

But the pretty princess was struggling on the screen against the urge to inhale the scent of a strangely beautiful blue flower. Continents away on a barren mountainside, Sabu and the betrayed prince watched through the marvellous crystal and implored her not to. We in the audience held our collective breaths and prayed that she would not fall for the sorcerer's trick, however seductive the flower's colour or its scent. I squirmed in my seat and held tight to my father's hand. Didn't she know she would forget everything, lose everything that ever meant anything to her? Didn't she know she would lose her one true love, that she could never find him again, not if he wore out seven leaden shoes, not if he tricked the ferryman, not even if he captured the pony with the fiery mane and remembered the words to whisper into its ear?

I pleaded for the princess not to fall for evil Jaafar's scheme, not to inhale the blue flower's noxious odour, to listen to me this once. I promised I wouldn't care what happened after that, so long as she walked away, just walked away. As long as she kept on going and didn't look back. The blue flower of forgetfulness was not part of the story. It had never been part of the story. There was no flower, no mountainside, the evil sorcerer had already, *pouf*, been dispatched. It was a Hollywood invention. But thinking back on it now, if there ever was a fairy tale that explained our lives, it was the one that I saw on that summer afternoon.

We all breathed deep of that blue flower. Under its spell we spent our lives building German autobahns and English gardens, chicken farms as good as the ones in Kentucky, shoe factories rivalling those in Czechoslovakia. Amusement centres named Luna Park, Ice Palace. Skyscrapers and Firestone tires, Hyatt Hotels. Dreaming dreams inspired by the blue flower of forgetfulness, we littered Tehran's streets with the names of surrogate lovers. Chattanooga, San Remo and Sorrento. Versailles, Berlin and Bavaria, Eldorado and Xanadu. Miami and the Metropole, Hyde Park and Hollywood.

Though I prayed, "Dear god, don't let this happen," we all forgot the country we loved.

36

At that early age I must have sensed that things were slowly, inextricably slipping away. So I resolved to remember. I resolved never to forget Sabu, to remember the words of every story. To remember the streets I grew up in, and the friends I grew up with, even the ones the teacher liked better. Exiting the cinema, I gave my father an unexpected hug, and resolved to remember.

I remember kissing my father goodbye on the day I first walked to school by myself, and turning around halfway down the street to see him still standing at the gate. I remember being passed by Firouz as he walked with a palpable sense of purpose to the American College. I remember Nazanin's sidewalk encounters, and the first time I recounted second-hand stories in Beirut. I remember my Los Angeles lessons and I still remember the smell of Tehran's streets first thing in the morning.

And I remember when everything changed. When oil prices surged out of all control and the nation celebrated its two thousand five hundredth year of uninterrupted monarchical existence in the deserts overlooking Persepolis. When the cast of extras included the Hashemite King Hussein, Haile Selassie the Lion of Abyssinia, Valery Giscard d'Estaing, Spiro Agnew, and bearded foot soldiers dressed up as Invincible Warriors. When Iran obtained the world's largest hovercraft fleet and Iran Air took out full-colour advertisements in Newsweek Magazine. When for the price of a faux-Swiss chalet in a desirable section of Tehran, you could buy Frank Sinatra's estate in Palm Springs with three kidney-shaped swimming pools. When Iran tied Scotland one-one in Montreal.

No longer in pony tails, I also knew that Madame Claude flew prostitutes in from Paris on Wednesdays and Sundays. That Chez Maxim's catered, from Paris, intimate dinners for some shepherd-turned-industrialist's two hundred fifty closest friends, and I somehow made the cut. Bursars found themselves examining and re-examining payrolls, only to be told what they thought was the total of all salaries was, in fact, my cousin Ali Akbar's monthly compensation. A Toshiba-dealership-owning merchant turned industrialist was worth more than John D. Rockefeller, I was informed over lunch by the bank president who held just one of his accounts.

Under the circumstances it was easy to lose one's bearings, it was easy to forget. The country collectively did, encouraged by the Padeshah who believed he could turn Iran into the fourth largest military power in the world. It was laughably easy to lose one's bearings. Even for the ones who knew better, the ones who presciently called it the Carnival.

Not for the Ferris wheels and bumper cars, the cotton candy, and the elephant ears, the faceless voice urging one and all, "Come on in and enjoy the greatest show on earth." Not for the stuffed animals and the tunnels of love. Not for the promises, "Step right up. Everyone's a winner." They called it the Carnival because they knew the day would come when the gypsies would pack up their red and white striped tents and move on. And still, even those who knew better stayed on for one more ride, for one last spin.

I've grown wiser since the day I went to see Sabu and ended up with stolen memories. Though I still find myself clenching for my father's hand, I know what to expect of Hollywood endings. And I know that somehow, despite my best efforts, despite the myriad recollections that continue to curse me, somewhere along the line we all breathed deep of that blue flower.

37

There was, however, at least one who was not intent on changing his lover into the vision of his misplaced desire. There was one, waiting for an imminent reply from above, who did not want her to change, ever. Who still made up make-believe excuses to brush imaginary eyelashes off her cheek. "Stay still for a moment. Here, I'll get it for you. You really must learn how to stay still. There, I think I've got it now, no moving..." One who invented excuses to make her repeat that quizzical look when she wasn't quite sure if he was joking, that playful frown on her brow, or the pouting of her lips.

He counted the minutes to when he would see her again, watched from the balcony for her white Peykan, sure each time he saw one that he could make out the blue beads dangling from her rear-view mirror. On closer examination they weren't blue beads at all, but pictures of prophets or pop stars. He would laugh and wonder how he could have thought it had been hers, until another white Peykan drove by and he detected the blue beads for sure this time.

Or he might imagine her car had broken down and see her walking down the street, recognize the movement of her hips, the familiar pink dress, convince himself that it was her, until the evidence swayed overwhelmingly in the other direction. And then he would laugh at himself again, pick some other vaguely similar body out from the crowd, and re-enact his self-deception all over again. When she did (finally) arrive, they would make love and speak of all the things they had saved for that moment.

Eventually, he would steer the conversation toward topics that would bring out the softness in her voice. There was a quaver he loved when she spoke as if she still lived among trees where you could see as far as the Caspian, clouds that reflected genies and bottles. The days when he was still throwing colossal boulders into fordable streams.

"Only beautiful things make me cry," she had once said. And though she may not have wept, she was always moved when commonplace things were turned into objects of rare beauty. When donkeys' foreheads were adorned with blue Egyptian-paste hippopotamus beads or plastic imitation ones. When water carriers carted the most exotic sculptures on their backs. When twisted trees were adorned with knotted prayers. When the display-case architecture of the camera obscura was more magnificent than all its dimly lit scenes of Paris, London or Rome.

Fereshteh loved the coffee-house paintings that depicted Imam Hussein's larger-than-life martyrdom, the Prince of Innocents naively depicted twice the size of his enemies. The often repeated scene where Zoleikha invites the ladies of court to her palace, hands them oranges and the knives with which to peel them. Upon a resplendent Yousef's entrance, the ladies are so distraught that those of them slicing oranges ever so serenely cut their hands. In this ingenious manner Zoleikha absolves herself from falling for a servant. After all, any woman in her place would have done the same. Fereshteh loved that the proof of this tale lies in the existence of blood oranges. Joseph's oranges they are called by the Arabs.

Fereshteh collected begging bowls and lions with twirled moustaches. Though it did not always bring tears to her eyes, she shook her head in wonder when reciting Molavi, and especially the poem that began:

The Beloved put a broom in my hand;
He said: Sweep dust from the surface of the sea.

Of all the mosques, the one she loved best was without gold, tile or faience. The one adorned in humble brick, in an endless array of patterns and inventions, each one of its hundreds of domes different from the hundreds of others. She fervently attended passion plays, taking great enjoyment when the tamed lion eschewed the Prophet's noble body, and picked out the murderer's instead—the king of beasts' natural recognition of wickedness aided by the less-than-discreet placement of a choice piece of meat on the evil one's neck. She was always moved when villains shed tears of remorse even as they engaged in the abominable acts that led saints to martyrdom. And she was enchanted that tears from the eyes of the faithful were captured in funny-shaped bottles for their healing powers.

It was not surprising that Nur ed Din loved her. Nor was it extraordinary that he never tired of steering the conversation to things of beauty. But they would sometimes, perforce, turn to more pragmatic matters. Fereshteh knew he had been waiting for a sign ever since his uncle's death, and knew as well as I that he would never engage in a career in engineering. She was convinced that if there was any chance of finding his place in life, he had to return to Kerman, where it all began.

38

Fereshteh had always known Tehran to be an aberration, the contradiction of everything Nur ed Din believed in. It was a city bent on consuming the countryside, a city of the displaced, the uprooted, the rootless, smacked down in the foothills of the Alborz mountains. From Rasht and Tabas, Sologhoon and Abarkooh, from cities, towns and villages the hopeful flocked to the nation's capital to seek their fortunes. The young and the defective came to this bastard city, hoping. To accommodate both innocence and imperfection we built them modern towers and moderne apartments, Swiss chalets and Spanish villas, white houses, ranch houses, townhouses, and plastic pop boutiques. We built them a city founded on their dreams of overnight riches. "You can't find spirituality in a city like that," Fereshteh told Nur ed Din, stroking his face.

Tehran had always been that kind of city, ever since Nasser ed Din Shah enlisted a vazir to fulfil his desire for Renaissance-esque defences. The vazir foolishly accepted to build the walls at his own cost on the one condition that any un-built lands encompassed within the mud and brick would come into his possession. Unexpectedly, but not surprisingly, he proceeded to build walls that extended far beyond Tehran's limits, making a vast fortune from the king's crenelated desire.

"I know she's right, but still it is my home," he confided to me one day, knowing how attached I was to the city. "I love wandering through the streets whichever way my feet may take me. Once, through a door inadvertently left ajar, I caught a glimpse of a courtyard, a blue-tiled pool, and a line of laundry left out to dry—one white undershirt, two pairs of striped pyjamas and seven pink nightgowns. Another time I saw a pomegranate tree and a patch of green grass. And a book of poetry that would not be read, a jug of wine that would not be drunk, and a blue hubble-bubble whose red-hot coals would soon turn grey. Where else in the world do you find that, Yassaman? You've travelled the world, you tell me, where?"

What could I say? I felt the same way. But Fereshteh knew that if there was a place for Nur ed Din, it was in the God-forsaken, wind-swept deserts of Kerman, in that vast expanse of rolling plains and jagged mountains where people are so small against the backdrop of the infinite. In the desolation where, in awe of the savage miracle of God's creation, we are constantly reminded of the transitoriness of this life.

And if the terrible splendour of the desert is not evidence enough of the vanity and futility of this world, you need only open your eyes to the crumbling fortresses and citadels of some great and forgotten dynasty, or the ruined homes not so terribly distant from your own. Fereshteh prompted Nur ed Din to move to Kerman, the mud-brick city punctuated with domes and crumbling wind-towers that had been home to so many prophets and poets. And more than one Sufi.

But she did not desire to have him retire from the world. Not unlike Victorian physicians who prescribed Umbrian holidays, she believed in the power of place. She also longed to build a garden. In that terrible desert, in that fantastic landscape, she wanted to create an oasis where you could appreciate both God's greatness and his grace. "Ever since I was a child," she said, "I was taught there are seven levels of hell and eight levels of heaven. I was taught to believe that God's terrible justice is exceeded only by His divine mercy."

Fereshteh wanted to build a paradise in the desert with Nur ed Din. It was not the first time anyone had undertaken such an endeavour. There is a heavenly garden built by a prince; the prince's garden it is called. It is a garden of towering plane trees, of weeping willows, tulips and oleander, daffodils and narcissus, of pink, white and red roses, of fig and cypress trees fed by a source deep from within the mountain. From a spring that gushes forth and cascades down the hillside, ice-cold mountain water pops up blue and sprays in splendid arcs out of the most ingenious fountains. Not far from the pleasure palace is a tea-house where the remnant of that same mountain spring runs through a gravestone-lined ditch where I once took a glass of tea before my encounter with the darvish.

There is no absence of garden paradises in Kerman. And even when there is but a flower or two, a couple of sprigs here or there, the Kermani love of the garden gives them license to paint in the roses and the nightingales, the fluttering of the butterfly and the fragrance of the evening breeze. Soon they begin to believe their own inventions, believe that there is more than a patch of dirt and a flower struggling against an unrelenting sun. Soon enough they hear the gurgling of water and the song of nightingales, detect the scent of hyacinths, freesia, roses.

At other times there is not even a patch of dirt. There is no land, no water. There are no real or imagined plane, fig or mulberry trees, no cypresses, no peaches, pomegranates or walnuts. No roses, no tulips and no daffodils. Then the residents of Kerman will do the most amazing thing. They will embellish their whitewash-walled rooms with a bit of colour. The carpet they put out may have birds and flowers, perhaps a tree of life, a goldfish, an antelope or a rabbit. But even when it does not, even when it is nothing more than swirling paisleys, it will, *abracadabra,* bring to the four bare walls some sense of the delicious coolness, of the brilliant colour, of the wonderful respite of a garden.

Naturally, the idea of building a garden in Kerman appealed to Nur ed Din. He had always felt a special affinity for the city of his birth, and loved the thought of creating a place where he and Fereshteh could live surrounded by beauty. Ever since she first casually mentioned it in conversation, he had approached ancient gardeners and arborists and heard the most incredible stories of pear trees grafted with the branches of peaches, apricots and plums so that one tree bore all four fruits at once. He was told that you could tell the time of day by the scent of the rose, and was informed matter-of-factly, "The rose's scent is strongest just as it is dying." He learned that the jasmine flower grows naturally in the mountains of Kerman, and that its perfume, distilled by the thin air, is unmatched.

But his interest was not in flowers, butterflies, and bubbling brooks. I know in my heart that his desire to create an earthly paradise was influenced, in part, by a story his uncle once told him. They had been on one of those early-morning walks that Uncle Mustafa engaged in every day when in Kerman. His favourite promenade was along the tree-lined street that led to the graveyard. Nur ed Din was probably ten or twelve at the time. He enjoyed the freshness of the air at the break of dawn, and the way his uncle would walk with his hands clasped behind his back, reciting poetry and telling stories. Every time they arrived at the graveyard, they were greeted by a dishevelled-looking man Uncle Mustafa addressed by name, and for whom he always had a kind word or coin.

Nur ed Din was overcome by curiosity. "Uncle, why does this man spend his days here, doesn't he have a home of his own?" he asked, searching Mustafa's face for an answer. "Did he lose someone very dear to him?" he continued, trying hard to find out why anyone would choose to spend his days in a graveyard. "Did he go mad with grief and decide to spend the rest of his days close to the one he lost? Was it his brother, his wife ... was it his lover?"

"No, Nur ed Din," his Uncle Mustafa replied, laughing. "It was not quite that, though it is a rather sad story. There may be a lesson in it for you, so if you give me a minute of your attention, I will tell you. The man you see at the graveyard was named Abolfazl, but they called him Hafez for his ability to recite the Quran. I knew him for his reputation as a brilliant student of theology. Forsaking all material possessions, he lived at the *madreseh,* and devoted himself to learning the Quran, reciting it by heart in the most melodious voice. Did I say he renounced all material possessions? Well he had, all except one. It was a little thing, a hat his mother had given him on the day he left home. A skull cap he wore every day, taking it off only when he went to bed.

"One day he woke to find his hat missing. Distraught, he looked high and low, asked everyone he knew, but was unable to find a trace of his one possession. He began accosting passers-by and questioning strangers, but to no avail. Finally one day he reasoned, quite correctly I might add, that the person who had taken his hat would end up at the cemetery. So he came to this graveyard to wait for the one who took his hat. Hafez has been here ever since. It is not quite the story of a broken heart or a lost lover, but I believe it is even more poignant."

Nur ed Din often thought of that tragic story, of Hafez's impeccable logic in waiting at the place we all end up sooner or later for the person who had absconded with his hat. And of the ridiculousness of such a proposition. More than a year had gone by since his uncle's death and every day he waited patiently; yet he had still not received a sign from God. So Nur ed Din was inclined to follow Hafez's tainted logic in creating a paradise on earth, a place God would have to inhabit sooner or later. What else could he do? All his requests and pleas had gone unanswered.

One day during a stroll through tree-lined streets Fereshteh argued her case. "We have the means, since your uncle (God rest his soul) passed away, to try to make a go of it wherever we want. Let us go to Kerman. Believe me, you will sigh a sigh of relief when you leave this city. You are distracted. In Tehran you will always be distracted. Wait until you wake up one morning, see that incredible yellow light at sunrise, and breathe the mountain air. Wait until you see the stars spread out like a blanket in the heavens. Then you will know."

As they continued to walk past the *maktab* of children reciting the Quran, swaying backward and forward in imitation of the Prophet on his camel, she stopped and described her dream with a passion that made him want to kiss her right there. "We will build a beautiful home with a courtyard, a beautiful garden with a stream that runs through it, a garden with fig trees, peach trees and cherry trees, with hyacinths and narcissus, with pink roses, red roses, yellow roses and white roses, single roses and double roses. We will build a garden where you will get drunk with the smell of roses."

He loved what she was saying, but still he was torn. In so many ways, Tehran was his home. As Fereshteh and Nur ed Din stood in front of the children, swaying even as they watched the lovers converse, she looked away for a moment with downcast eyes and then looked back. "How could you not be tender when surrounded by roses?" she asked.

That settled it. They informed their friends of their imminent move to Kerman.

39

"What do you want, Nur ed Din, what are you looking for?" friends asked, dumbfounded. "Businessmen are flocking to the country looking for contacts and representatives. Yesterday I had dinner with the chairman of Pays Bas. Had you told me, I would have made an introduction and you could have struck a deal. But don't worry, he'll be back in two weeks. And if you can't wait that long, I'm lunching with the president of Barclay's tomorrow."

"What do you want, Nur ed Din, what are you looking for?" they asked in cocktail parties and intimate sit-down dinners. "You could make a fortune overnight with a well-placed investment. I know you're not interested in the possessions of this world. I've always known that. But there is no harm in putting aside a little something. If not for yourself, then for Fereshteh. You never know."

"What do you want, Nur ed Din, what are you are looking for?" Firouz asked, as shaven-headed boys splished and splashed down a turquoise-rock river. "Tell me what it is, and if it is in my power, I will do it. Just say the word and I will arrange it for you. Is it that sign from God you are waiting for? Believe me it is not my strong suit," he said with a smile, "but if it will keep you here, I'll try to intercede for you in that matter. In the meantime, there are a couple of opportunities I think you should seriously consider." Nur ed Din could not bring himself to entertain the possibilities. But he equally could not bring himself to tell Firouz that he intended to surround himself with tenderness in Kerman.

Firouz knew more than he let on. I had told him weeks ago, "It is obvious to anyone who cares to open their eyes that their place is elsewhere."

"Are you sure? Do you know this?" Firouz had asked.

"As well as I know that you walked away from a wonderful life in America," I replied, revealing an intimacy that was not often spoken.

Though he knew in his heart of hearts there was nothing to be done, he insisted on arguing with me. "What can Kerman offer that we do not have in Tehran? Here Nur ed Din can do whatever he wants. I'm not saying he has to be a banker, a lawyer or an engineer. I'm just saying that in Tehran he can write his own ticket."

It was true. Those were the days when I was offered the position of Assistant Dean at the Faculty of Beaux Arts one week, and when I politely declined, they offered me the

Dean's own position the following week. In a country ruled by one thousand fabled families, the wealthy and powerful were all connected in one way or another, and we took care of each other.

Once when my passport was misplaced, the Minister of Foreign Affairs sent over a signed, blank one with the gallant note, "Fill it out as you like." When I needed to get on a plane and the flights were completely booked, all I had to do was make a call and a ticket was waiting for me at the airport. There I was guided to the VIP lounge while airline staff handled the nuisances of customs and immigration, reminding me of the days convicted Bakhtiari khans sent their henchmen to do the time for them.

It was the Carnival and we were in the middle of the three-ring circus. We all knew the strongman and the bearded lady, the trapeze artist and the knife thrower, the juggler and the clown, the lion-tamer and the lion. The man in the top hat, red jacket and black boots. We knew the voice behind the mike urging one and all, "Come on in, come in and see the Greatest Show on Earth." We knew the man shot from the cannon and the diver who plunged into a bucket of water. We knew the dancing pig.

We knew the Senator who lived with both his wife and the Admiral she had chosen for her lover. The newspaper publisher purported to be the Shah's love-child. The bank president with a habit. We knew the Minister of Education inclined towards mysticism and the Minister of Interior who never recovered from his only son's tragic death. We knew the Ambassador who saw an Englishman every time he looked in the mirror. We knew (and some of us were related to) the fabulously wealthy Governor who moved to Switzerland rather than endure accusations of graft. We knew the merchant who made a fortune stockpiling snow tires, and the Admiral whose wife made the mistake of wearing a diamond ring obscene even by the standards of Iranian society in the Seventies. We knew them and they knew us.

40

I frequented those restaurants, hiked those mountain valleys, lived those halcyon days. I knew what it was to be young and burning with desire. I knew what it was to want to build shining white buildings, a brilliant white city. I knew Firouz, I knew Nur ed Din and Fereshteh. I knew the ones they grew up with, and grew up with the ones they knew. I knew them and I knew their stories. I witnessed the denouement from across living rooms, across dance floors and at so many seated dinners. I watched, I remembered, I wrote and I forgot. I played my part.

Firouz continued to play Gary Cooper. Strong, silent, and square-jawed, he was what was known in the Old West as a square shooter. He was a man who would give you a square deal. The kind of man who would look you square in the eyes, a man you could depend on to get things squared away. He had advanced, geometrically, from the straight line to the square. And in Iran in the Seventies he was a square peg in a round hole.

He played Gary Cooper in his professional and in his personal life. Unshakeable in his principles, he wore a tin star and a pair of six-shooters, lit matches on his stubble, and slept with his boots on. Like so many cowboys who live in the unrelenting force of the sun, he squinted (especially when dragging deep on a cigarette) so it looked like he had Chinese eyes. I knew better. The almond eyes could actually be ascribed to a Mongol ancestor, passed down from the time when the country was overrun by Tamerlane.

And women loved him. Maybe it was the force of his conviction, the strength of his belief, the beauty of his commitment. Maybe they felt he could love them with the same devotion, with the same unquestioned and unquestioning desire, with the same unwavering fidelity. Maybe they thought they had finally found a man who could be true. Or perhaps it was the challenge of replacing Iran in his desires. Recognizing that he did not have eyes for anyone else, that he could not even contemplate, for a second, devoting his life to a woman the way that he had devoted his life to his country, they were, perhaps, propelled to want to possess him.

Knowing that we were close, that we took walks together, they would corner me at cocktail parties. After engaging in pleasantries, after speaking of the weather and asking after the health of mutual friends to bring his name into the conversation, after I assured them "we are just friends," they would complain, "Don't you find him ridiculous in his unwavering devotion to this damned country? He should be worshipping me, instead. Believe me, I would give him a reason to spend the rest of his life in worship. I would give him something that he could devote a lifetime of devotion to, believe me, I would."

"Only have affairs with married women. That way you avoid complications," Shahriar advised, blowing smoke out his nose. He need not have wasted his breath; Firouz was the married one. The one who would only have fleeting, surreptitious affairs that would not detract from his one true love.

Sensing this, his provisional lovers were only incited further to possess him. There was one in particular who kept calling. "Please Firouz, can't we see each other? I need to see you. I'm not asking you to slay dragons for me, just to share a cup of tea. If you no longer want to see me, just say so. But couldn't we get together for old time's sake? I'll join you at a cocktail party, a dinner, a ribbon cutting, any one of the functions you attend every night of the week with people who don't even care for you. I miss you."

Though Iran never said "Yes" even with her eyes, Firouz could devote himself to no other. He was wed to a country that would only lead him on, claiming ignorance of his affections, feigning not to recognize him. A country that said "Nice to meet you" each time their paths crossed. Pretending not to remember, not to have enjoyed each and every one of his advances, each time he had firmly put his arm around her waist and cajoled her into walking down his path. Each time he had held her face in his hands, looked into her eyes and kissed her with the abandon that he never once exercised in any other part of his life.

Despite the reckless kisses, despite the way he threw caution to the wind, each time he had to seduce her all over again. It was as if he had never kissed her before. As if she had never been kissed before.

"Don't be this way, I know you say you're not sure about me, about this, that you need time. No, of course this won't detract from you, why would you say such a thing? No, you're not like all the others. There are no others. We've been through this before. There is no one else for me. I love you, I have always loved you." And then with only a hint of exasperation, "Don't you remember the last time we made love?"

Believing I was his confidante, women would ask, "Why should such energy be wasted on a fickle country?" Maybe it was their desire to lure him from his infatuation that made them pursue him so. Or maybe they saw in him the warrior, the general, the hero their fathers once had been.

Never once did he falter. Never once did he stop loving the country that would not love him back. She never offered more than a noncommittal shrug of her shoulders, a toss of her hair, an occasional kiss. But it was obvious she enjoyed his attentions, his advances, his embraces. It was obvious that she kept his love letters, and late at night read them one more time. In a moment of truth or weakness, tossing and turning at four in the morning, she may have admitted that she had once loved him, had once written a response she had intended to send, until her good senses prevailed and she tore it up, writing instead the more reasoned letter that lay in the bottom of a box in his closet.

She may have admitted that she had been attracted to him—love was too strong a word. But in the same breath she also would have said that her path lay elsewhere. She would not be strong-armed by a man who, though he didn't have the slightest clue as to who she was, was sure who she should be. What she should look like and how she should act. In the kitchen, in the parlour and in the bedroom.

Against all indications, against all the evidence, he hung his hopes on winning her heart and her hand. Believed that she could not help but be compelled by the sincerity of his intentions, the diligence of his effort, the magic in his kiss.

Somehow he convinced himself that her glances and laughter were directed towards him. That she just needed time, that she would come around, that she could not help but admit it to herself and confess it to him. And so he continued to pursue her fervently and devotedly through the go-go years, through the revolution and even after he had been betrayed, exiled and forgotten. Through it all he continued, in his way, to love her.

41

Iran was changing. Firouz desperately believed it was in response to his imprecations that she was finally wearing the French perfumes he found enchanting, the mod hairdos he found so fashionable. He hoped she would soon come around to sporting the dresses that salesgirls with not even remotely similar builds modelled for him in boutiques of European capitals. He desperately wanted to believe that Iran was as good as any Western country, and Tehran as modern as any Western city.

Not so long ago, Tehran had been surrounded by walls with one hundred and fourteen towers, one for each *sureh* of the Quran. Walls of mud-brick that never served as a defence against invaders. Nor could they hold back the astronomical growth of the city. No, that's not quite right. Exponential would be the more appropriate term, because god knows the expansion was much more mathematical than it ever was celestial. The walls were abandoned almost as soon as they were built. First in favour of other walls, and then for boulevards and highways, cloverleafs without a single reference to the

Quran or its one hundred and fourteen *surehs*.

"*Besmellahe rahmane raheem,* praise be to Allah, Lord of the Worlds, the Beneficent, the Merciful, Master of the Day of Judgement, thee we worship, thee we ask for help; show us the straight path," the first verse reads. In Firouz's Tehran, the references were no longer to beneficience, straight paths or small kindnesses, to the One who raised the heavens without pillars that you can see. The references were to Detroit and Paris, to Berlin and Los Angeles, London, Queens and Las Vegas. The Orient no longer jostled with the Occident for supremacy on Tehran's streets. As we built residential districts and business centres to accommodate the city's growth, the Occident had won hands down.

It was not just the architecture. Girls in beehive hairdos wore miniskirts and young men with Jason King haircuts sported bellbottoms. Rooftop restaurants served chicken kievsky, cinemas played the latest Double O Seven films, and chubby Iranian comedians implored go-go dancer sidekicks, "Give me a James Bond kiss." Trinity, the spaghetti-western cowboy, was more of a success in Persian than he ever was in Italian. Not only could he draw, slap his opponent, replace his six shooter, draw and slap his opponent seven times before his adversary extracted his gun from its holster, but even more amazingly, he managed to deliver punch lines without ever moving his lips.

At times the larger, bolder and more-colourful-than-life posters for these cinematic pearls or those starring Louis De Funes or Bruce Lee were juxtaposed with domes and spires, women in black chadors. It only served to accentuate how out of place the domes and the women in black were. There was very little of Tehran that spoke of anything other than a western and modern city.

It was just that the Iranians in the foreground failed to live up to the backdrop of modern Tehran. For the most part they wore the right costumes and sported the right haircuts. But then, to Firouz's chagrin, they would picnic with their samovars on highway medians. They would wander the streets buying old suits. With progress and affluence they no longer walked the streets chanting, "I buy coats and trousers." Persisting in their line of work, they used pickup trucks and microphones instead. Which was extremely poignant while making love on a torrid three o'clock in the afternoon.

Even if the residents persisted in baffling Firouz's attempts at Westernization, by the mid-nineteen seventies almost all of Tehran was new and Western. It was a rather simple calculation. Arithmetic, not mathematics. In 1873, one-hundred-and-fourteen-*sureh* Tehran had a population of one hundred thousand. By 1970 it had grown to "three millions" as Houshang was fond of saying.

Tehran was exactly what might be expected from any self-respecting, forward-looking capital city. Stone and glass houses gave a wink and a nod to Mies, concrete office buildings mimicked Gropius, and villas found their inspiration in Le Corbusier. There was a student of Frank Lloyd Wright who succeeded in creating a Persian Prairie style, and I achieved a vicarious popularity for Lautner in the foothills of the Alborz mountains that he had not yet encountered in the Hollywood hills.

Not all of Tehran's buildings embraced the modern. Some were simply Western. There were ranch houses, chateaux, and chalets. Moorish fantasies and the occasional Kublai Khan pagoda pleasure palace, equally Western concepts.

Firouz and I often walked the streets as bakers fired early morning ovens, as taxi drivers waited for passengers to queue up, and tea-shop owners handed out hubble-bubbles and two cups of tea, one sweet and one bitter, to mimic life.

"The desires of a society are expressed in the brick and stone, the concrete and glass, the tile and the faience of the buildings lining the streets," I told him, pointing to the Achamenian-style bank.

"But that is the past, Yassaman. Our future is in the planned new town laid out on the west end of Tehran," Firouz pointed out. "It has two soon-to-be-built shopping malls, an international school and a village of highrise apartments."

"How do you know that?"

"I've bought a couple of lots out there. The terms are excellent, and land in Tehran cannot help but go up. I strongly recommend that you buy as well. If you like, I'll make an introduction. You know there's a waiting list."

I almost invested with Firouz in *Shahrak-e-Gharb*. Best translated as *The Diminutive City of the West,* it renounced all associations with the East. But for a few highrises named after dead poets, there was not a hint of anything Iranian.

42

But I didn't care, not until the day I saw the City Theatre. Thinking back now, I vaguely remember having heard that a brilliant young graduate of the Beaux Arts had received the contract, but I thought no more of it. There were so many contracts being handed out, so many brilliant young architects. Around the corner from the sidewalk where I had spent so many memorable moments, the City Theatre was not off the beaten path, nor was it on my regular circuit. So I never got to see it as it went up. I did not pass by to see the structure and the skeleton, to guess at how it would all play out. I did not attend the ribbon-cutting, though, to my astonishment, Firouz later informed me matter-of-factly that he had.

One day, not long after the ceremony, I happened to pass by. "Stop. Stop right here," I told the driver abruptly. It took a while to get up the courage to get out of the car. To circumambulate the building as the faithful do the Kaaba, casting stones at the devil. To strike up the courage to see if the promise of the exterior was actually fulfilled on the inside.

Upon entering, I was the princess who yawned, stretched and asked, "Have I been asleep long?" On that day I understood that I had been wasting my time designing buildings as good as the ones in Paris or LA. I was the beggar who cast aside doubts, picked up his mattress and followed a stranger in flowing robes. The lines of its broken arches, the rhythm of its columns, and the faience covering its walls revealed a modern building that had understood the Islamic tradition without a single reference to the domes and spires of Safavid mosques or Saljuq palaces. An architecture that understood them all, dissected spaces and forms, applied new materials, turned everything on its ear, reinvented itself and miraculously succeeded.

I rushed through my commitments, declined every new project, closed my office and spent the next six months walking the streets of desert towns, sketchbook in hand. I devoted pages to the streets of Natanz, the residences of Kashan, the bathhouse of Kerman. I sketched flowing gardens, domed bazaars and dilapidated caravanserais. Mosques and minarets, palaces and ruins, recumbent lions and rising suns, the name of God in so many flowing scripts.

And when I returned I insisted Firouz walk with me through Pamenar and Chaleh-Meidoun, through Nasser Khosrow and the twisting and turning streets surrounding the bazaar. I was giddy designing houses around blue-tiled pools that reflected the ever-changing sky. Wind-towers that captured the breeze. And how they were so brilliantly reinterpreted in the Museum of Contemporary Arts.

Eager with anticipation, I walked the streets of Tehran looking for those buildings that, even unsuccessfully, engaged in the debate between our architectural tradition and the modern. I passionately spoke of designs, technologies, and the genius of the City Theatre.

But Firouz did not care. More than architecture, he cared about the Tehran where houses were built with corrugated iron roofs and cooking oil tins. The *bidonvilles* that received the detritus of the city as it flowed downhill. The houses washed away every time there was a decent rain. The slums meant to be replaced by new towns that never got built, by apartments shipped over in prefabricated concrete pieces that never got assembled. The shantytowns built of cardboard and leftover scraps of metal. Cities of tents and tins without water and plumbing. Cities not featured in bridges of turquoise picture books.

Firouz cared for the Tehranis who watched their hopes evaporate even as everyone else got richer. The ones who left their villages, the fruit un-plucked, to build houses they never could afford to live in, drive taxis they could never afford to purchase, walk through streets buying and selling secondhand suits.

43

I often saw Firouz and prided myself that I knew better than any one else how he felt. So I was quite surprised when on one of our walks he announced, "Yassaman, you would be proud to know that I am no longer reading travelogues. Given our current circumstances, I am devoting my attention exclusively to fiction." Allowing a dramatic pause for the full impact of his statement to sink in, he continued, "I am currently reading *The Thousand and One Days* and *The Perfumed Garden*. I will soon devote myself to *The Unveiling*. As it turns out, for our country, there is no understanding of the histories without the fiction."

He had finally found the images that flavoured the visions of every westerner who ever set foot in Persia and "many who never did, but still insisted on writing a book or two. Do you know, Yassaman," he pointed out, waving his hands, "they are all romances."

Of course they were. Star-crossed lovers dying entwined in each other's arms. Princesses unlocking forbidden doors and fishermen casting magic nets. Men and women who did not have the bravery to fight but did have the courage to starve. Veiled prophets with thirsty swords and husbands who pursued veiled women into dead end alleys, only to find their own wives. Servile monarchs and superb mendicants, crippled conquerors and content porters. They were oriental entertainments. Of course they were all romances.

"What is truly remarkable is that a good number of these books were written by the people responsible for making significant decisions for the French or the British Empires," Firouz pontificated. "Isn't it amazing that Gertrude Bell, the person single-handedly responsible for choosing Feisal to rule Iraq, was also the woman who wrote *Persian Pictures?*" Producing one of his little black books, he proceeded, "Listen to this: 'Every day I meet our aged kalendars and ladies who I am sure have suits of swan feathers laid up in a chest at home, and some times when I open a new jar of rose water I know that instead of a sweet smell, the great smoke of one of Suleiman's efreets will come out of its neck.' Can you believe that was written by the woman making decisions on the future of a nation?"

Of course I believed. In disinherited princes and prophets who cast no shadow. In the dewdrops of mercy, in the torches and encounters in the garden. Princesses who wept rubies and laughed gold. Pearl divers and little black fish. And I knew that Firouz still clung to the lion-hearted crusaders and one-eyed admirals of his youth.

"You do know that Feisal was strung up and decapitated, his body dragged through the streets and defiled by thousands. But that is really no reflection on Gertrude Bell. Arab despots have often been treated in this manner." Believing he was on a roll, he took a deep breath. "It is not without precedent," Firouz continued as we walked down avenues named for Persian poets and alleys for European capitals. "Though it sounds absurd that politicians, historians and archaeologists would devote themselves to fiction, it is not without precedent," he said as if coming to a significant conclusion. *"Hajji Baba of Ispahan,* Morier's account of a scoundrel and a nation of scoundrels, was actually based on his diplomatic missions to Iran. It is still touted by historians as the most insightful and accurate account of Persia and the Persian character, and remains required reading for every traveller, diplomat, and Orientalist. Have you noticed there is not one single redeeming feature in any of his characters? Not in the avaricious king, not in the calculating chief minister, the self-serving and ignorant mullah or in the rogue Hajji Baba himself. I have known scoundrels in my day. Believe me, I have my own misgivings about the Iranian character. And let me tell you, the rogues I have known always have something to recommend them."

Of course I knew; after all, Sabu was my first love. I still remember the scene where, with a wink to an unseen god, he stole the flying carpet from the white-bearded one. "Allah, take him by the hand, the old man does not need a carpet to come to you. But if I am to save the prince I will need to take flight now," he said with a mischievous look.

Nor did I need fictional characters to remind me that scoundrels have their redeeming features. I needed look no further than Farshad, Firouz's green-eyed classmate with a permanent five o'clock shadow and a soft handshake. Giggling girls outside school gates used to whisper that his vocation in life was to take his classmates to the red light district. The young men invariably came back with remarkably little to say, except for how Farshad was greeted by name and with respect by everyone from the pimps to the sellers of single cigarettes. And how each prostitute prominently displayed Farshad's framed, signed and dated photograph on her bedside table.

There was even a story that on one occasion, he picked up a young streetwalker and took her to a deserted house where he was soon apprehended by the gendarmes. Not missing a beat, he asked for their indulgence. "Gentlemen," he said, "could you wait a just little while longer? I paid for two."

But Farshad was the first on the scene when Nur ed Din's uncle passed on. I don't know what words he used to get past the housekeeper under strict orders not to admit anyone. Perhaps the ones he used on recalcitrant prostitutes. But she let him in when she had turned so many others away. He was the first to offer his condolences and comfort to Nur ed Din. Farshad was a knave, but for what he did for Nur ed Din, he held a special place in my heart. I knew scoundrels and I knew bastards, and I knew better than Firouz that the real bastard in the story of *Hajji Baba of Ispahan* was the author.

44

In his search through Western fiction, Firouz did a peculiar thing. Though he seldom read them, he acquired every edition of the *The Arabian Nights* he could find. He collected *Stories from the Arabian Nights, Tales from the Arabian Nights,* and *More Tales from the Arabian Nights.* He collected *The Portable Arabian Nights* and *The Supplemental Arabian Nights.* He owned versions recounted by Lane and Payne, Galland, Housman and Lang, editions illustrated by Maxwell Parish, Moreau and Wyeth. He scoured bookshops and auction houses, the antiquarians in Quai Saint Denis and Portobello Road, left calling cards for booksellers who never called him back.

He owned the *Mille et Une Nuits* in French, and he owned them in German. The only one he actually read was Sir Richard Burton's *One Thousand Nights and a Night.* Though the stories could not keep his attention, Burton's footnotes persuaded him to read the entire eleven volumes. "The amount of research and documentation is incredible, Yassi, and in itself an indication of the degree of misinformation on the Orient. And Burton's editorial comments are a constant source of pleasure. Where else could you find a footnote that explains, 'Yet Eastern medicine consists mainly of two parts: the first of general prescriptions, and the second of aphrodisiacs, especially those *qui prolongent le plaisir* as did the Gaul by thinking of *sa pauvre mere.*'"

In reading the footnotes to the Arabian Nights, he finally understood what motivated orientalists like Morier, Gobineau and Bell to come to Iran. He also came to understand what motivated those who never had and never would. Why Arnold, who did not know a word of Persian, had bothered to rhyme, in English, stories of Rostam and Sohrab, Iranian heroes that he did not, could not know.

Firouz read his Oriental Romances and learned to recognize references to the albino hero Zal, who at birth had the hair of an old man. He knew that Rostam's beard was forked and that Belgheis was the beauty of all ages. He learned to know the One who bids and forbids, the Destroyer of Delights and the Sunderer of Companies (and the Living One who dieth not). He caught the references to Tobias and his angel, to Solomon's flying carpet and to the worms that gnawed away at his cane until they revealed that he had been propped up for years while others ruled in his stead. He knew that the awaited one, solid as a mountain, would arrive on the clouds. So when Nur ed Din finally confided that part of his move to Kerman was his desire to create a paradise with Fereshteh that God would have to notice, Firouz could not resist the urge to quip:

A Persian's paradise is easily made.
'Tis but black eyes and lemonade.

45

In a sense it was as simple as that. Nur ed Din had no use for the endless stream of *houris* promised to the faithful followers of the one true Prophet. No need for cities of gold, tables set with exquisite *pilaus* and sumptuous *sherbets*. Tables groaning under the weight of abundance that were replenished even before one rose to rest one's head on a lute-playing *peri*'s lap. All he needed was a pair of black eyes and a mole on his angel's cheek. He could have skipped the lemonade.

He wanted to watch her lying next to him at the first blush of dawn. Her face to be the last thing he saw before closing his eyes to dream dreams he would not remember. He wanted to watch her meticulously arrange the morsels on her fork and the morsels on her plate, keeping the very best for last.

He wanted to see her smile as she did so, knowing that when she looked up she would be certain her eyes would meet his. He wanted to see her give all the money in her purse to the first beggar she encountered. He wanted to spend the hours with her in lovemaking, in conversation, in Kerman.

But there was this matter outstanding of constantly waiting for a sign. He had repeatedly petitioned but had not yet heard from his God. So he decided to build a paradise that God would have to inhabit. And if God would not reside in his paradise, then at least it would prompt a reaction. It was not without precedent. It had happened before in a story I knew well. And if I knew it, then I am sure Nur ed Din must have heard it at least once. Maybe even from Uncle Mustafa.

Ibn Shaddad, an impatient man who had been assured a place in heaven, had decided, nonetheless, to create a paradise in this world. A garden and many-pillared city in the desert. Ibn Shaddad spent twenty years amassing the coral and amethyst, the gold, ebony and ambergris encountered in descriptions of Eden. He devoted his vast fortune and the wealth of the nations that bore him allegiance to the creation of a paradise on earth. He named it Eram, and in the books that told the story it was called the many-pillared city of Eram.

Ibn Shaddad did not stop there. He equally devoted himself to the creation of a hell because, he reasoned, there is no heaven without a hell. He sent *jenns* to collect the most terrible creatures on the world's surface, the black scorpion, the forked-tongue serpent, the gnat. When all was ready, he went forth to inhabit the city without equal in this world or the next.

But God struck him down, sent a terrible flood to destroy the vanity and arrogance of a man who could not wait until death to inhabit a promised paradise. God struck down the man who thought he could rival the divine in this world. Eram was obliterated, Ibn Shaddad and his retinue destroyed. To this day people search without luck for traces of the city that Ibn Shaddad built and God destroyed. Nur ed Din could take consolation in the fact that at least God had taken notice. At least God had responded. And that, in Nur ed Din's particular situation, was encouraging.

I do not believe Nur ed Din was seeking to rival the divine. He was not going to create a heaven of gold and amethyst or scour the globe for creatures to inhabit his hell. Nur ed Din was not interested in competing with celestial territory, or infernal for that matter. He was just trying to call attention to his petition by building a place that God would want to inhabit. It was a simple proposition. No cornelian or lapis lazuli, not a single pillar. Just a bubbling stream, oleander, tulips and jasmine, a weeping willow and a grassy, shady spot where one could make love.

46

Fereshteh had an innate appreciation for flowers and fruit trees. She knew that in Iran, before there were cities, there were cities of gardens. Behind brick, stone and adobe walls, there were plane trees and weeping willows, cypresses and pomegranates, apricots, peaches and apples, walnuts, mulberries, figs, and sour cherries, horse chestnuts and poplars. Secret wells, grasses that only sprouted one week of the year. Arbours where one might recline, leaving the wine untouched, the *ghalyoon* unsmoked, the book of poetry unread.

Fereshteh loved gardens and loved to surround herself with flowers, trees and running water. And while Nur ed Din's Garden of God might have satisfied Allah, it was not quite what his angel had in mind. She wanted to grow roses. She wanted to plant roses as far as the eye could see. Pink ones and white ones, red ones and double red ones, the ones named Dusky Maiden, Child's Play, and Fantasy, Double Delight, and Scentimental, Brilliant Pink Iceberg, and Raspberry Swirls. The ones named after Miss Flippins, the Princess of Wales, the Duchesse de Brabant and the Souvenir de Malmaison. Aunt Ruth, Elizabeth Taylor, Linda Campbell and Barbara Streisand.

Roses that spoke a language all to themselves. Coral for desire, lavender for enchantment, yellow for joy. "I care," "Welcome back," and "Remember me." White for reverence and "Keep a secret," dark burgundy for unconscious beauty, dark pink for thankfulness, pink for "Please believe me," and light pink for grace and joy. She wanted to be surrounded by roses, to harvest roses and sell them to gardeners, lovers and florists. Fereshteh had always felt that union with the divine was to be achieved in creating things of beauty. What could be more beautiful than roses?

She believed, she insisted in believing that this would be their path. She loved Nur ed Din and she had faith in him. She knew he would receive a sign. But saw no need to put life on hold until things became manifest. What if somehow they had missed or misinterpreted the mumblings of thanks from a beggar, a pattern of windblown leaves on the sidewalk, a rhythm in the poplar's branches. Any one of them could have been the sign he had been waiting for, any one of them could have held the key.

She knew that more than building a paradise, Nur ed Din had to devote himself to the day-to-day. Trying to avert an imminent future where he would reach for a worn and tattered photograph, a folded and re-folded letter, trying desperately to avert that final black and white scene where he would reach out, in an angled shot, oversize shadows painting the walls, for the one thing that was good and pure, she decided to build on Nur ed Din's love of gardens.

She knew that for Nur ed Din spirituality was not to be achieved by looking at ripples in the lake, examining the shifting sands. She knew he found his spirituality in the day-to-day. She had seen it a million times. Nur ed Din telling jokes about Bedouins and camels to policemen and street sweepers. Talking soccer with the grocer and reciting Rumi with the baker, discussing literature with the pool attendant. She had seen him laugh resoundingly as he smiled and pointed his finger at an unseen God. Once, late for an engagement, she went out to find him on the street corner in a heated discussion with taxi drivers and passengers who had delayed their departures to hear him out.

"I have a devout friend who says his prayers five times a day just as the Prophet prescribed," Nur ed Din explained to the group of curious bystanders. "Except he does so religiously at exactly forty-five minutes after the appointed hour. 'Everyone else is praying at dawn,' my pious friend says. 'God is too busy to really pay attention to what I have to say. That is why I wait until after the rush.'" The taxi drivers laughed and shook their heads in wonder.

He had a sense of humour that found expression at the oddest moments. Once, when they had gone together on a trip to the Caspian, Fereshteh had been frustrated to find that she had brought two bikini bottoms and no tops. Learning of her predicament, Nur ed Din consoled her, "Darling, please do not be upset, your packing was absolutely right. It is the destination that was wrong. We should have gone to St. Tropez."

She loved him for it. It was at moments like these that she wanted to bear his child. On days like this she would write him unexpected letters that started off, "The grocer is giving me a lecture on the merits of vegetarianism, as I am picking out bunches of white grapes and thinking of you." It was at times like this that she would catch herself wanting to write, "At the perfume seller's this morning, there was the most beautiful child. He had your eyes. He even tilted his head that certain way that you sometimes do."

She loved him, but had tired of waiting for a sign. She knew of signs, and she knew that miracles were not quite what they were made out to be. A poem she had encountered quite by chance summed it up for her. It was about a girl swimming naked in the sea, and a bearded man walking on the water, and a question. A question, or rather, an assertion about the miracle of miracles, the marvel announced from on high. It was written by a Frenchman.

47

Fereshteh knew of marvels, she knew of miracles, and she knew of flowers. Nur ed Din was swept away by the force of her conviction. He too found reason to want to plant roses. In their quest for a place to grow roses they searched through the city of Kerman and they searched the outlying villages. They looked in *ziaratgah,* the place of pilgrimage, *lolo,* the pearl, *bagh bala,* the upper garden, and *bagh paeen,* the lower garden. They looked in the mountain of the upper garden, *kooh-e bagh bala,* and in the mountain of tulip fields, *kooh-e lalehzar,* where they briefly resolved to grow tulips. They searched for a home among woven flowers, and in the field called the lady's house. They almost found it in Rostam's well, and in the lions' lair. They searched in couples' mountain, in the place of pomegranates, and among the willow reeds.

They instinctively loved a land named after pearls and pomegranates, after heroes and the lions they hunted. They knew they were on the right track, but despite all their wanderings through mountains and plains, through fields and villages, months later they still had not found their place.

And then as the sun was setting, they came across a village in the shadow of a mountain that reminded Fereshteh of a reclining Indian chief. She pointed out his barrel chest, his abbreviated neck, the jutting chin, the proud lips and nose. Nur ed Din thought it bore a resemblance to the profile of Robert Mitchum and told her so. It was a village like any other, with mud-brick walls and ancient walnut trees. It had dirt streets and smelled the honest smell of a village. In the distance an impregnable citadel sat on an impregnable mountaintop. Ice-cold water ran through ditches. Sour cherry and quince trees extended their branches over crumbling walls.

But it was entirely deserted. Or at least it seemed so as they looked for someone who might tell them what it was called, why the trees were overgrown, the fields untended.

They wandered through winding dirt streets, under entangled branches, past stone and mud brick walls, irrigation ditches and green pools where water flowed in and water flowed out. In their wanderings they encountered a house with geraniums, powder-blue curtains, and a neatly-tended garden. Still there was no one in sight.

Finally they turned a corner and arrived at the top of a hill. There they encountered an old man and his over-laden mule. He walked right past them, not questioning for a moment what the young lovers were doing in the middle of the deserted village. Intent on learning the name of the village, Nur ed Din offered the old man a firm good afternoon, and having managed to gain his attention for a moment, inquired, "Uncle, why is it that in this beautiful village with such abundant water and such wonderful fruit trees, you are the only living soul we have seen?"

Watching the mule continue down the hill, he shook his head and replied, "Ten years ago this village suffered an earthquake. After that everyone left."

"But how could they desert a village like this?" Nur ed Din persisted.

"Young couples like you had already begun moving to the city. They took it as a message from God. Some come back to pick fruit or to picnic on the weekends, but I am one of the few who stayed."

Watching the donkey disappear down the path the old man hesitated, then began again, as if he needed explain further, "I couldn't leave. The ones who are dear to me are buried in this land." He scratched his white beard and smoothed his hair before putting his cap back on. "You will excuse me, I have to deliver this load of thistles to the next village and get back before dark. Tonight is a moonless night."

"We had not meant to keep you from your work, uncle, but tell me, what is the name of this village?"

The old man's voice drifted up the dusty street, "We call it Bolbolouieh."

48

"What a funny old man, and what a funny name for a village. Bolbolouieh. He did say Bolbolouieh, didn't he?" Fereshteh asked.

It had a nice ring to it. Bulbul, as the British transcribed it during the Victorian era, is the fabled Persian nightingale. "Bulbul" they wrote in their entertainments, evoking images of songbirds in gilded cages, of plain, brown birds singing the most enchanting melodies. And roses, for there is no nightingale without a rose. The bulbul pouring out its heart in song, wings caressing petals, while the rose gently sways this way and that. The bulbul turning the white rose blood-red, singing like water bubbling from a silver jar, its breast pressed against the thorn.

Bolbolouieh. Bolbol meaning something more than a nightingale. Bolbolouieh, the place of the bolbolou, as the Kermani call it in their lilting, lethargic accent. It would also be the place of the rose.

Beyond its evocative powers, Bolbolouieh had much to commend it. It was far enough, but not too far, away from the city. Largely uninhabited, it had abundant water, fertile soil and was watched over by a horizontal Apache. On top of that, there was very little risk of desolation or disaster. God had already destroyed this particular paradise once.

So they set their hearts on finding their place in the village of Bolbolouieh. They walked through the streets looking for a house and walked through the outskirts looking for fields. They found a mud-brick house encircled by mud-brick walls, with a turquoise blue-tiled pool reflecting the ever-changing sky. It had the most delicious stream of water cascading through the garden, and ancient plane trees provided the most delectable shade. Damaged by the earthquake, long cracks ran through its walls, endearing it to them even more. Like a broken vase glued back together by a child. Like a dog with a crooked ear.

The house they chose had a roof where they could spend the night under the blanket of the stars and a balcony from which they could watch the sunset. A stream filled the turquoise-coloured pool and ran through the garden. Of course there was work to be done to make it a place to live, but the essentials were there. Rectangular rooms and whitewashed walls, a pool, a garden and the sound of running water. The warble of nightingales was sure to follow.

Fields abounded. Fields fed by irrigation ditches and subterranean channels that brought waters from far-away mountains into the village. Fields delineated by stone walls and mud-brick walls, fields where wheat and barley, beets and turnips had once grown. So they bought the house and a few small pieces of land and set themselves to creating their gardens. The few remaining villagers thought they were mad. Stories of ascetic, slightly less-than-complete ancestors notwithstanding, they could not believe that an educated couple would come to live in a place destroyed by God and deserted by its inhabitants. But Nur ed Din and Fereshteh were earnest and intent in their purpose. With Nur ed Din's inheritance, they were able to attract day-labourers from neighbouring villages who tilled and fertilized the soil. Men and women who planted the roses Fereshteh painstakingly chose and had transported to the village in the back of a brightly painted lorry inscribed with the words, "Life is beautiful, but ..." an infinite melancholy captured in those three silent dots. Day-labourers cleaned the irrigation ditches, pruned the roses, fought off aphids and mould, and created by the end of the year two fields of roses in Bolbolouieh.

The best Fereshteh sold in the flower bazaar to be placed in vases, arranged in bouquets, or exchanged by modern couples—"Under dowry please specify one stem of a rose, and one stick of rock candy." The petals of the ones she did not sell, she scattered on paths, floors, tables, and between sheets. She placed rose petals in the hubble-bubble and would occasionally take a puff just to watch them dance in smoke and water. She marked her favourite verses of Hafez and Molavi, Rilke and Prévert, placed rose petals on dashboards, altars, breakfast and tea trays, on pies and cakes. She made rose-petal jam. Their lives were filled with roses. Their lives over-flowed with roses. They had almost run out of things to do with roses, and then one day Nur ed Din went away to return, a week later, with the most amazing contraption.

49

Years later, after having forgotten the names and faces of the ones who first made their hearts go pitter-pat, the dreams they tried so hard to forget, they would remember the day Nur ed Din brought the pipes and vats, the contraption that took the rose through fire and water and from which rosewater emerged. Floating on top was a layer of essence so delicate it had to be extracted with a feather, so precious it was worth far more than its weight in gold.

Nur ed Din put together his marvellous device of copper and steel based on various entries under the term "distillery," rudimentary drawings, and a simple principle. But no mat-ter how simple the principle he explained to the villagers as they gathered around to watch fragrant drops emerge from the copper pipe, it never ceased to amaze them. And it never ceased to amaze him.

The distillery was rather basic, a shed with a huge vat filled one day of the year with boiling water. On harvest day, for those brief hours before dawn when roses are most fra-grant, the forsaken village of Bolbolouieh would be populat-ed with more than a thousand men, women and children in coloured scarves, patterned shirts and patched pants. After picking the roses they would place shovelful after shovelful in the boiling water.

From the vat a copper pipe ran through a pool where water flowed in and water flowed out. As the rose-scented vapour went through the water, it condensed, drops forming on the sides of the copper tube, little drops that would emerge from a funny-looking funnel and end up in bottles. A simple process, but it never failed to amaze Nur ed Din. Something about Bolbolouieh resulted in the most amazingly fragrant roses, more fragrant, more powerful than Kashan and Ghamsar whose names are synonymous with roses and rosewater. Mullahs, pastry chefs, perfumers, lovers, soap and powder makers clamoured for the bottles that bore a line drawing of a ringed hand delicately holding a single rose. It was named after the Prophet's daughter, for Zahra who was more than any other the true flower of the Prophet Muhammad.

The popularity of Zahra Rosewater soon prompted Bolbolouieh's mostly absent landowners to action. One plot after another was devoted to the cultivation of roses, roses sold to Nur ed Din and Fereshteh to be plucked once a year between four and six in the morning.

The landowners would check with Nur ed Din on the types to plant, how to fertilize and prune them, how to breed and cross-breed them. "Plant the Prophet's flower. Plant the rose beloved by Muhammad, and do the things beloved by Muhammad," he told those who inquired. By way of explanation he would continue, "On the day the Prophet (may peace be upon him) ascended into heaven on a winged horse with the face of a human, a creature whose legs reached as far as its eyes could see, on that day, as the Prophet rode off to heaven, the sweat from his brow fell to earth and from the sweet sweat of the Prophet's brow sprang the white rose."

If he was in a good mood, Nur ed Din would continue, describing the crown on the winged creature's head, the dark eyes and the soft ears, how the *buraq* said to the Prophet, "Ride on me today, but do not forget me on the day of intercession." Or he might tell stories to overly erect villagers and fidgety children of how Saladin, when he expelled the crusaders from the mosque of Omar, purified it with five hundred camel-loads of rosewater. Of how Ayesheh's innocence was proven when an angel instructed the Messenger of God to cast yellow roses into the pool and see if they changed colour. Nur ed Din had a line of poetry for every circumstance, an anecdote for every occasion. These he would recite punctuated by his resounding laugh, while pointing a finger at an unseen God.

The villagers loved his eccentricity. When bored, they would make a point of asking to borrow some implement. Nur ed Din, knowing that he was being set up like a teacher whose students wish to avoid the lesson at hand, would laugh his laugh and proceed nonetheless to tell the story of how Mullah Nasr ed Din was approached by a neighbour who asked to borrow his mule.

"'I would give it to you if I could,' the Mullah lied, 'but unfortunately I lent my mule to a friend in the neighbouring village.'

"At that very moment the mule in question began to bray, which the rebuked borrower did not fail to bring to the good Mullah's attention. 'But Mullah, how can you say your mule is not here. I can hear it braying.'

"'Who are you going to listen to,' replied the Mullah without a moment's hesitation. 'Me or that mule?'"

The villagers knew the story well, requested it often, and enjoyed it immensely when a newcomer would ask to borrow an implement. They would stop work for a minute or two, smile and gather round to hear Nur ed Din tell the story of the mullah and the mule one more time. Nur ed Din had a story or a line of verse for every occasion. Sometimes it seemed he only spoke in stories.

He knew each villager by name, even the ones who only came once a year. He took pride in knowing the villages they came from and in remembering the convoluted relationships that characterize any Iranian family. "How is your cousin, Ali," he would ask solicitously, his questions a mark of his interest and concern. "You are Gholam Reza's son, aren't you? How is your father? How was his pilgrimage to Mashhad? Tell him I have a thing or two to discuss with him," he would say though there really was no business to transact.

"How is your sister doing? Is she still the top student in her class?" he would inquire of the mischievous twelve-year-old with bright eyes and a shaved head. The boy would mutter some polite confirmation.

"You could stand to learn a thing or two from her," he would advise the boy. Turning his back as if to walk away, he would spin around abruptly to catch the young rascal pointing to the heavens.

Trusting in Fereshteh and Nur ed Din, the villagers returned one by one to Bolbolouieh. They came because they heard stories of young lovers who had transformed a ruin of a village into a place where roses bloomed and nightingales sang out of season. They came seeking happiness, but stayed because, more than happiness, Bolbolouieh offered them the promise of happiness.

50

Every day Nur ed Din waited for the sign that did not come. Every day, without fail, he prayed to his God and asked for a sign. And though he never received a response that he could discern, he continued to love his God. He loved his God and continued to long for the *moazzen's* call when he would wipe the tears from the corners of his eyes, wash his face, his hands and his feet and prostrate himself toward Mecca.

He loved *Eid-e Ghorban,* the Feast of the Sacrifice, and the story that accompanied it. When his uncle told him for the first time of the burning bush and God's demand of Abraham and Isaac while handing out choice cuts of meat to the needy, Nur ed Din inquired indignantly, "How could a kind and compassionate God ask for such a thing? And how in the world could Abraham ever attempt to sacrifice his own son?" before rationalizing, "But it all turned out all right in the end." After that conclusion Uncle Mustafa pulled him aside to tell him, in a voice that spoke volumes, "Never seek to test others. Not your friends, not your loved ones, and especially not your God."

Nur ed Din found these words perplexing, but continued to have faith, and on *Eid-e Ghorban* continued to go through the village with offerings and kind words for Hassan, Abdulhussein and Reza, for Fatemeh, Massoumeh and Bibinaz. There were days he looked forward to and days he could not bear to miss. He still loved the ceremonies in honour of Hussein's martyrdom and continued to lead the procession in black for the "Prince of Innocents'" death. As he did, he thought back to that day when a girl with a mole on her cheek signed six four nine four nine while beating her breast.

It disturbed him that he had not yet found his Mount Qaf, had not even been visited by a man named Gabriel, let alone an angel. Beyond the miracle of the bumblebee, he had received no indication of God's greatness. No fiery chariot, no shooting star, not even an alighting dove. It was especially troublesome when a member of his flock travelled all the way from Tehran to ask Nur ed Din to assume his duties or to reproach him for having abandoned them. To these individuals Nur ed Din would calmly respond, drawing on poetic license, "On the day he died, I asked my uncle, 'How will I follow in your footsteps?' and do you know what he said? He said, 'Ask your God for a sign; He will give it to you.' Every day I ask for a sign, and every day I wait for it to come. What is one year or ten years in the scheme of things? Have patience. All things will come to pass as is Allah's will. But stay with us for a day or two. Tell us of how things are going in Tehran, of your family and our friends. Come, let me show you the garden."

Nur ed Din devoted himself to his paradise and waited patiently for the sign he never received. As the weeks, months and years passed, the pain of waiting no longer troubled him so much. He was preoccupied with the workings of the garden and the rose fields, the comings and goings, the day-to-day decisions. Besides, he invented all types of justifications.

My favourite was a story he had heard from our friend Nasser, and adapted to his own circumstances. At the age of fourteen, Nasser had written a love letter to the girl with the pretty pink overcoat and the charming laugh. "When we are all dead and buried beneath mounds of earth" were the lugubriously romantic opening lines taken directly from Napoleon's letter to Josephine. With those borrowed lines, Nasser had written his first love letter. He carefully folded it and carried it around in his shirt pocket, waiting for the moment when he might give it to the girl in the pink overcoat, acquaint her with the perfection of his love and extract a kiss from those charming lips.

Except the letter always seemed to stay firmly in his pocket. There was the time on the bus when he could have given it to her, but she was leaning against him so serenely that it would have been a shame to disturb her. And there was that other time when they were suddenly alone in the parlour, except she had asked him to play ping pong, and how could he refuse?

Missing opportunity after opportunity, Nasser carried that letter around for months. And then, as a reminder of his first in a string of unrequited loves, he would place it in his inside pocket, no matter what coat he was wearing. Perhaps God was no different. Perhaps God too was waiting for the perfect moment, the perfect opening to give Nur ed Din the letter that would begin, like Napoleon's, "When we are all dead and buried beneath mounds of earth, then you will know the extent of my love."

Even as Nur ed Din waited, he continued to love his silent God and to love his angel with the beauty mark. He loved the paradise he and his lover had created from a deserted village. He loved the tenderness brought about by roses. He thought about God's letter less and less as he increasingly preoccupied himself with Zahra's rosewater. But sometimes late at night, God's silence would nag at him like an itch on an amputated limb. And then he would rise, dress quietly, splash water on his face and walk off into the hills.

While Nur ed Din had come to Kerman with the preposterous notion of building a paradise God would have to inhabit, Fereshteh had been intent on escaping Tehran and filling their lives with beauty. But those were not her only goals. She knew he prospered in his interactions with others, expounding theories and pointing to an unseen God. She knew there was a market for the roses they would grow in Bolbolouieh. She knew they could sell their roses, rosewater, and rose essence in Kerman and in Tehran. She knew they could sell in Japan where no wedding is complete without an arbour of roses, in India where roses are eaten raw by the lovelorn, and in Mecca where the faithful anoint themselves with rosewater as they circumambulate the Kaaba and cast stones at the Devil.

She was not wrong. Not only were the lovers intoxicated with the smell of roses, they also prospered. They made money growing roses. They made the villagers money growing roses. And while Nur ed Din's intention had never been more than to create a paradise, he found himself devoted to an endeavour that prospered. This was new to him. He had never been involved in the business of buying and selling.

No one in his family had ever gone off to Bombay to broker tea or to Ceylon to buy it in bulk. He had never given outrageous prices with a straight face. He had never been sent, like a somewhat round classmate later to be an even rounder businessman, to collect an unpaid debt. Nur ed Din had never been taken out of school to sit in the debtor's shop every day from the time it opened to the moment it closed until the debt was repaid. He had never had to sit as full glasses of tea were brought in and empty glasses taken out, silently enduring the barbs cast in his direction until the debtor became so irritated at the sight of the vapid-faced boy every morning as he opened his shop and every evening as he closed it that he finally paid just to be rid of him. At that point the round boy could no longer go back to school, but he did not need to; he had learned a vital lesson in human character.

The round classmate learned that lesson and learned it well. Nur ed Din never did. Yet somehow, he and Fereshteh made money. They were fortunate, they had a product they loved and that people wanted. They also had a place that had achieved a certain mystique. Bolbolouieh.

51

The friends who came to visit were astounded by the beauty of the garden, the beauty of their lives. Overcome, they would quote the lines first recited to Mughal kings in the gardens of Shalimar, "If there is a heaven on earth, 'tis this, 'tis this, 'tis this."

Nur ed Din would smile, thank them for their kind words, and wink, "What are you waiting for?" to an unseen God.

At the evening hour, when light softens the edges of mountains, for a moment their friends imagined living out their lives in Bolbolouieh. Friends who had found the meaning of life not caring what Nietzsche, Nehru or Walter Cronkite had to say. Friends who found it very, very beautiful, though not quite so beautiful as Tangaloo. Friends who could have lived there with the bottoms of their trousers rolled up, their feet in the water and their hands on the earth. Lived out the rest of their years under the shadow of a reclining Apache, to be buried in unmarked graves on unnamed hilltops.

But they never stayed. Though their lives were spiritually and emotionally bankrupt. Though they lived beyond their means, over-expending against an emotional asset already mortgaged and refinanced to the point where they could no longer live long enough to see it paid off. Though they could no longer make the payments that barely covered the interest and never ever touched the principal. Though they would leave their moral and spiritual bankruptcy as a legacy to their heirs. Though they found solace and sustenance in the beauty and tranquillity of Bolbolouieh and briefly replenished their depleted spiritual reserves, they never stayed for more than a week or two.

Firouz was no different. He would fly in for an occasional weekend, partake of village meals, play songs about the days of wine and roses, and take photographs picking the Apache's nose. He would walk the fields and utter exclamations of approbation. *Bah bah!* A simple exclamation that carried for me the additional weight attached by my uncle from Qandahar. "Years ago," he once told me, "I would go with my friend Sheikh to the garden by the Caspian. You know, Omid's father. We would sit on the veranda on a starlit night and watch the silver moon dance across the waves. The scent of orange blossoms filled the air. We sat in silence, listening to the pounding waves pound, drinking ice-cold vodka and eating pickled cucumbers, the tips of our cigarettes glowing in the dark. Every now and again he would shake his head and break the silence to say *bah bah*. And I would nod in agreement."

On his visits to Bolbolouieh Firouz sometimes exclaimed *bah bah,* but it did not carry quite the same meaning. He never could sit still. A day or two after his arrival the moment would come when he would pack his bag (it took him no more than four or five proud minutes) and head back to Tehran. Fereshteh would insist that he stay, Nur ed Din would cajole, "C'mon Hercules, let someone else carry the weight of the world for a day or two." I might say, "Look, there's a tree wearing lipstick for her lover. And a more forward one who has shed all her clothes." But it was no use, Firouz never stayed. There were things he needed to do. Plans and policies to be implemented; schools, airports, dams and roads to be built.

It was as if only Firouz could see the secret door invisible to everyone else. As if he held the key and knew the precise moment when the sun streaming through rose-coloured windows would reveal the words on the stone archway needed to revive Iran to its ancient glory. As if he was the one who knew the secret James Bond button that would catapult Iran firmly into the twentieth century. Or perhaps he thought that he could save Iran by a sheer act of will. That his all-consuming desire to transform the country, if applied honestly and assiduously, would bring about the results he so desperately desired.

One theory says it is the land and not the people who determine what becomes of Iran. That the land has always determined its own fate. That it is a land that has always given hope and a land that has often betrayed. According to this theory, the rich topsoil of educated, sincere young men and women was no more than a thin layer in a desert of shifting sands, a desert that would inevitably destroy all planted in its tragically thin and rich layer.

But Firouz never heard this theory, or if he had, never believed it. So he seldom stayed in Bolbolouieh for more than a day or two before rushing off to an important meeting, an important project, some book he had to sign on some summit.

52

In spite of Iran's aloofness and indifference, Firouz continued to pursue her from various posts from which he would resign when asked for a favour that he never could perform in good conscience, and they, in good conscience, never should have asked. He continued to pursue his desire, not realizing what every woman in the room could tell with one glance. That the one he loved so desperately would never give herself to him, even if she loved him in turn.

We all knew Iran was only good for a waltz, a cha cha cha, a twist. He would never dance her outside, undress her while holding her close, lead her up the staircase and into the waiting bedroom. But he continued to pursue her with fervent adolescent desire. His long-past-adolescence friends encouraged him: "Don't look now, she can't take her eyes off you." "She wants you." "Firouz, don't ask me how I know, but I am sure tonight is the night." With exaggerated enthusiasm they awaited reports, exclaimed, "Excellent, well done," at propitious moments. "And then what happened?" they asked though they knew his desire was not to be fulfilled. Not on that night, nor on any other.

They knew that in more ways than one he was like our stammering friend on the day he went hunting. After trudging through mountain passes for what seemed like hours, the guide pointed, "Shhhh, quietly now, there's a herd of ibex there under the cypress tree." Fumbling the latch on his rifle, dropping his glasses, crushing them underfoot, and searching frantically through his pockets for a handkerchief to wipe the sweat running down his face, our friend managed to scare off the herd without firing a single shot. "Ssssorry I didn't hh-hhit one," he offered a bemused guide. "Sir, why apologize? That was far better than hitting one," came the response.

The ardour of Firouz's attentions was far more attractive than "hitting one." Pursuing Iran with all his desire, he arrived at the office before anyone else and left well after everyone else was gone, just to elevate himself in her eyes. He pursued her in conferences and symposia, dinners and cocktail parties that bored him to tears. He entertained people he could not bear to see. Men who predictably repeated the same tired stories. And a woman who astounded him by confessing that years ago she had divorced her husband because she found herself falling for him.

He had never known. She had never intimated a single word. "How am I to be held responsible for the divorce of a woman I scarcely saw, who never once professed her love?" he asked me.

"Firouz, falling for a man other than her husband meant, quite simply, that she was not in love with the man she had married. In her book that was cause enough for divorce," I argued. "And who says love needs scented letters quoting the great lovers of the world. It is something that shines, like honeymooners on an Aegean cruise. Surely you must be able to see that?" But he never did.

In his attempt to seduce Iran, Firouz attended meetings that only led to more meetings. When he was younger he used to walk out, just as he had when the assistant to the ahem ahem Assistant to the Minister of Agriculture had lectured him with his back turned. With age, Firouz had learned to extract himself with a discrete phone call, even if all present knew it was invented.

So he surprised them when, quite unexpectedly, he stood up in the middle of a meeting, recited a few lines of poetry, and walked out for good. He even surprised himself. It was not something he had premeditated, not something he had been planning. He was an impatient man, but not an overly impulsive one. When he had sat down at the table, it was a meeting like any other meeting, a day like any other day.

53

He did not quite know what prompted him to do it. Reflecting on it years later, Firouz would say the week had started off like any other, with long hours and late night engagements. But if he was in the kind of mood where he might end up balancing a tea-glass of vodka on his head, reliving the New York snow, Nur ed Din and the statuesque blonde, and if I reminded him, "Wasn't that the week you received the call from the woman next door?" then he might revise his statement and say, "The only peculiar thing about that week, not that it had any bearing on my actions, was that one night I returned home late, and began to loosen my tie when I received a telephone call. It was rather late, but I picked up the receiver, thinking, 'Maybe it's just a call from someone in Europe, like the time Healey called me, drunk and sentimental.'"

But it wasn't. The call came from his neighbour, Madame Gharagozlou. In her youth she had been a most striking beauty. Her beauty had faded, but not her charms. She was famous, in circles where they still kept track, for declining every single suitor no matter how rich or handsome. Seldom sitting through candlelit dinners to the end, she always accepted watches and sent back rings. For some reason, she and Firouz struck up a friendship. In his busy schedule of meetings and engagements, in his mission of building the hospitals, dams and hotels he seldom saw after ribbon-cuttings, I think he took pleasure in being able to extend a tangible courtesy to an aging beauty. At times he helped her navigate the morass of bureaucracies or assisted in managing her assets. What to sell and what to keep, whom to trust.

He enjoyed being of assistance and was tickled that she maintained an imperious attitude even when asking for help. Like the time she had requested that he accompany her to the Stock Exchange. Though he had a car and chauffeur available, she had insisted on a taxi, and then insisted on paying. "How much do I owe you?" she asked the driver, who responded with a rate that was a throwback to the days when she was still breaking hearts. When Firouz finally convinced her to let him pay, he offered the established sum to the driver, who responded with a smile, "That was for Madame. For you it is double." Firouz paid it willingly because the scoundrel of a driver had been chivalrous enough to establish a rate "for Madame."

Firouz enjoyed his little expeditions with Madame Gharagozlou, the satisfaction of taking care of whatever chore seemed to have overwhelmed her. Nonetheless, he was surprised to hear her voice long past bedtime.

"I'm sorry to disturb you at this hour, Firouz Khan, but you must come and help me right now," she started with the self-assurance of those who need not introduce themselves. And then with a whisper, "Someone has moved into my apartment, and I simply can't get her to leave."

"What are you talking about, Madame Gharagozlou? No one has moved into your home, that is just not possible," Firouz responded, slightly taken aback.

"But I tell you she has moved in, and I cannot get rid of her," she persisted.

"Who is she?"

"At first I thought she was an old classmate. But she was singularly unsociable. That's when I told her she would have to leave."

"What did she say then?" Firouz asked with a slight sense of foreboding.

"That's the whole thing. She didn't say a word. Firouz

Khan, I'm at my wits end. I don't know who else to call." And then with the hint of a plea, "You must come at once."

Firouz slipped his jacket back on, tightened his tie, splashed water on his face to freshen up and eau de cologne to cover the smell of stale cigarettes, and walked down the stairs. He seldom took elevators and always avoided moving sidewalks. He found Madame Gharagozlou waiting for him at the door in a powder-blue dressing gown. After all these years her famous skin was still impeccable. He found himself wondering again why she had never found a suitor she could learn to love. Madame Gharaghozlou greeted him and then bolted the door firmly behind them.

"I don't know how she got in," she began immediately. "I always keep the windows and doors locked. Look for yourself," she continued, walking him through the apartment. It was true, every window was secure. She had even gone to the effort of placing furniture against doors. "I have done my best to trap her," Madame Gharagozlou said, responding to his unspoken question as she proceeded to lock and unlock imitation Louis XIV doors. "Look for yourself, there is no way she could get out of these rooms. I was sure I had captured her in this very one, but somehow she escaped."

"It was more secure than Alcatraz," he told me when recounting the story with an unexpected flourish. "Harry Houdini couldn't have extracted himself. Even Steve McQueen couldn't have escaped. The doors and the windows were secure. There was no other means of exit. If someone had, in fact, been in the room, they never could have extricated themselves."

Firouz and Madame Gharagozlou went through the rooms one by one, locking and unlocking doors, but they did not find a single soul, nor in Firouz's estimation did they find any sign that the house was inhabited by anyone other than an evidently normal in every other way, but obviously somewhat demented, Madame Gharagozlou. On the piano they did encounter a wonderful signed black and white photo of Madame Gharagozlou with Bette Davis eyes.

"It is quite a beautiful photograph," Firouz offered.

"Don't look at me now," she responded running bejewelled fingers through silver hair. "I broke a heart or two in my youth."

Not quite sure what to do with this particular piece of information, Firouz broached the subject that had been on his mind, "Madame Gharagozloo, you certainly have done an excellent job of securing your home. I must commend you. No one could ever get in or out of these rooms." He continued gingerly to ask the question that had been nagging at him since he entered her apartment. "But do tell me, where is she hiding?"

"Ahh, now you understand how she has been tormenting me, eluding me every time I finally think I have her trapped," she said, unlocking the door to her boudoir. "This is where I saw her last. I don't think she has been able to escape. There she is. We have her now."

For the life of him Firouz could not see a soul. Just a room with flowered wallpaper, an art deco mise de toilette, and a pink love seat. He and Madame Gharagozlou were the only ones in the room.

"There she is. Ask her why she is tormenting me like this. Tell her she must leave right now. Tell her to answer me. Get her out of here." Madame Gharagozlou pointed a shaking finger at the mirror.

Firouz looked around the room one more time and felt a sinking feeling, like he had on the day they threw Cassius Clay in jail. Her own face. She did not recognize her own face.

How many times had she sat in front of that mirror, putting on or wiping off her "face," drawing or removing a mole from her cheek? How many times had she looked into that mirror, putting on or taking off her creams and lotions? He was about to laugh and say, "Madame Gharagozlou, there is no one here. That is not a person, it's a mirror. It's just your reflection in the mirror." But something about the way she was looking at him made him catch himself.

And then Firouz did what for him was the most extraordinary thing. I was never quite sure why—maybe it was something about her, or something about himself that made him say words he never would have uttered otherwise. "Madame Gharagozlou," he said taking her by the arm and leading her toward the door, "you should have called me sooner. I know exactly what needs to be done. But it is not something I can take care of tonight. Please have patience and wait just one more day. I will come back tomorrow and take care of it personally. I can assure you, you will never see her again," he said, getting the words out just before his voice faltered.

The following day, under the pretence of securing the premises, he removed all the mirrors and that was that.

Firouz later shared the story at a cocktail party, leaving out names to protect the innocent. To his amazement all he got in response was laughter. They all laughed at the vain woman who could not recognize her reflection. "Imagine that, she spent her whole life in front of the mirror, and now she can't recognize herself. That is priceless, Firouz, truly priceless." More than slightly perplexed, he repeated the same story to a different group. The results did not differ.

It was one of the most poignant, disturbing, and yet in a certain way most beautiful experiences of his entire life, but when he told the story everyone laughed. It was not the way he told it. He never could deliver a punchline. But everyone who heard the story of the cracked lady and the mirror had the same callous response.

54

The following morning while shaving, he caught himself examining his reflection. He seldom looked at himself, except when tying his tie, brushing his teeth, or as he pushed and pulled his skin taut to get the shave that is only achieved by another set of hands and a straight-edge razor. But sometimes he would find a full length mirror placed firmly at the turn of the staircase, or encounter stainless steel elevator doors. Then he never self-consciously feigned interest in a chandelier, a plant, the pattern on the carpet. He always met his reflections head-on.

But as he lathered on shaving cream with a British boar bristle brush and extracted an old Gillette razor, he found himself studying his reflection. First he examined each feature, his face a passport photo. Finding no definitive answers, he flashed his winning smile, frowned, and simulated surprise. Lathering on the white beard that God would give him in a few years, he remembered the way Madame Gharagozlou had looked at him. Somewhere behind the terror of the unfamiliar, was there a recognition that this was who she had become? Did she need to have him play along with her massive self-deception? "Of all the self deceptions, hers was harmless," he said to himself. "She hurt no one."

As he pulled his face taut and pushed his tongue against his cheek to achieve a closer shave, he thought of his own path. He had always taken account of his actions and could justify each and every one of his moves, each and every one of his steps. He was confident in what he had done and in what he had failed to do. He could sketch his trajectory, the curve of his marvellous ascent tied together not only by the promotions (he never once accepted a lesser position), but by the results—this loan obtained, that dam built, that highway completed.

But standing in front of the mirror, he remarked that with oil money raining down, all the rules he lived by had vanished. It had been all right as long as Iran had a GNP close to that of Pakistan or Albania. Then it was obvious that villages had to be provided with piped water, people had to be housed in decent, sanitary buildings, schools had to be built and staffed, roads constructed, dams, airports, and factories. There was not much debate on the measures to be taken.

"Serviceable architecture consists of no more than two and a half good ideas," my UCLA professor used to say to anyone who would listen. For the development of Iran you didn't need to come up with a single idea. What was needed was the miraculous ability to actually make it happen. Firouz had it. The earnest desire that overrode all the irrelevant objections and unfathomable excuses. The patience to endure invented problems and delays, to suffer abuses and insults from lesser men.

To be able to deal with blasé officials and suspicious villagers, despondent engineers and corrupt administrators, with the ones who raised objections at every turn, who wanted bribes and studies, payoffs and statistics, but who more than anything wanted to place sticks in his spokes, make him fail just to show that they could. It took far more to implement the solutions than to invent them. To surmount obstacles, to pacify objections before even embarking on the projects vital for the nation's advancement. Which was why it had never been accomplished before.

Somehow things were easier in the early days when everyone agreed on what needed to be done. When if there was a choice, it was what to do first. No discussion of building new towns in deserts and ski resorts in the mountains, no question of creating the world's largest hovercraft fleet, no question of acquiring more F-14s than anyone in the Middle East, or soccer teams to tie Scotland one–one.

But when petrodollars arrived overnight, everyone became fantastically, beyond-their-wildest-dreams rich. They could buy the projects they never could have built. And since they were all rich, they must have been wildly successful. Everyone was a success, everyone was brilliant, everyone's wife was beautiful.

For Mohammad Reza Pahlavi it was not just a question of bank accounts and brides. The king of kings and light of the Aryans was richer than the rest. He was more handsome, more intelligent and righter. He had more beautiful wives. By all accounts he also lived a charmed life. He had survived point blank assassination attempts. He had foiled the Communists in Azarbaijan, preventing a secession everyone else thought imminent. He had returned to popular acclaim after being ousted by Mossadegh. He had defused coup d'etats. He was visited regularly in his dreams by Imam Ali. Of course he saw greatness within his grasp.

Surrounded by Rockefellers and Onassises, Fords, Cabots and Lodges, Henry Luces, Henry Kissingers and an occasional Golda Meir, he was certain to catapult Iran into the twenty-first century and properly take his place alongside Roosevelt, De Gaulle and Churchill. To which a tenth grade student who hardly knew him and was just beginning to find herself remarked acerbically, "If he is a Churchill, then I am Sophia Loren." And for a moment, for more than a moment, she was.

55

As he stood in front of the mirror reflecting on honesty and self-deception, Firouz found himself declaiming a quatrain by Khayyam:

> A Shaikh beheld a harlot and quoth he,
> "You seem to be a slave to drink and lechery."
> And she made answer, "What I seem I am.
> But Master are you all *you* seem to be?"

It took him by surprise. Even with the tea-glass of vodka balanced on his head he would not have admitted reciting those verses to himself. Talking to oneself (silently or out loud) was a definite sign of a feeble mind. It was not even one of his favourite quatrains, it was Houshang's. If he were to have recited Khayyam, he would have quoted this quatrain for its impeccable logic:

> While Moon and Venus in the sky shall dwell,
> None shall see aught red grape-juice to excel;
> Oh foolish publicans, what can you buy
> One half so precious as the goods you sell?

Even balancing the tea-glass of vodka, he would not have quoted the Shaikh and the Harlot, nor would he ever have shared the thoughts that went through his head on that morning. Though he was often painfully honest with others, he often treated himself like a stranger, standing on ceremony, somewhat stiffer than with a friend or an acquaintance. Not loosening his tie, not taking his coat off, and definitely not putting his feet up. If he were close to you and in the mood, then at best he would make a veiled reference that he hoped you might catch, like a man who introduces you to the woman with whom he is having an affair, with the unexpressed hope that you will put two and two together.

But on that morning he shaved, searched the mirror for a sign of recognition and finding none, quoted Khayyam, "And she made answer, 'What I seem I am. But Master are you all *you* seem to be?'" He then splashed on his 4711 and dressed himself in a suit and tie as his father had every day of his life whether working or not. It was the only other thing he reluctantly learned from his father.

First he put on his socks, pulling them up over his calves. Then he put on his shoes. Having done so, he put on one of his famous white shirts and buttoned it from the top down. Only then did he put on his trousers, one leg at a time.

Having dressed, he got into the waiting silver Mercedes to be unnecessarily waved through the red light by that rogue of a saluting policeman. It was a day like any other. The sun rose as on any other day. When it was over, the sun set as on any other day. As on any other day he walked his habitual route past the hotel with the revolving rooftop restaurant, stationary since the day it was installed, past the cinemas screening dubbed versions of *Scarecrow* and *Dr. Zhivago,* past the handicraft stores selling sheepskin coats favoured by Twiggy and silk scarves favoured by the Queen. He passed the National Iranian Oil Company headquarters and the neon red-white-and-blue bottle-top encouraging passers-by to drink Pepsi in Farsi script. He mused that in Saudi Arabia they suffered from an alphabet that lacked the letter P and consequently had to drink *Bibsi.*

As on any other day he passed the streetsweepers who scratched their heads and wondered why in the world a man of his stature and obvious importance didn't have a car and driver. He walked past Swissair with its floor-to-ceiling Alps-in-spring wall paper, and past the only store in Tehran with shopping carts. Several blocks later, he arrived at the office where as on any other workday he saluted his cook's second cousin—the guard in a grey uniform and a hat inspired by a French kepi. He took the elevator to the top floor, greeted his secretary and sat down at his desk, at which point a glass of tea and one lump of sugar magically *pouf* appeared just as he lit a cigarette and reviewed his obligations for the day. Not finding anything pressing, he returned phone calls and headed across town to his first meeting at the Prime Minister's office. "If you're not five minutes early, you're late," Joe Coles had taught him in Chicago. It was a code Firouz lived by, even in Tehran where rigour in matters of time and arithmetic can only cause heartache. There was not much he could do about it—more than waiting, he hated to make others wait. The meeting started half an hour late.

Looking around the room, he noted the Minister who had spent a career at the United Nations meticulously taking exception with the reports that crossed his desk, and the banker recently turned real estate developer who no longer needed to preface his comments proclaiming his allegiance to "my direct superior, His Imperial Majesty." The Minister who spoke Farsi fluently but, due to a German military school upbringing at a tender age, had difficulty reading and writing in his native tongue, and the banker who even from his college days only made loans to people with money. From the looks of it they might never get out.

But then Firouz realized that there was at least one chance the meeting might end at a reasonable time. The representative from the oil company was present, and on one occasion Firouz had personally witnessed, he had actually ended a multi-million dollar negotiation early. "They're right," he had proclaimed. "Their demands are entirely reasonable, pay them what they are asking," he said to the amazement of those involved, including the contractors.

Looking around the room at the assortment of Churchills and Disraelis, Gladstones and John Foster Dulleses, Firouz reflected that among self-deceptions, Madame Gharagozlou's did not even register. She was just a vain old woman who could not or would not recognize herself in the mirror. Her self-deception was not harmful. Not in comparison with these men who purported to run the nation, who believed themselves to be wildly successful economists, financiers and administrators but never once argued for what they believed should be done for the advancement of their country.

These so-called Ministers who never once stood their ground, never once disagreed with the pronouncements from above. Deferring to the Shah's every directive, they never once argued for what they believed to be true, to be necessary for their country's advancement. Never once disagreed, never once proposed a more workable alternative.

And with their every "as you wish," the Padeshah's edicts became more and more outlandish. "I know more than these so-called economists," he would assert, and they would all scrape and bow and agree. "These goods are overpriced," he would proclaim, and they would all nod their heads in agreement as the Shahanshah went about establishing the correct prices for hamburgers and dishwashing liquid, pastries and chewing gum.

Madame Gharagozlou's self-deception was nothing in comparison with these so-called Ministers and Excellencies. It was nothing compared with Firouz's, who had set out to live his dreams and woken up to find himself playing a supporting role in someone else's fantasy.

56

As the Prime Minister entered and the meeting began, Firouz realized it was physically impossible for him to sit at the polished imitation Louis XVI table with the oversized bouquet and the pitchers of ice water. A tired Rosa Parks, too exhausted to go to the back of the bus, he stood up. He stood up not to fight injustice or incompetence but because he was overwhelmed by the burden of twenty years of meetings, the devotion of his youth and vitality to a nation that was being steered by another man and in another direction.

The men around this table had already abdicated their responsibilities, deferred their judgement in favour of the man who called himself the king of kings. Firouz could not, and so on that day when he could no longer sit still he stood up. It was not a question of ideals and principles, but a burning desire to get out of the room, an irrefutable, unquestionable realization that he could not stay a moment longer. While he could graciously and unexpectedly play along with the delusions of a faded beauty, he could not bring himself to continue to humour these supposed statesmen and financiers. Or maybe it was just the overwhelming tiredness of a man who was exhausted, spent. The tiredness of a man who had depleted not only his own energies, but energies he did not have.

Whatever the reason, and there was speculation as to what it might have actually been, the fact is that he stood up, recited two lines of poetry, made his apologies, and to everyone's astonishment, walked out of the room. He smiled his most knowing smile as he walked past the secretary, loosened his tie as he passed the doormen, guards and invincible warriors, and with a noticeable bounce in his step, continued past the parking lot where his chauffeur and silver Benz waited, into the streets of Tehran.

57

He'll be back," they said. As if he had stepped out for a minute or two. As if he'd gone to the balcony to have a smoke. "Mark my words, he will come back," they said, not being able to fathom that anyone could walk. But he did not come back. He walked out of that room and he kept on walking.

He finally admitted that he felt old and tired beyond his years. "It has been a tough twenty years, but they say only the first hundred years of life are hard," he remarked to himself, barely managing a chuckle. He had lived only half that long. Yet in that brief period he should have realized that it would play out this way. How could he have imagined that it was the dawning of a new age, a new and modern era when things would be better, when things would be different? How could he have believed that this time it would not end with a despot lulled into fantasy by sycophantic Kaa-the-snake advisors hissing sibilantly, "Trust in me, just in me." Whispering in his ear, looking hypnotically into his eyes, proclaiming in receptions halls, board rooms and Senate chambers, "You are the one, the anointed one, the awaited one. You are the only one."

It was a story he had often transcribed in his own crooked hand in little black books. A simple story with a simple lesson. But he had not learned the lesson he transcribed, and he had not listened to the story. Even after it was all over, after it all crumbled and fell apart, he debated events and circumstances, the could-have-beens and might-have-beens, wanting desperately to believe there was something more to it all than a tragedy in two acts.

On that fateful day he walked up the street named Kakh after the palace it led to, down to the street named Shah, and right onto Pahlavi, the street of arching and intertwining branches that led to the mountains. He passed the street that led to his office and the streets that led to friends' offices. At the street that led to mine, he made a detour and walked the few short blocks to the glass curtain-walled building where I worked.

"I'm afraid she is in a meeting," my secretary replied to his inquiry. Sensing a certain degree of urgency, or perhaps realizing Firouz's need, she inquired, "If you like, I can pull her out for a moment." Sima had a good sense about these kinds of things. Firouz, who did not, considered her proposal for a moment, thanked her and responded, "No, I was just dropping by. I thought if she was not preoccupied, we might go for a little walk together." Which, my secretary remarked later, seemed a rather pleasant thought for the middle of the morning in the work week.

I sometimes wonder how things might have turned out had I not been in meetings, had I been called out, had I joined Firouz on his walk. Would he have confided more than the same old stories of water pitchers and oversized vases? Would he have gotten past the quirks of ministers and their deputies? Would he have finally gotten to the heart of the matter?

But I was in a meeting and he was not inclined to interrupt. Without me he walked back to Pahlavi Avenue and he kept on walking. Without me, he walked past neon drops turning into allegorical seas, past the Eldorado Ice Cream stand, past the Ice Palace, past caged flamingos and the Golden Age kabab shop. Past beggars and bureaucrats. The ones who worried about where their next meal would come from, and the ones who believed the One who gave you teeth will also give you bread. And he kept on walking.

Though he was spent and exhausted, he could still walk, and he did, all the way from the Prime Minister's office to the square at the foot of the mountains. Though he was tired and spent, he walked to Tajrish, which was as far as the street named after a dynasty went. Noting a crowd gathered near the bus station, Firouz crossed the street to see what the hullabaloo was all about. He found a strongman lying flat on his back, and a Peykan with six smiling passengers being driven across his chest.

There were at least a hundred idle passers-by gathered round to see this marvellous feat. And though he could not figure out how it was the strongman could withstand the weight of a full-sized, fully loaded car, it did not stop Firouz from thinking that it was still the middle of the day. Didn't these men have anything more pressing, more vital, more important to do than stand around and wait for a strongman to lie down on broken glass, a clown to stumble over oversize feet, a charlatan to show up and give them something to fill their time?

It was as if for these able-bodied young men in the renascent Persian Empire, time was to be passed idly waiting for an obese man to waddle by, a car to break down, the fruit seller to be caught overcharging a customer. A gypsy fortune-teller to put out her charts, an unusually dark-skinned man to show up with a scorpion and packets of coloured powder, a young rascal to endeavour to engage a woman his mother's age in conversation. As if time were to be filled with the drama enacted between a cat and a crow.

58

He was astonished that people could live like that. That they could spend their days waiting to be distracted. Without a greater goal than for day to become night and night to become day, day after day, night after night. How could they not want to build a house one resolute brick at a time, reach a mountaintop one determined step after the other?

Even after Firouz understood that everything he built would be dismantled piece by piece, destroyed in one fell swoop or maliciously left to deteriorate from neglect, he still believed. Even after he came to see that what he built during the day was taken down at night. Even then, he could not comprehend that one could live a life just letting day pass into night and night into day.

After the years in exile in progressively smaller apartments, when he planned his days around trips to the bank and the dry-cleaners, he still believed. Even after he found himself watching the six o'clock news and the nine o'clock film no matter what was showing. When asked, "How was the movie?" his friend Abolghassem always answered "It was average," which bothered Firouz since Abolghassem was a mathematician. "Surely some of the films are better or worse than average," he countered with his irrefutable statistical assertion, his impeccable logic. But in exile, films defied statistics—they were all worse than average. It made no difference. He watched them religiously, every night at nine o'clock.

After all that, he still believed. Even after recognizing that it had always been this way, that everything created one day would be dismantled the next, he never suspended his belief. Though he did realize, somewhat late, that this state of affairs was not new or unfamiliar, that it had happened to our parents and to our parents' parents. That there never had been any stability for more than a couple of years until the Shah was assassinated, usurped or replaced by another who would start all over again, embarking on grandiose plans only to rapidly lose his perspective, abdicate his judgment, be murdered, or worse, be exiled.

Despite having read the histories, charted the timelines, documented the events, he believed in the value of the struggle. Even after he knew that what he had contributed, that what he had achieved was in the final analysis no more than those idle men who stood around waiting for a charlatan to occupy their minutes or hours, he still believed, believed that it could work. Not only in America, but also in a country like Iran. Against the overwhelming evidence of irrelevance and futility, he still believed.

59

The following day he rode the silver Benz to within blocks of his office, saluted his cook's second cousin, listened to his recordings, checked his appointments, scribbled his usual letter of resignation, cleaned out his desk in less than fifteen minutes, said his goodbyes, and left.

No one even asked why. Feigned expressions of surprise only served to underscore the fact that they knew him better than he knew himself.

"Did they know that I could not have sat there for another minute, did they know that too?" he wondered out loud. "How was it they did not tell me sooner, did not pull me aside and ask, 'What are you doing here?' 'What are you thinking?' 'Who are you kidding?' Yassaman, tell me, did you know as well? Was it that obvious? Why didn't you say anything?" he finally asked.

I averted my look, and for once he did not belabour the point.

He found himself at a loss for what to do next. There were opportunities, there was no end of opportunities. The Carnival was in full swing. He could take any position he wanted, make money hand over fist, live off the income from the boards and foundations he chaired. He could establish the charity he had always talked about, write the book he had been mulling over for years. He had published only one volume, and that a translation of Walt Whitman Rostow's theory of the Take-Off. Taking inventory of his life, he thought back to the Chicago professor who had told him, "If you want to help people, sell them shoes." But he had never wanted to sell shoes, either literally or metaphorically.

He had been propelled by the fervent desire to use America's successes to reanimate the slumbering country that was once the Persian Empire. And though each of his endeavours was a smashing success, the overall outcome was a resounding failure. The roads and dams had been built, schools and universities constructed, but the culture of building roads and dams had not taken root.

There never had been a Persian "Golden Age;" that was a Greek phenomenon. Instead there were periods of greatness when, shackled by the merciless will of a conquering despot, we feverishly built mosques, palaces and gardens, produced poetry, miniatures and calligraphy. Under the indomitable will of a tyrant, Iran produced things of great beauty, things of incalculable value, creating a shooting-star magnificence that ever so briefly and brutally lit up the sky until the king went insane, poisoned his brothers, blinded his sons and castrated his enemies.

A Persian Golden Age is what Firouz aspired to, what we all pursued, forsaking the comforts of a house and two-car garage in Ann Arbor, Salt Lake City or Bethesda. When Iran was still a poverty-stricken, backward country we came back. But when money poured down like rain, all that was forgotten. Our purpose was forgotten. No one could accept that the fairy-tale lives we lived were not what we aspired to. No one ever bothered to ask, "Tell me, just between the two of us, is this what you wanted, is this where you wanted to end up? No one else is here, it's just you and me. And I wanted to know, if you had it to do all over again, is this how you would choose to live your life?"

No one bothered to ask that question. Instead, they all subscribed to some dubbed-over version of who we were and what motivated us. As if we were Peter Fonda in the final scene of the only slightly censored *Easy Rider* that played in our cinemas. As if we were all a young, rebellious and impossibly handsome kid on a chopper, in that final scene where he gives the truck driver the finger.

Not quite sure what to do with that particular gesture, ingenious censors inserted dialogue where there had been none. And so the truck driver, without opening his mouth, asks Peter Fonda, "How many people did you kill?" And Fonda, displaying his middle finger instead of moving his lips replies, "Just one." At which point the truck driver reaches under the seat, extracts a shotgun and blows Peter Fonda away.

In "translation," the movie was not just lost, it was destroyed. The words inserted into Fonda's unmoving mouth may have explained the flourishing of Fonda's finger, but in the process managed to somehow justify the indiscriminate brutality of the truck driver, leaving everyone in the theatre scratching their heads. "When did he kill someone?" "Did you see him kill anyone?" "Who did he kill?" "He was killing me," they remarked on sidewalks and in sidewalk cafés.

He had not killed anyone, nor said a single word. But we were accustomed to words being said without lips moving, as we were to lips moving without words being said. The movie-goers left the cinema scratching their heads, much as they would when we, who had grown a-thousand-nights-and-a-night rich and beautiful beyond anyone's wildest dreams under the Shah's reign, marched down the streets to overthrow that same king.

60

Everything suffered in translation. It suffered from Farsi to English and from English to Farsi. There was a shop in Tehran that summed it up for me. The yellow neon storefront sign read, in blood-red Latin letters "Sang Flower." *Sang* means stone, and when combined with *Gol* (flower) becomes *Gol-e Sang* which means flower of stone and signifies "moss." There is a beautiful and plaintive song my father would sometimes sing that says (in almost literal translation):

I am the flower of stone,
I am the flower of stone,
What can I say of my aching heart.
If you do not shine on me like the sun,
I am cold and colourless.

It rhymes (and works) in the original.

Somehow the shop owners opted to name their store neither *"gol-e-sang"* nor "flower of stone," nor "moss" for that matter. They christened their shop *"Sang* Flower" and achieved neither the poetry of the flower of stone nor the accuracy of moss. We also failed to translate accurately, and suffered immensely in the process.

Take Firouz's beloved bureaucracy. We joked that in Persian it was more aptly named *zooreaucracy*. Haim's Shorter Persian English / English Persian Dictionary defines the noun *zoor* as "strength" or "power." When combined with the verb "to say" it signifies "to force" in the sense of making people do things they do not want to. *Zooreaucracy* might best be rendered in English as "coerce-aucracy." It was not only words that suffered in translation.

Our failure to translate accurately or even compassionately pervaded every facet of life, from storefront neons to newspaper headlines. There was even a carpet weaver who spent fifteen years creating the most exquisite Isfahan carpet in red and blue hues. At the top he inscribed in English, *Live is beautiful,* followed by his name, Seyed Abolghassem Kashani. When Firouz saw it at one of the Expos he occasionally attended, he had been outraged at the English text on the Persian Carpet, and even more so by the mistake. When the poor man proudly inquired, "Sir, isn't it beautiful?" Firouz was exceptionally blunt. "Having been fool enough to insert English into the fabric of an Isfahan carpet, why were you such an idiot as to misspell it?" he assailed the ass of a carpet weaver.

The ass of a carpet weaver got it wrong. But even when we got it right, we still got it wrong. We came up with shops that sold Leathern Goods and fruit stands that referred to themselves as Fruiterers, both of which are Oxford English Dictionary-correct. But you will never encounter a leathern goods store, nor a fruiterer in the streets of the English-speaking world.

Often we did not bother to translate, transliterating instead, with unexpected results. Nima's Leather became Nima Charm Company while Technical Printing or *chap-e-fanni* became Funny Chap. Hans became the *Ons* or Friendship pastry shop but only after the revolution when the baba au rhum fell out of favour. In post-revolutionary Iran there was also the Ministry of *Jihade Sazandegi,* of which only the first two words were translated. Why even attempt to translate into English an institution that would be best rendered as The Ministry of the Holy War for Constructiveness?

We translated, transliterated and fumbled through it all with mixed results. Desperadoes literally became "those who have washed their hands of life," which was a funny title for an Eagles song. For those of us who were trying so earnestly, everything suffered immensely. It was especially painful when western terms were first transcribed in Farsi and then written in a Latin alphabet, resulting in street signs like *Jandark* which was meant to signify a 15th century maiden warrior who led a nation in war and was burned at the stake. Or *Berguer,* which was supposed to represent a meal in a round bun.

Though we could cast knowing glances, roll our eyes or simply laugh out loud, we knew the ideas and the principles we attempted to convey were misinterpreted. It soon became painfully evident that the Western culture we believed in, the Western principles we trusted in, suffered hugely in translation. Meritocracy failed miserably as a concept, honesty maintained the flexible status it had always enjoyed, and accuracy in figures never did quite reach the elevated situation for which some had hoped. One-eyed in the kingdom of the blind, we were amply misunderstood. No amount of explanation could remedy that. No amount of patient understanding could remedy that.

In 1970s Iran, the Shah, the man who had abolished political parties in favour of a resurgent one party system, was the Father of Democracy. "And why is that," the teacher asked of the student in the back of the room, after others had intelligently and eagerly responded to her inquiry with names like George Washington or Benjamin Franklin. "Because he is screwing the mother of democracy," came the punchline from the back of the room.

6I

Everything suffered in translation. Since it did, Firouz went back to the originals. Before we took to the streets, before he took to the streets, he went back to the sources. "I never tire of reading Curzon. Each time I do, I find something new," he told me unconvincingly as he searched through dusty collections. Reading the same old tomes time and again for some insight into why it had all gone so wrong.

In search of the answer to that particular question, he read the story of Ibn Shaddad and the city that rivalled the divine. Sackville-West's story of how she came upon a wonderfully fragrant white flower and asked of her Iranian hiking partner what it was called. "The snow flower," he responded. "But as he was wrong about everything else, I suspect he was wrong about this also," she observed to Firouz's infinite joy. He read the tale of Mullah Nasr ed Din and the contradictory donkey. And the story of how the Mullah searched under the streetlight for lost money. "Where did you lose it, Mullah?" a helpful passer-by ventured. "I lost it over there," replied the Mullah, pointing across the way. "Then why do you search for it here," the poor soul inquired. "Because the light is so much better," came the Mullah's response.

He read foreigners' accounts, madly scribbled their quotes into his little black book. Scribbling (madly), Firouz noted their insights into the land of roses and nightingales, the land of the lion and the sun, of the peacock throne. He read foreigners' accounts because there really were no Iranian histories. How could there be in a country where crumbling palaces bore testimony to the transitory nature of it all. Where the arrogance of leaving behind a legacy was disabused daily. Where the message was never, "Preserve the past," but always the one on Alp Arsalan's ordinary gravestone:

Thou hast seen Alp Arsalan's head in pride exalted to the
   sky.
Come to Merv and see how lowly in the dust that head
   doth lie.

Where British poets were able to actually embellish that
cautionary tale, inventing legless trunks of stone, Pasha's gates
were embellished with the refrain "Only God is Great." Sig-
net rings engraved with "Solemn words and these are they:
'Even this shall pass away.'" Rendering potters and hands
that writ, wine taverns and clay (gently brother pray), they
managed to write verses that exhibited a genius in capturing
the futility of it all.

There were Persian poems and Persian epic poems. There
were Persian verses and Persian quatrains, Persian doublets
and Persian stanzas. There were Persian poems, not in iambic
pentameter but with any number of meters and penta-meters,
with any number of rhythms, rhymes and rhyming schemes.
There were Persian poems. There were Persian poets. But
there really were no Iranian histories.

My aunt, whose eyes could barely see, whose ears could
barely hear, who used to say with a smile, "The gifts God
gives you, He takes back," who when she dyed her hair never
seemed to notice that it took on a purplish hue, who could
no longer listen to the radio, who could no longer watch TV–
played a game for hours on end in which she would quote a
verse and her opponent would in return have to quote a verse
that began with the last letter of the verse just recited. She
loved to play it, and was exceptionally good. She could go
on for hours, outlasting even the most erudite of her opponents. Except she had none. She would spend the hours of
the morning after she awoke and before she rose lying in bed
quoting verses back and forth. Knowing, before she finished,
the verse that would be given in reply.

But Firouz was not interested in poems. He read histories. He read accounts. Which were almost always written by
foreigners. Trying to unravel the threads, he read the books

that, he felt, dealt with his particular predicament. He read the books that, he felt, might shed light on his particular situation.

And though he learned many things, he did not learn why it was things had turned out as they had. He received no insight that would prompt him to strike his forehead with the palm of his hand saying, "What was I thinking?" Exclaiming, *"Yaftam!"* which translates directly as "I found it," but is best expressed by the word "eureka."

He read the books under his preferred lamppost.

62

Firouz continued to keep up appearances, wore a suit and tie every day of the week, excepting only those occasions when he sported his white turtleneck and the blue blazer with anchor-emblazoned gold buttons. He attended the dinners and the cocktail parties, always the second to leave, like his technocrat friends who bought Buicks when they could easily have afforded Cadillacs. When people asked, he replied with a wink, "I'm between jobs." But they already knew he spent his days reading obsolete histories. They thought they knew the call he was waiting for—the one from Kissinger or from the Shah himself. But they were wrong.

For the first time in a long time he felt distant from it all, as you would on a fall day when leaves are changing colours, when first smoke is spiralling out of chimneys. When everyone else is going back to class, choosing courses and schedules, buying books and chatting in line with friends and acquaintances. When everyone else was doing what Firouz had done for years. Except this year he would not. He would not go back to school this year, nor next year, nor the year after that. Though he could see them from across the street, he would not be joining them in reading rooms and quads, in lecture halls and on playing fields. It was a misunderstood Firouz who one day walked out of that meeting, made a small detour to my office and continued toward the mountains, though he did not reach the summit and did not sign the book. A misunderstood Firouz who took inventory of where he was, trying to understand how every resolute step had led him farther away from his desire. "Yassaman," he confessed, in an uncharacteristic moment of weakness, "I'm not quite sure how, but I've ended up with a zigzag life."

It was true. Having failed to seduce the princess, his quests were no more than meanderings, his wanderings no more than excursions. Had he awakened the nation with a kiss, his absurd Tale-of-Two-Cities principles, his abrupt two lines of verse would have been understood. But the one he had tried so hard to seduce, to dance outside or upstairs had not been swayed. In the face of such a failure, his straight line life could only be considered a zigzag path toward the one certain destination.

Lawrence of Arabia once noted in a passage Firouz duly transcribed in a little black book that in the Middle East the shortest distance between two points was not necessarily a straight line. Aqaba by land, he also advocated. But any schoolboy can map the fastest way around the town square, and they all know it seldom has to do with geometry. There never was any challenge in figuring that out.

The challenge lay in making the shortest distance between two points a straight line. That was something one could devote a life to as a schoolboy and well beyond. To make the principles of geometry apply to our day-to-day lives. To institute the straight line in a society that has always meandered or taken the most drastic turns. A society where mathematics and geometry fail to predict any particular outcome. A society in which arithmetic fails to explain the results in anyone's life. Where you could add it all, tally up the columns, the assets and liabilities all night long and still not get the answer in the back of the book.

63

In Iran the challenge lay in making the straight line the shortest distance between two points, in making it all add up. Firouz devoted a lifetime to this simple equation, walked a straight line every single day, and ended up with a zigzag life.

It perplexed him. So when he had a chance, he sequestered himself with his books, spent his time reading the volumes he had missed, the ones that had eluded him. Not finding the answers he sought, he pored over the travelogues and histories one more time, hoping to detect the open-sesame panel that would explain it all. Hoping to find the abracadabra words that would explain how it was that he had fervently and steadfastly pursued his desire and found himself impossibly far away from fulfillment.

As if he were the brother who, distracted by riches, had forgotten the words that would let him out of the thieves' cave with whatever treasures he managed to stuff into his bulging pockets, discarding silver for gold, gold for rubies, rubies for diamonds, diamonds for black diamonds. The brother intoning, "Open poppy. Open aspic, open balsamic. Open caraway, open coriander, open cumin, open cardamom. Open allspice."

As if he were still there, frantically reciting words when the thieves returned to find that something was not quite right. And then he would be impaled, a head on a stake left to warn others what happens when you try to steal from thieves.

But he was not the brother with a faulty memory. He was not the one distracted by riches, by ill-gained loot, not the one they would apprehend. He was not one of those the robbers would find frantically mumbling whatever mumbo jumbo might get him released. The words Firouz sought were not to save his head.

He devoted himself to finding a greater truth, a timeless truth about Iran. He had forgotten the profit and the loss, had removed himself from it all. But he made the regrettable and understandable mistake of searching for the answer in the hundreds of accounts written from roughly the middle of the fifteenth century onwards, when a Spanish ambassador was sent to attempt to forge an alliance with a Mongol king and left behind a book unequivocally entitled *Narrative of the Embassy of Ruy Gonzales de Clavijo to the Court of Timur at Samarcand.*

I tried to get him to look elsewhere. Joked, "Had I known it would come to this I would never have sent you that copy of *Queer Things About Persia.*" Still he insisted on searching for answers in the same dusty tomes. I told him he was reading the wrong books. What I could not say, what I could never say, was that the authors, like him, were outsiders. They would be equally baffled by the turns of events, equally astonished with the outcome, equally puzzled about the directions their lives and their efforts were taking. They would be equally at a loss to explain a country that had captured their hearts but eluded their minds. Had I known it would come to this, I never would have sent him the travelogue that prompted the search for an answer he would not find, that he could not find. I would have sent, instead, a picture of a hat and a copy of *The Little Prince.*

64

Firouz persisted in searching through leather-bound books for the answers that lay elsewhere. He spent his days in a coat and tie, leafing through ancient volumes for the one quote he so vividly remembered failing to note. Between books, he walked the streets of Tehran as he always had. Sometimes I accompanied him.

"Maybe I'll take a trip," he ventured, "I'd love to go back to Beirut. I don't think I've ever told you this, but one of my favourite memories from those years is the time we went to the beach. At one point we swam out together, past the place where the green sea turns blue. I turned to say something only to find you floating on your back. And I envied you because, try as I might, I could never manage to float. But you just lay on your back without giving it a second's thought, floating there in the aquamarine sea."

I did remember the episode, the beach, and Firouz's laughable attempts at floating. I remembered the peppermint-striped changing rooms, taking off my bathing cap and floating in the Mediterranean.

"Wouldn't it be wonderful? I would check into the St. Georges, and spend a week just lying on the beach and walking the streets. Or maybe I'll go back to Chicago and find out what became of Mary Helen. Do you know I got a card from the bookseller in Paris. There's an important auction coming up, and he thinks I might be interested. But before I head out, I think I'll just drive down to Bolbolouieh and surprise Nur ed Din and Fereshteh." He never went to Beirut, with or without me. Nor did he look up Mary Helen or any other real or imagined girlfriend. He didn't make it to Bolbolouieh. He spent his time reading books and keeping up appearances.

One night, after a particularly tedious dinner, he found himself buying a cigarette from his habitual sidewalk vendor. It was a pleasure he had not savoured in years. The pleasure of buying one pleasure at a time. Not a box of twenty pleasures, not a soft pack of twenty pleasures, and especially not a carton of four hundred pleasures. But on that night Firouz decided on a whim to buy just one cigarette.

As the vendor struck a match that flared up blue and yellow, Firouz felt an intimacy with the man selling cigarettes, chewing gum and lottery tickets, the kind of intimacy one feels with silent taxi drivers and talkative priests. On the spur of the moment he turned to the man who had just sold him one single cigarette and lit it, cupping his hands. Blowing out smoke, Firouz confessed, "I've made a complete mess of my life."

The man who had held the match to the Winston until Firouz tapped once with his index finger to indicate with a certain degree of intimacy that it was lit did not say a word in response. The man who had watched Firouz come and go for years remained silent. Thinking the vendor had not heard or appreciated the full impact of his statement, Firouz repeated, "I've made one huge mess of my life, how about you?"

The man struck the same red and white (soft) pack twice to get one to pop up. He took a cigarette, lit it with cupped hands, looked up at Firouz and exhaled. He did not say a thing. It was as if he had not heard. Or as if he had heard it not once, but a million times. He sold lottery tickets and cigarettes, sometimes a pack at a time. And having done so for too many years, he knew enough to know that it had to do with a woman.

His own cousin had left a job with prospects to go back to the village. They had all told him, "Forget her, she's not the one for you," but their words had fallen on deaf ears. His cousin had persisted in wooing a woman who accepted his presents and his attentions, asked for more time to consider his proposal, and ended up marrying the butcher with the Honda Two-Fifty. There was something about the man in the suit and silk tie that reminded him of his cousin. He couldn't put his finger on it, but there was one thing for certain. He knew that if the gentleman in the blue double breasted pin-stripe suit were to engage in such a confession, it was because the one he loved was slipping through his hands.

He knew, yet the cigarette vendor did not say a word. It was a shame, because he could have asked Firouz exactly how it was that he had managed to mess up his life. He could have asked how it was that a man in Firouz's position could feel so despondent. How he could find himself on a street corner confiding in a man he had often seen but with whom he had seldom spoken more than a few perfunctory if kind words. He could have asked how it was that a man who was envied by so many could find himself confessing to the vendor on the streetcorner that his life was in shambles.

But he didn't. He just sat there smoking his cigarette, feeling an unstated complicity with the man with the loose tie around an open collar. He could have said anything, it would not have mattered what, and kept the conversation going. He could have commented on the weather and Firouz would have kept on talking. He could have sighed and Firouz would have told his story. He could have coughed and Firouz would have spoken the words I longed to hear. But he preferred to sit there silently stoking the ember at the tip of his cigarette as if it were the fire that burned in his heart.

65

Had he asked, he might have understood why a few weeks later, ostensibly without any reason, Firouz took to the streets. Why, without any ostensible reason, a nation spontaneously took to the streets to overthrow a Padeshah who had made them fabulously rich and beautiful beyond their wildest dreams.

He might have understood what prompted Firouz to join a swelling ocean of people demanding something more. Or maybe it was just something else. Bankers, bank tellers and bank guards. Teachers and substitute teachers. Cooks, chefs and sous-chefs. Singers and dancers. Workers and day-labourers. Automobile mechanics and apprentices to automobile mechanics.

The same engineers, taxi drivers and pastry chefs who had become incredibly rich and beautiful during the Padeshah's reign. After all, it was not just the bankers and lawyers who acquired fairy tale lives. There were carpenters and shopkeepers, colonels and bureaucrats, contractors and cooks, people who had the good fortune of buying or inheriting land, opening businesses, stockpiling tires, or buying shares in any one of the companies traded on the Tehran Stock Exchange. As the somewhat round businessman used to say to cover up his own out-of-all-proportion prosperity, "When it rains, everyone gets wet." In the course of a few scant years there had been the kind of deluge that attracts Arab desert dwellers to

Hindustan during monsoons to sip cardamom-flavoured coffee in arcaded hotels.

Perhaps the cigarette vendor with a penchant for Humphrey Bogart silences would have gleaned what it was that motivated an entire nation to take to the streets. A nation that had turned ugly-duckling beautiful in the course of a few short years. The same Persian Question nation that for years had been viewed not in the exclamatory or in the imperative but in the interrogatory. As if Persia needed to be followed by a question mark.

But in the 1970s Persia was being unequivocally stated in the affirmative. Americans, Englishmen and Germans were climbing over each other to live in Iran, to be in Iran, to work in Iran. Multinationals were racing over to build cars and toasters, to sell insurance and gold-backed securities. I. M. Pei was proposing hotels and Louis Kahn was designing embassies. The competition for the Pahlavi National Library read like a veritable who's who of the architectural world, with a jury that included Phillip Johnson and me.

In 1978, after Iran had become sought after and things Iranian had become chic, those same chic Iranians with the now-wonderful complexions and the now-beautiful eyes, with the now-fascinating culture and the recently discovered poetry in their lives, took to the streets. We took to the streets to demand change.

"How is my serve?" I once asked our friend Mehdi, who always was a more accomplished tennis player. "The serve is fine," he said in what I felt at the time was a flippant reply. "The player has to change." In revolutionary Iran, the player, too, had to change. To be more precise, both the serve and the player had to change. The country took to the streets demanding that they change. We took to the streets demanding that the entire game change.

We wanted a game where the lines were clear and the goals even clearer. Where uniforms told whose side you were on and who was paying the bills. Where flags went up when players strayed offside. Where yellow cards were handed out for blatant fouls and red cards for dangerous ones. We wanted a new team, a new referee, one who could not be bought. We wanted a new game. We wanted the game where the player who was one with the ball danced down the field, weaving, feinting, striking, knowing which way his opponents would move even before they did, and the goalkeeper leapt like a trout up a waterfall. We wanted *o jogo maravilhoso*. We wanted the beautiful game.

66

When it came right down to it, there was no need for the poor cigarette vendor to sigh, cough or gather the courage to ask, "Excuse me sir, but exactly what do you mean?" There was no need to inquire because, when the nation took to the streets, there were no questions. The questions would come later, with the regrets.

When we poured into the streets and the squares, it was obvious. I will go even further: It was self-evident. It was Thomas Jefferson self-evident. It was Thomas Paine "We have it in our power to design the world over again" self-evident. Martin Luther King "I have a dream" self-evident. JFK "Not merely peace for America but peace for all men and women; not merely peace in our time but peace for all time" self-evident.

When the entire nation took to the streets, it was more than self-evident, it was palpable. You could feel it in your gut and you could feel it in your heart as a people marched together, chanting, "The Shah must go. The Shah must go." You could feel the excitement as a nation united, Marxists, Islamists and Centrists, the shopkeeper down the street and the retired school teacher who taught English for the day when he would regretfully write on the blackboard in a flowing script "Time is Gold." The political ones and the ones who knew nothing about affiliations, but had always abhorred the imperfect, unjust or mean.

It is a sight to see: When a people demand justice from their God, when a people demand a voice from their King. When an entire city spontaneously converges on a single street. When a people decides to stop watching from windows and balconies, stops standing on sidelines and finds itself running through alleyways to catch up with the crowd. A nation throwing on coats and hats, forgetting scarves and gloves, forgetting to turn off the kettle, to join the crowd shouting out loud what they had felt for years but had never even whispered in the privacy of their own homes.

Following a hum in the streets that could be heard from blocks away, a hum that draws you as you fumble with your coat button, a hum that mounts in volume until you turn a corner and find that it is the sound of thousands of voices shouting in unison, chanting in unison. Words that are at first indiscernible, but as you listen, as you hear the rhythm, you begin to make out four incredibly courageous words. And it comes to you that thousands of voices are stating, demanding, urging what you had always felt but never uttered. And you are swept away by the throngs of people asking to be heard, demanding to be heard. "The Shah must go, the Shah must go." You join the crowd, adding your voice to the thousands. Or walk along in silent solidarity, your jaw set in quiet determination.

Had you been there, had you heard that hum, you might understand why the best and the brightest came to participate in the marches that led down Eisenhower (soon to be Liberty) Avenue to Shahyad (soon to be Liberty) Square. You might understand how it was that we might be swept up in the euphoria of a people demanding Liberty (soon to be the Islamic Republic), a nation demanding justice, and not just in the next world. Demanding justice in this world from a king who had been accountable only to his God. Removing the pomp and the glory to reveal a man who, like all men, had his faults, who, like all men, had his weaknesses, who like all men, had made his mistakes. Removing the ceremony to reveal a man who, like all kings, could be held responsible for the dissolution of our dreams.

We had always wanted to play our part in the birth of a nation founded on decency and democracy. But that particular avenue had been barred to us when we first returned, and then we had been swept up in the day-to-day that consumed not weeks but decades, until we woke up in the middle of one night to find that it had been years since we had even thought of the goals we had once believed in so fervently. So you might understand how we who had worked for our country, a country of the poor, illiterate and oppressed, would feel compelled to walk down the streets in solidarity with a silenced nation chanting, "The king must go, the king must go."

You might understand why those of us who had come back to build a country might enjoy the opportunity to become Gandhis and de Tocquevilles, Benjamin Franklins and Nelson Mandelas. How we might choose to see unicorns, eagles and lions. How we might choose to see stallions, white stallions, winged white stallions.

You might understand how the flower of the nation would take to the streets. Why a man who had already removed himself from it all, who had resigned himself to his failures, a man who had finally learned to care and not to care though he never did learn to sit still, would take to the streets to demand justice in this world.

Firouz had walked away from it all, sequestered himself with his beloved books, and resigned himself to his own less than spectacular failure. He wanted no more than to understand how it was that he had arrived at this particular place in life. But you still might understand how even he might throw on his jacket and hurry out, forgetting to lock the door.

67

At the end of it all Firouz found himself disinherited, maligned and exiled. But he already knew that. He did not believe it, but he knew it. He did not need two thousand five hundred years of history to give him a clue as to where things were headed. The past sixty were indication enough. Sixty years enough to show that from one Shah's reign to the next, those in favour one day were out of favour and dead the next. You could imagine what would happen with the change from a monarchy to a system that turned out to be, after all the struggles and the suspended disbelief, the Islamic Republic of Iran. And if the lessons of Iran were not enough, he could always refer to history. Revolutions have always eaten their young.

He should have expected that even if we succeeded in doing the impossible, we would be expropriated, exiled or executed. He knew it, but he did not believe it yet. It would take a while for it to sink in. In the meantime Firouz was swept away by a nation demanding a voice.

I was swept away by a nation demanding something more. And the first thing on our list was that the Shah must go. "The Shah must go, the Shah must go," we shouted in unison with communists and centrists, Mojaheds and the old timers from the National Front, with the ones we would later call Hezbollah, as we marched toward the Parliament, as we walked past the American Embassy. Thousands of voices shouting the same incredibly brave words. Thousands of voices defying tanks and bayonets, defying the secret agents who walked beside us, forgetting for a moment prisons and torturers, the implications. Forgetting for a moment the welfare of mothers, sisters, brothers, sons and lovers.

And if a nation could forget the implications, then Firouz could forget his history. If we could believe in a cause that cast us against the might of a monarch, then the least that he could do was join in. And though we did not beat swords into ploughshares, we did manage to turn guns into vases by placing roses and tulips, hyacinths and freesia, narcissus, daffodils and jonquils into the Kalashnikovs and M-14s, into the hands and helmets of the clean-shaven soldiers who lined the streets. We arranged bouquets in gun barrels, corsages in buttonholes of immobile young men, garlands in the nozzles of Chieftain tanks.

We walked the streets and we did the impossible. The Shah kissed the ground, got on his plane and left with a handful of Iranian dust as his father had done before him. But Reza Shah had been removed by the British, and his son by his own people. Therein lay the difference. Mohammad Reza Shah was removed by the Iranian people, and it was not the first time. The people had walked these very streets before, had overthrown this very monarch once before.

68

So, when the time came, Firouz and I walked the streets together to remove the Shah of Shahs, the King of Kings. Firouz needn't have. He had quoted those two lines of verse and removed himself from it all. But when the time came, he marched with the millions, knowing all along that it would be his undoing, sensing that it all would unravel. After all, she had betrayed him before. But he set his beliefs against his judgement, his ideals against a sinking feeling of how it would all play out.

What could he do? He had devoted his life to the pursuit of those simple principles he had learned first with the Presbyterians. Standing straight and thinking straight. Living the stories of truth and justice. Being that ordinary person rising to face extraordinary challenges. The Presbyterians did not teach him of scorpions and frogs, Cain and Abel, Darius and Alexander. Yet, all he needed to know of treachery and deceit, he could learn from his own family, as I would remind him painfully.

When his father's father had died, there had been a strongbox. It was a Russian strongbox adorned with coins and inscriptions, and could not be opened without a ringing sound as the key was turned. Within it calligraphy, deeds and decrees, marriage certificates, *farmans,* and poems, wills and titles. Along with the Quran that was brought out every New Year were titles to properties already given to the daughters, properties coveted by the sons. On the night the patriarch died, as the grandfather clock struck midnight, one of the sons contrived to turn the key, ingeniously opening the ringing strongbox, and silently removing the documents giving title to his sisters. He stole land from his own sisters. Or so the story went. It was a story repeated at late night gatherings, over one too many cigarettes, after one too many bottles of *araq,* after the story of Firouz's parents' marriage.

Firouz still owned the melodious Russian strongbox. It was the only possession of his father's he kept other than a straight-edged razor. But it did no good. He never did listen to the sound of that particular bell.

69

I'm no longer quite sure if Le Petit Poucet left a trail of breadcrumbs or if he broke branches along the way. If Hansel and Gretel offered the witch a twisted twig or a chicken bone. Was it the door at the end of the hall that was forbidden to Bluebeard's wives, or the one from which a key dangled? Were the moon and the stars to be found in the tail of the fiery stallion, or in its mane? Did the words *amatal nastre* bring forth the dragon's breath, or send sentries into restless slumber? There are any number of ways to remember oft-repeated tales.

The way I remember it, when we returned from our studies, the nation had not been ready for us. And when the revolution happened, we were not ready for it. We were industrialists, entrepreneurs, doctors and architects, statisticians, adjustors and comptrollers. We were idealists who had clothed a nation with Barak clothes and Bella shoes, washed a nation with Darugar soap and a nation's laundry with Snow and with Sea detergents. We had never been politicians; that particular avenue had been closed to us.

We had been in universities in Kansas and Kentucky when a nation took to the streets to support a populist Prime Minister who believed in Iran, a parliamentary system, and that monarchs should govern and not rule. But he also believed that Iranians, not the British, should own the resources beneath Iranian soil. He believed in nationalizing the oil industry. For that he was ousted.

In the turmoil that ensued we were never quite sure of the facts. Had we known for sure that Mossadegh had been supplanted by a coup conceived by the grandson of an American president, we never would have devoted our lives to building a nation where coups could be staged, Shahs instated and removed, governments changed, injustices perpetrated at the whim of even a great nation thousands of miles away.

We had always known our kings and prime ministers could be changed at the will of a Lord Curzon, a Lord Sykes, or a Winston Churchill (third son of the seventh Duke of Marlborough). But never a Roosevelt and an Eisenhower. We believed, as so many before us, that during our own brief lifetimes we were witnessing the dawning of a new era, that the stars were finally aligned. There could be no doubt—it met with every term and condition of the prophecies, signs and premonitions. We had seen the clouds move across the moon, noted the shift in the tides of power, and knew that we were part of the dawning of a new and wonderful American age. An age when the weak and oppressed of the world would be heard and we would encounter justice in this world.

Years later, after this age turned out to be like all that had come before it, after all the sordid facts came out, Firouz took great exception with the full-length portrait of Eisenhower on

the turn of the stair of the Columbia University Library. Going so far as to write a letter to the Chancellor explaining how
that very library housed the documents that established in no
uncertain terms why a portrait of Ike, even in civilian clothes,
was a disgrace to an institution devoted to higher ideals.

Roy Mottahedeh, a man who taught at Princeton and
Harvard, but never at Columbia, a man whose father left
Iran behind forever, tells a story that Firouz transcribed in
a crooked hand in one of his numerous black books. The
story of a mullah who, somewhat late on his way to prayer,
is splashed by a dog relieving itself. Knowing dogs to be im-
pure, and not wanting to be further delayed by going home
to change his clothes, the mullah refuses to look directly at
the animal, and consoles himself, "God willing it's a goat."

There was no need for marginal notes to understand the
meaning of that passage—just the bare outline of our lives.
We returned from our studies in the United States, in Britain, in France, in Germany, not looking the dog directly in
the eye. Not abandoning our paths, not changing out of our
pin-striped suits, we went back convincing ourselves that it
was not a dog. It was a donkey, a mule, a camel, a very small
camel. "It was not relieving itself at all." "It was relieving itself
but it did not splash on me." "There really was no splash—this
is a wine stain from last night's dinner party, it's not even wet.
Here, touch it and see. No, I assure you, touch it. It's just a
wine stain."

By the seventies we had to acknowledge that we had been
betrayed. We knew how we had been manipulated. We knew
who Kermit Roosevelt was and what he had done. We knew
we had been bought and sold.

But we believed, against all the evidence, that while Iranian kings and prime ministers had been purchased in the
past, things had changed, the stars were now aligned. We
were a force to be contended with, a nation with a voice, and
the voice of an entire nation could not be silenced. They
could not bribe, bully, trick, or cajole an entire nation. They
could not fool an entire nation. They could never squeeze an

entire nation. Though they could buy the big people, they could never buy all the little people of the world. We believed that this time we would take fate into our own hands, that we would oust the king who had been foisted on us all those years ago. We would exercise the beautiful principles of self-determination we had learned so thoroughly, we had believed in so fervently.

We walked because we knew he was not the one we had chosen. His father was not the one we had chosen. We knew it instinctively, and later we took the time to search the archives at Kew Gardens, to document through forgotten correspondence, check stubs and memoranda what every man on the street had suspected for years—that Reza Shah had been installed by the British. We would also go through the Dulles brothers' papers to establish that Reza Shah's son had been reinstated by the CIA. But we had already known that more than instinctively by the Seventies. And knowing that, we took to the streets to remove a king who had been placed on the throne by someone else. We took to the streets to demand a ruler of our own choosing. After twenty-five years of the reinstated Shah's reign we took to the streets, finally putting to use that part of our hearts, that part of our souls we had removed and left in a drawer all those years ago, when we failed to look things squarely in the eye.

But we were technocrats, not politicians. We were contractors, doctors and writers. And when it came right down to it, we were outmanoeuvred. We were marginalized by a clergy that had itself been outmanoeuvred and marginalized once or twice over the course of the past hundred years, and knew enough not to let it happen again. Swept away by euphoria, believing that finally we could create the Great Society to which we had always aspired, we walked the streets and we lost.

I'm sure others will tell the story differently, with different heroes and different villains, and certainly with other beginnings. As I said, I am no longer quite sure if it was a trail of pebbles or gumdrops, breadcrumbs or broken branches. All I remember for sure is the ending.

70

We took to the streets and we lost. We who were willing to do the far-far-better-than-anything-we-had-ever-done-before thing. We who did the unthinkable when the Shah-anshah kissed the ground, took a handful of dirt and left. Not long thereafter we too left, when the king we had helped overthrow was replaced by the kingdom of God in this world. A kingdom of God in which we were branded idolaters. We left after we realized, in the popular idiom, that we had loved a revolution that did not love us back.

There were no cameras, no symbolic handfuls of dust. There was no kissing of Persian soil. Those of us who still could, got on planes, waiting anxiously on the runway as the Revolutionary Guard pulled passengers off. Those in danger of losing their lives walked across borders to Turkey or Pakistan, leaving their dreams and their homes behind. They ended up in Los Angeles and London, in Berlin and Toronto, and in those apartments they had bought in Nice. Some were heartbroken, but not Firouz. He was no stranger to unrequited love.

Firouz took the five minutes necessary to pack his bags with his trademark white shirts, the suits he insisted on wearing even in forced retirement, and enough pairs of socks that he would not need to hang them on the washstand on alternate nights. He packed the oversize boxer shorts, the Gillette razor, and a pair of striped pyjamas. He packed the little black books filled with two and a half decades of other people's words, and left his collection of travelogues with an obscure friend he had always trusted completely and implicitly. He said his goodbyes and left to spend the next twenty years in progressively smaller apartments in Los Angeles and London. He left, and within days, I left.

But what of a man and a woman who had no interest in the kingdoms but only in the paradises of this world? A man and an angel who had devoted their lives to tenderness. Nur ed Din and Fereshteh continued to do what they had done since the day they set foot in the village named for nightingales. They grew roses, they harvested roses, and once a year between four and nine in the morning they distilled rosewater. Later that day, as villagers gathered round with bated breath, they extracted rose essence with a feather. They did as they had always done.

Though they heard the rumblings, they really did not experience the tumult of the revolution. Their lives were untouched by the walks and the protests, by the events in Tehran, Isfahan and Tabriz. They lived in a small village on the edge of the desert, they grew roses. Firouz urged them to take up the banner, to strike the gong. He told them time and again, "Forget your gardens and your rosewater for a moment, for just a moment, and come help us make history. What are gardens when revolutions are happening?" Nur ed Din and Fereshteh heard the euphoria, the sincerity and the unmistakable passion in their friend's voice. And they stayed away from it all.

Though Nur ed Din could tell Firouz that revolutions did not interest him, he refrained from saying that until Firouz had worked the earth, planted the shoots, and clipped the vine, he could not know why Nur ed Din refused to walk, chanting, down Liberty Avenue. Reflecting on the gardens that grow, distant from dynasties and revolutions, Nur ed Din realized that when it came right down to it, he had no desire to participate in these momentous moments that seemed to roll around with shocking regularity every so many years. He had found his lover, and through her he had found his place in this world. "I love us," he would tell her jokingly. But it was true. He loved her first, but he also loved what he had become. He loved what they had become.

It was only at times that he wished they were elsewhere. And when he did, it was not in revolutionary Tehran, but anonymous in the streets of Rome or Paris. Once, in his youth, he had seen a couple embrace by the Geneva airport baggage carousel. More than any Hollywood scene, it was the most sensual kiss he had observed in his entire life. There was an intimacy in their bodies melding through coats, gloves, hats and scarves that spoke of ease, intimacy and desire. Though he felt he was intruding on the most private of moments, he could not bring himself to look away.

There were times he regretted that he could not kiss Fereshteh in a park or a metro, by a fountain or a theatre. He regretted that her lips remained unkissed except behind closed doors. He wished that they would take a trip to Rome or to Paris so one time in his life he could embrace her with the kind of public intimacy afforded only by anonymous airports and crowded streets, behind Romanesque churches, at street crossings.

But they did not leave Bolbolouieh. Their public intimacies were limited to the times he stroked her arm superfluously in rose fields, or asked her to stay still as he removed an imagined stray eyelash from her face, as most of the children with shaven heads or colourful scarves shyly looked the other way.

She had found him, and through her he had found his place in this world. He had found his people. Though he did not guide them through the travails of life, he did admonish them to plant the Prophet's flower. Those who followed his advice flourished. At first he had felt some trepidation in suggesting that they invest in a far from proven venture. But he had been compelled to tell them to plant the flower favoured by Muhammad, the rosebush of the garden of Islam and the nightingale of the lofty heavens. Nur ed Din had felt passionately enough to suggest, though he could not presume to know better, that they might benefit from such an endeavour. It gave him no end of pleasure to see them prosper.

Bolbolouieh was his world. He had very few reasons to go anywhere else. There certainly was no reason to take to the streets demanding change, to breathlessly follow the crowds chanting, "Bakhtiar, Bakhtiar, *nokar-e bi ekhtiar*"—servant without power. Nur ed Din had no desire to follow the struggles between one faction and the next.

He did not follow as the clergy consolidated power, embracing and then methodically decimating the National Front, the Mojaheds, the Communists and the Cheriks. He did not lament as one candidate was defeated or another elected. When the time came, he did not register and he did not vote on the question: "Should Iran become an Islamic Republic, yes or no."

He removed himself from it all, stayed away from it all, like a monk in some charterhouse (of Parma). But still, Nur ed Din, who never once took to the streets, who never once uttered a single slogan, lost just as much as his friends who walked, chanted and soliloquized. You might even say he lost more. After all, he had more to lose.

71

Nur ed Din may have removed Fereshteh and himself from the machinations of this world, but the world was coming to him. There was no stopping it. Old mud-brick walls were being torn down to make way for boulevards and villas. The remote village that had once been idyllic Bolbolouieh was being engulfed by the city. As roads were built, subdivisions developed further and further away from the centre, as speculators sought the next desirable address to sell to city dwellers with a penchant for the old ways. The ones who loved ancient walnut trees and running brooks of water, if only on weekends. And land in Bolbolouieh was beginning to command extremely attractive prices.

It made no difference to Nur ed Din and Fereshteh—they had no interest in cashing in on Bolbolouieh. And though they knew better than most that the bloom of the rose is fleeting, they tried to stay on. Though they knew that the silkiest rose has its thorns, they hoped, against all evidence, that they would not be pricked. They refused offer after offer. Others who had no such luxury informed Nur ed Din and

Fereshteh apologetically, "We did not want to sell, you have been so good to us, but we have children who want to marry well. They need our support now, not when we die. It is for their sake, not for ours, that we sold."

Nur ed Din and Fereshteh nodded their heads in agreement. "You were right, you have your families to think of. And who knows, perhaps the new owners will continue what you started," they stated hopefully, knowing full well that whatever the new owners did, they would not plant and harvest roses. Though roses and rosewater had been profitable even lucrative, though roses and rosewater had paid the bills for years, they could never compete with the windfalls to be had from development.

So Nur ed Din and Fereshteh watched their dream slowly erode, until one day, some time after the crown had been exchanged for the turban, the chief of the gendarmerie showed up to request, "Mister Nur ed Din please be so kind as to accompany me to headquarters in Kerman City. Please excuse the inconvenience, Mister Nur ed Din. I assure you it is merely a formality, but it is one that I am obliged to perform. It should take no more than a few minutes."

When he arrived at the gendarmerie after a long and silent drive during which the chief gendarme smoked almost incessantly, Nur ed Din was asked to step into a "waiting room." Three windowless walls and one mirrored one, decorated with a sofa, a love seat and a telephone. Here the chief informed Nur ed Din that he would soon be joined by an official from the Ministry of the Interior. "Mr. Akhavi will join you in a moment," he excused himself, begging off to attend a prior engagement he had been unable to reschedule.

Nur ed Din, somewhat displeased at the chief's departure, resolved to put his best face on and go through whatever formality he was to be subjected to. It wasn't long before Nur ed Din began to have severe misgivings about having made the trip. Finally, after a wait of fifteen or twenty minutes Mr. Akhavi entered the room. Wearing the party-line attire of a collarless shirt buttoned to the top and a trimmed three-day beard, he greeted Nur ed Din and ushered him into an office. There he took up his place behind a desk cluttered with papers, pictures of the chief gendarme's family, and a faded calendar-view of the Matterhorn, compliments of Toblerone. Nur ed Din was offered a singularly uncomfortable folding chair that bore a strong resemblance to what one might find in a rural classroom.

"Would you like a cup of tea?" Mr. Akhavi asked Nur ed Din. Not an offer, but an insult. It is a matter of course and a sign of respect that tea is brought whether the guest wants it or not. Tea appears without having been requested. If the guest is not interested, he or she will often take it from the waiting attendant to recognize the courtesy, pose it on a table, and simply not drink it. "No thank you," Nur ed Din politely declined.

Having duly insulted Nur ed Din and dispensed with formalities, Mr. Akhavi began the questioning. "Doctor Nur ed Din, have you lived long in Bolbolouieh?"

"Ten years," Nur ed Din replied, not taking exception to the gratuitous promotion which, again, was more an insult than a sign of respect. Nur ed Din was not, nor had he ever been a doctor, medical or otherwise.

"And what is it that you do in Bolbolouieh, Doctor?" the man behind the desk continued in his most affable, conversational tone.

"I grow roses. I grow roses and produce rosewater. You may have seen it in the bazaar, it is called Zahra rosewater." Nur ed Din began to take a very guarded approach to his responses.

"You grow roses, you say. I have not seen your rosewater, though I am sure it is excellent. But am I to understand that you came all the way from Tehran to Bolbolouieh to grow roses? Is that correct? You, an educated man, an extremely well connected individual, an engineer educated abroad came all the way from Tehran to grow roses."

"Yes, that is what I did. That is what I do."

"You would have to agree with me that it is rather odd, wouldn't you. You really cannot expect me to believe that you,

Doctor Nur ed Din, an engineer, a man with infinite possibilities would leave Tehran with all its amenities, to grow roses in Bolbolouieh," the man with the smirk continued, revealing what it was about him that had bothered Nur ed Din from the moment he had entered the room.

"I have rose gardens, I grow roses, and I produce rosewater," Nur ed Din responded curtly, and then offered, "I would be glad to give you a tour."

"That will not be necessary," came the reply. "But you still have not given me a satisfactory answer about your activities in Bolbolouieh."

The first thought that crossed Nur ed Din's mind was that he was being accused of something, though he was not sure why. The second was to wonder if he knew someone well-connected enough to get him out of this situation. "As I said, I will be glad to show you the roses and the facilities, I grow roses. I have grown roses and distilled Zahra rosewater for the past ten years. If you do not feel like going out there, please ask Mr. Husseini, the chief gendarme, he knows what I do. And Mr. Akhavi, it is Mr. Akhavi, yes? If I am not growing roses, then exactly what is it that you think I am doing?" Nur ed Din continued, tiring of the innuendos. "Exactly what is it that you are asking me, and why? If I am being accused of something please tell me what it is. If not, I think I am ready to leave this meeting now."

"Mister Nur ed Din," Mr. Akhavi proceeded, rapidly dropping the "Doctor," "I just have a few more questions and had hoped that you would cooperate. I understand that you have a religious following. Is that true?"

Racking his brain as to where this would lead, Nur ed Din replied with the easiest response he could come up with. "Yes."

Smiling, Mr. Akhavi leaned forward. "Would you please tell me if you yourself are a *mojtahed,* and if not, which religious leader you follow."

Nur ed Din was entirely unprepared for this line of questioning. But he knew it was a trap that he could not afford to fall into. If he subscribed to one of the Ayatollahs of the current regime, he would be forced to follow that Ayatollah's pronouncements. And if he denied following an Ayatollah, it would be practically an admission of apostasy.

Taking a deep breath, he responded, "You are correct, I do have a following of sorts, Mr. Akhavi. I also subscribe to an Ayatollah." He paused. "The Ayatollah Yazdi," he said, naming a respected spiritual leader who was conveniently dead. Convenient because Nur ed Din could espouse a leader but act independently of pressure from the existing religious establishment.

It was no use explaining that he did not really have a following, that he was waiting for a sign that had not come. It was no use explaining that his uncle had died without giving him an answer, but only a request that had gone unanswered. In fact, it made no difference what Nur ed Din answered. It was irrelevant that Nur ed Din had dodged the bullet of his religious leanings. He had only managed to worsen things by besting Mr. Akhavi. Mr. Akhavi was simply collecting evidence to further thicken the file. If Nur ed Din had been summoned, if the chief gendarme had excused himself from the meeting, then the fix was already in.

Realizing there was very little that he could do, he said, "Mr. Akhavi, I have an appointment with my wife and she will be waiting for me. Please let me call her and tell her I am running late."

"Of course, Doctor Nur ed Din," came the response. "What is the number, I will dial it for you myself."

Nur ed Din gave the number and Mr. Akhavi dialed it amiably. Fereshteh answered the phone, and from across the desk Nur ed Din could hear her voice, "Allo, Allo, who is it?"

Mr. Akhavi hung up the phone. "That was your wife," he proclaimed with a smile. "Now, where were we?"

72

Without the benefit of a telephone call, Nur ed Din was taken away that same day. They put him in a car, drove him to Tehran and threw him in a cell.

When he did not return that evening, Fereshteh began calling the friends he would have stayed with if he were indisposed or too tired for the drive back. When one after the other expressed ignorance of his whereabouts, she picked up the phone and called the chief gendarme. His rehearsed response confirmed her fears. She immediately got into a taxi, went to his house and confronted him.

"Where is my husband? What did you do with Nur ed Din? I entrusted him to your hands," she accosted him when he opened the door.

"Madame, you have honoured us, please do come in," he attempted.

"I have no desire to come in. All I want is to know where my husband is. How could you have stooped so low as to drive him off? He trusted you." And then almost as an afterthought, "Who are you to speak of honour."

"You are distraught, dear lady. Please come in and sit down. A cup of tea will do you good. Would you like a cigarette? It might help to calm your nerves."

"My nerves will be fine if you would just tell me where he is," she persisted.

"Like I told you when you inquired over the phone, all I know is that I was asked to bring him in for routine questioning. I dropped him off and left to take care of other business. I have just made a number of calls on your behalf, but none of my associates saw him leave. Please have some patience, I will find out when he left the gendarmerie and with whom. I cannot imagine that anything would have happened to him, though I must say I was surprised that they came all this way to ask Mr. Nur ed Din questions. After all, he raises roses.

You are not aware of anything that he might have done, are you? Any information you might be able to provide would help me to locate him."

Cursing him for a coward and a bureaucrat, and wondering what kind of an idiot he took her for, she stormed off. Confronting her worst fears, she asked the taxi to take her to the morgue.

"Madame, surely your husband will show up. There must be a simple explanation. There is no need to search for him among the dead," the taxi driver tried to reassure her.

Rejecting the well-meaning reassurances of this particular stranger, she insisted, "I know my husband. If he has not called, it is because he cannot. And I know these bastards too. You never know what they will do."

"Madame, don't talk like that" the taxi driver implored, "please don't talk like that."

But the taxi driver knew she was right. There had been a number of people who disappeared, only to reappear, weeks later, wrapped in white. Finally handed over to family, friends and lovers who had gone from police stations to gendarmeries to prisons, their inquiries met by blank stares, vapid reassurances and rote responses. "Sister, it will be all right, surely he will show up. Maybe he had to attend to some private business."

Confronting her worst fears, she went to the morgue, wondering what it was they could have wanted from him. He had never done anything. In that short distance between the gendarme's house and the morgue, she imagined finding his body, immobile, on a stone slab. And saw herself wandering the city with a tattered letter that coiled off to the moon. She saw herself with distraught, flowing hair and frayed, threadbare kimono, holding on to the one thing that she had left.

Except he had never written that one definitive letter to keep in the bedside drawer and read every night like a prayer. He had never written the letter that would be discovered years later by someone looking for a pen, a book of matches, a scrap of paper. He had never written the letter that said it all. But at least he had kept her letter. If nothing else, she could walk the streets reading her own ragged, tear-stained letter, creased from all the foldings and unfoldings. At least she had that.

She did not find him at the morgue. She sighed a sigh of relief, and immediately berated herself for being so ridiculous. However ridiculous she may have been, she still did not know why he had not called. She still did not know what had become of him. There was no plausible or even implausible explanation for his absence and his silence. She had tried them all.

During her brief kimono-clad, tear-streaked search, she went to the shops across from the gendarmerie. There she encountered the fruit seller.

"Sister, please do not waste your time. They've taken him away," he offered, looking over his shoulder.

"Where have they taken him, where is he, what do you mean 'they?'" she breathlessly asked.

"Madame, you've certainly lived here long enough to know what it means to be 'taken away'," he said, rearranging the quinces. "They put him in a car and drove off. It was a black Mercedes, and they came down all the way from Tehran. He won't be coming back, not for a while."

"But where did they take him," she continued, wanting desperately to have someone else say it.

"Madame, do I need to spell it out for you? They took him away. He's been locked up. He won't be coming back soon."

"What has he ever done to be put in prison?" she finally said the words out loud.

"Sister, I don't know you, I don't know him, and I don't know what he's done. It's none of my business. But look, it was important enough for them to send someone down in a black Mercedes. I wouldn't be surprised if he were in Evin," he said, and wished one more time that he could just sell his shop and move somewhere else, maybe to the boulevard they were building. Maybe there he could make a quiet living selling fragrant peaches, apricots tinged with a pink blush, bruised figs.

Fereshteh left that same day for Tehran. How could she have been so blind, of course that was it. Had any other misfortune befallen him, she would have known by now. He had been taken away. There was no need to further accost that bastard of a gendarme, no need to call family and friends. No need to place an advertisement in the paper to run with a picture of Nur ed Din at his most formal, and text that read, "Lost. Last seen on Wednesday, September 25 in the vicinity of the gendarmerie wearing a blue suit and a white shirt. Reward for any information leading to his return."

Nur ed Din used to joke about taking out just such an advertisement for Firouz during prolonged absences. She had never found it funny. She had seen too many faces in the bottom right hand corner of the back page of evening editions. She had seen too many unreadable faces of runaway husbands, kidnapped children, abused wives. But in her reluctance to laugh at Nur ed Din's joke, she had never imagined that the faces in the evening paper had been driven off by black Benzes with special license plates. She had never thought about what happens to those faces last spotted buying pumpkin seeds or leaving the restaurant after a meal of stewed lamb, a glass of sweet tea and a cigarette.

That very same day she packed her bags and without explanation entrusted the house and the gardens to her foreman. Trying hard to convince herself that she would not be staying long, she took only the bare essentials, four outfits (ensembles, he had jokingly called them), three pairs of shoes, four bras and six pairs of underwear, her toilette and a nightgown. She did not pack the black manteau that masked her curves and the scarf that hid her hair—she would be wearing them every single day.

As she packed, she reflected that for the first time since he had gone off to come back with that absurd contraption, she would be spending the night without him. For fifteen years they had scarcely been apart. They had woken up together, they had slept together. Their lives had been one. Looking around the room they had shared for so many years, she imagined him off in his cell, four bare walls and a stark lightbulb, a sink in the corner. Trying to picture him with his head

shaved, she suddenly found herself fighting back tears, swallowing hard to stop the swelling in her throat, biting her lip
to stop the trembling. She thought of him innocent and lost,
and bit harder. She heard finality in the clanging of an iron
door, and could no longer hold back the tears.

At first she sobbed long silent sobs, moaning like mourners do. And then she cried like the ones who cry for their own
dead. Sobbing, rocking back and forth, striking her face and
pulling her hair, holding herself tight. Like the ones who cry
for their own dead, she swayed back and forth oblivious, like
them, to the only words of consolation that could be offered,
"May it be your last sorrow."

Distant from the tender and merciful touches that wipe
away tears, that hold convulsing shoulders, she wept incon-
solably. She wept for Nur ed Din who removed imagined
eyelashes from her face and laughed when he made love. She
wept for Nur ed Din who climbed a Damavand tree and reported on events along the Caspian coast. She wept for the
man who walked down the streets beating his breast, and had
happened to look up at a balcony on the second floor. She
wept for Nur ed Din, she wept for herself, and she wept for
Iran. She fell asleep on the bed, moaning softly, not knowing
what time it was or how long it had been.

73

Arriving in Tehran unannounced, she went directly to her
brother's house. She was welcomed as one who needs not
explain. But Farhad was naturally perplexed by her unexpected, solitary arrival. He did not have to wait long for an
explanation. "They've taken Nur ed Din," she began, scarcely
taking off her coat. "On Monday the chief of the gendarmerie came to our house and they drove off together. When
he didn't come back by evening, I began to call around but
no one had seen him. I went to the gendarme's house, and

he confirmed my fears. The fruit seller said Nur ed Din was driven off in a black Mercedes with Tehran plates, number 81118. He said he remembered because only important officials get numbers like that."

Her brother held her, kissed the top of her head as their father did, and told her not to worry. "Leave it to me," he said. "We'll find him and we'll find a way of getting him back. Everything will be all right." Later, he found the ones who had loved ones imprisoned, the ones who sought sisters, brothers and lovers, the ones who had been behind bars themselves.

The idealistic bureaucrat discovered with a cache of arms in her basement, the government official whose superiors still walked the streets with impunity though he spent five long years paying for unmentionable crimes, the wife of the money changer and the money changer himself. Even the ex-Minister of the Interior and the grey-eyed Director of the Plan Organization. The banker who continued to have tea once a month with old colleagues and once a week with old cellmates.

"You really have no choice," the ex-Minister advised her after hearing the fruit seller's story. "You must go to Evin and ask to see Nur ed Din. They will say he is not there. Do not be dissuaded. No matter what they say, you must persist. They will tell you to go elsewhere, to direct your inquiries to police stations or at some downtown office. Do not be dissuaded. You must insist on seeing him. If you can, get in to see Colonel Ahmadi on the second floor. He's the thin one with the salt and pepper hair and the moustache. He is really a very decent fellow. Don't ask for him by name, but try to position yourself so he is the one who handles your inquiry."

To give her consolation, the money-changer's wife added, "It's really not as bad as you think. Evin is a place like any other. Nowadays it has nothing to do with politics and ideology. They just want money. Fifty millions they wanted from us. They had him confused with the other Mohsen Moghaddam. We told them we were from Tabriz, that we were not one of those Moghaddams, that we did not have that kind of money. After six months of negotiating we paid seven and a half million tomans. After all, what is money when compared with a person's life? In any case seven and a half million really isn't worth what it used to be, isn't that right, darling?" she said, turning to her husband. And from across the room the other Mr. Mohsen Moghaddam nodded his assent.

The next day Fereshteh went to Evin. And every day that followed. Every day she went to the prison, and every night she came back empty-handed. Every day she went to the prison with the ones who had lost brothers, wives and lovers. Every day she watched and waited with others who watched and waited. She sat with the ones who had lost sons and the ones who had lost daughters. She sat with the ones who were foolhardy enough to speak out against the regime right outside the prison gates, and the ones who never once said a word. She sat with the ones who brought children, carpets and flasks of tea, and the ones who walked around with folders, documents and files.

She watched as widowed wives were dragged off by brothers and sisters, shouting and screaming, cursing the bastards. Not caring anymore. Not giving a damn. She watched as others quietly took loved ones by the elbow and walked step by broken step to the waiting car. She never found Colonel Ahmadi with the thin moustache, the man she dreamt of at night and wondered in the morning if he would look like the man who appeared in her dreams.

She arrived first thing every morning to make the same request of whoever happened to be behind the desk. "I want to see my husband, I know he's here," she would begin as if to convince them by the strength of her conviction to open otherwise closed doors. She might have been telling the taxi driver, "Take me directly to the Ritz, and don't take any diversions, I know the way." In response, the individual behind the counter would ask her husband's name and matter-of-factly inform her that they had no record of such a person. Had she checked at the gendarmerie? What made her think he was imprisoned? What had he done that would convince her that he had been incarcerated?

Informing her there was no one there by that name and that she was slightly ridiculous if not outright paranoid to be wasting her time at Evin prison, they would try to send her off to make her inquiries elsewhere. But she refused to go, restating her position time and again as she had seen others do, "I want to see my husband, I know he's here, I will not leave until I do." When it was obvious she would get no satisfaction on that day, she would say, "If you will not let me see him, then at least find it in your heart to do a good deed and give him this bottle of rosewater, it is from the roses in our garden. I know, I know, you say he's not here. Then please give it to some other poor prisoner."

Neglecting the expressions on the faces of guards who had never seen a rose garden large enough to extract rosewater, she would continue, "My husband always said the Prophet Muhammad (peace be upon his name) believed roses were sacred and the scent of the rose a gift from the heavens." The guards would act annoyed at the impudence of her request, watch her walk away, and casually take the rosewater from the counter.

Having exhausted their patience, she would sit outside the gate with the others who had exhausted their patience, with the ones who may have lost as much as she, and the ones who had already lost more. The reluctant fathers of communists and uncomprehending mothers of Mojaheds, the loyal brothers of monarchists and their outspoken sisters. She sat there as the bald gentleman with the thin smile joked that he worked longer hours than the guards did, and laughed to herself as one guard turned to the other and said, "Get a time card for Mr. Lari so that he can clock in and clock out like the rest of us." She smiled to herself every time he arrived earlier than they, and every time he stayed later. She sat there as others dutifully went off to ministries, gendarmeries, hospitals, morgues and police stations, and watched as they returned weeks later to sit with her outside the gates.

She watched the ones who like her went to the desk day after day and said, "I have come to see my brother and I will

not leave until I do." Who showed up day after day, who resolved not to leave until they got what they came for. Who
sat there impassive, uncomprehending as they were told time
and again to go away. The ones who responded with the for-
mula, "I know what I came for, and I will not leave until I
have got it." She watched as a young woman with dyed blonde
hair was dragged away wailing and screaming, "What did he
ever do, what did he ever do wrong except to love this damn
country. What did he ever do to you? I curse you, I curse this
government, and I would curse this damned country, but it
is already cursed."

She shed tears as prisoners were released into waiting
relatives' hands, and was amazed when an elderly gentleman refused to leave. "I will only go the same way I came,"
he said matter of factly. "When I was brought here, I wore a
gold watch. I will not leave without it."

"Dear sir," an idle bystander pitched in, "you are free. Go
home. They have told you the words we are all waiting to hear.
You are free to go. What is a watch or a pen when people are
losing their lives? Go and thank God you are free."

"When I came to this place, I wore a grey suit and a gold
watch," he replied. "They can keep the suit, it no longer fits me
and I suspect it is out of fashion. But I will not leave without
the watch. I won't do it," he persisted. "They can go ahead
and lock me back up."

"But you have been freed, we cannot lock up a free man,"
the guard argued.

"Give me my watch or put me back in my cell, it is number
four hundred and seventeen. I stayed there for two years for
no good reason, I can stay there for another two for a better
purpose," the elderly gentleman responded to the amazement
of all present.

When a clean-shaven guard reluctantly produced the
watch, the old man wound it, held it to his ear, and uncon-
vinced, finally agreed to leave.

74

Every day Fereshteh went to Evin prison, and every night she returned empty-handed to her brother's house. Every night she had tea with individuals who maintained they were related through marriage to the speaker of the house of parliament, and with people who maintained they were related by blood. She met people who could certainly get the job done, but only if she would first deposit funds into a bank abroad. At times she wondered how her poor brother could bring these charlatans tea, ask after their families, exchange pleasantries. How could he offer them fruit and cream puff pastries, optimistically listen to their lies? How could he tolerate these people who made their livings from other peoples' miseries, these bastards who lived off misplaced hopes?

Every evening she had tea with them, nodded her head and agreed, "Of course I will be glad to transfer funds to your account. But on the condition that first you do one thing for me, a very little thing. It is really nothing to ask of a person with your contacts and obvious abilities. I am embarrassed to bother you with such a small request, but I have no one else to turn to. Just deliver a letter to me, written in Nur ed Din's hand. Then I will instruct my bank of the wiring instructions."

Every day for more than a month she had written him a letter and mailed it to Evin prison. And though none of her letters were ever returned "undeliverable" or "unknown," she had not once received a reply. Still she wrote of the sunrise and the waning crescent moon, and wondered if he had seen it too. She told him of the crows with white striped wings that inhabited the plane trees, of the cats that never tired of trying to make off with one of their young. She told him of the woman with two dots and one thin line tattooed on her chin, and of the guard who smiled at her and remembered Nur ed Din's name.

She told him of the crippled beggar who sold lottery

tickets outside the prison walls. Despite the beggar's imprecations, "Madame, try your luck, who knows what might happen," she never drew a brightly coloured piece of paper from
his fan of tickets, but always gave him coins far in excess of
a ticket's value. She gave him coins from her purse, and she
gave the rest to the beggar who sat with his hands over his
face to hide his shame. She told Nur ed Din of the Kurds
in their oversized turbans who sat against the wall smoking
slender cigarettes and of the Azarbaijani women who were fair
and had blue eyes. She told him of the children who played
soccer in the courtyard and piled into one huge celebrating
heap no matter which team scored. She told him of her days
and she told him of her nights.

Every morning before sunrise she wrote him a letter, addressed it to Evin prison and sent it off. Since the recipient
and address never changed, each time she tried a different
stamp. She tried stamps with images of mosques and images
of martyrs, and for several weeks the one with the image of
the Iranian soccer team. Having seen a film or two, she imagined her letters were no different from those addressed to the
North Pole, the wish lists that ended up in post offices taking
up space. But in movies, at least, there was always a post office employee to take pity and send the letters to Santa, even
if it was only the one in Macy's.

75

She never received a miracle in Evin prison, nor on Evin
Road. In fact, the only miracle she ever received was in
the form of a telephone call from Abbas, the Bolbolouieh
foreman. "Madame, I have been searching all over for you.
Thank God I was able to locate your brother's number. You
must come back immediately. They put a *hokm* on your door
and a seal on the lock. Mister Nur ed Din has been accused,
and they say the State is confiscating your land. Madame, we

can fight them. We are not as feeble as they think. But you must come back." Hanging up the phone, Fereshteh finally understood what she was up against. Realized to free Nur ed Din she had to return to Bolbolouieh. That, at least, was miraculous.

The following day she arrived to find everything exactly as Abbas had described: The seal on the door, the letter in the window, the roses in full bloom. He welcomed her back and immediately asked "How is Mr. Nur ed Din's health?"

She looked away. Could not bring herself to say, "I do not know. Two months after his disappearance I still do not know if he is alive or dead." Could not explain, "For two months I have gone to Evin prison every day, and for two months I have had tea every evening with people of dubious intent and questionable abilities, but I still cannot answer your question."

Abbas understood immediately. "What kind of world is it where they can treat a man like Mr. Nur ed Din in this way," he lamented, before giving comfort. "Do not worry Madame, we will find a way of getting Mr. Nur ed Din out." Only then, with a hint of reproach in his voice, though reproach is far too strong a word, he offered, "Madame, had I known sooner, perhaps I would have been able to help."

Biting her lip and acknowledging Abbas' claim on her husband, she inquired, "Tell me, who is trying to confiscate our property?"

"They came one morning," he replied. "An official and a couple of ordinary soldiers. They placed the notice on the door and informed us the property had been confiscated. They gave no reason, except to say that Mister Nur ed Din was a criminal, and that his property was in the possession of the State."

They wanted Bolbolouieh, she had suspected as much. It had nothing to do with what Nur ed Din had or had not done. It had nothing to do with principles or ideologies, who he had spoken to or what he had said. It had nothing to do with his political leanings or his old-regime friends. They had imprisoned Nur ed Din to take Bolbolouieh, it was that simple. "This is what the revolution has come to," she reflected to herself.

At least now she knew what she was up against. At least she could find out who to pay, and how much. She was a pragmatist and always had been. They had Nur ed Din and she wanted him back. She had Bolbolouieh and they wanted it. She asked Abbas once again who had confiscated the property, who had their eye on the rose garden. "They have made their arrangements," he replied. "The government will confiscate it so they can turn it over to one of their gang to develop into villas and make a profit. I don't have a name yet, but we don't need one. We won't let them do it."

"Forget the property, how will we get Nur ed Din out of prison?" she asked.

"Madame," he responded, "Do not look at me like that. I am not without resources. I have lived long enough to have learned a thing or two. At least in this corner of the world we know what is what, and who is who."

It was true. Abbas and the villagers of Bolbolouieh had been part of the Revolution. They had sent off children one by one to defend the nation against Saddam Hussein. Some had risen in the ranks and others had not come back. They had friends and family in the Revolutionary Guards, in the Revolutionary Court. Friends and family who had gone on clandestine missions to Beirut and begged to serve in Bosnia. They were the parents, the brothers and sisters, the husbands and wives of martyrs with streets named in their honour. They had made the kinds of sacrifices no one could ever ask of any other human being.

And Bolbolouieh was not that far from Rafsanjan. Forty kilometres as the crow flies. Forty kilometres (as the crow flies) separates Rafsanjan from Bolbolouieh. And Rafsanjani was the turbaned leader of the nation. Some of his relatives had been admonished by Nur ed Din to plant Muhammad's flower. Some of his relatives, with shaven heads or flowered scarves, had been told that white roses sprang from Muhammad's sweet sweat as he ascended into heaven on a beast that placed its feet as far as its eyes could see. They had planted roses and prospered. They had listened to a man who pointed to the heavens, invoking an unseen God. They were not without resources, they could make one small request, a request that could not be refused in Kerman, and would equally be honoured in Tehran, and in Evin.

They made their requests. In parlours and in offices, over glasses of sweet and glasses of bitter tea they patiently made their inquiries and persuasively made their requests. Knowing what to say, how to say it, and who to say it to, they were able to secure promises of Nur ed Din's release. But it would take time. There were powerful people who wanted him imprisoned. Powerful people who felt they had suffered enough during the reign of injustice. Who had stood outside during allegorical roller coaster and carousel rides, who had not come up with the cost of admission. People who had more than the cost of admission but had stood outside the gate as the faceless voice urged one and all to step right up and enjoy the greatest show on earth. Watched from behind the fence as others won teddy bears and King Kongs. People who felt that it was finally their turn on the carousel.

For the ones who spoke up on Nur ed Din's behalf it was not a question of this regime or that, of whose turn it was to ride the merry-go-round. The sacrifices they had made were not for a spin on a unicorn twirl in a tea cup. The sacrifices they made could not be repaid with a handful of tickets to be traded in for a chance to throw balls at bottles, to shoot bull's-eyes on red white and blue targets. Though the idealism of the revolution had long since faded, no one had the heart to tell them that at the end of the day they had sacrificed sons and daughters for a chance to win a stuffed gorilla. No one had the heart to tell them, and so those in authority listened to Abbas and the villagers' requests: "You must release this man who has committed no crime, who has always been decent and correct in every way. I will personally vouch for him." As the parents, brothers and sisters of martyrs, they had paid enough to be able to ask for this one small thing. And, after all, Bolbolouieh was not that far from Rafsanjan.

76

Though Bolbolouieh was no more than a stone's throw from Rafsanjan, it was not the villagers who secured Nur ed Din's release. At least one version of the story says Firouz accomplished that particular feat. We had just returned to his apartment from a walk in Hyde Park when the phone rang. It was Ali Akbar who rapidly dispensed of formalities to inform Firouz, "Shredded Wheat, I do not know if you have heard, but Fereshteh is living outside the gates of Evin prison. Yes, I saw her with my own eyes. Believe me, I have made inquiries, and unfortunately they have only served to confirm my fears. Nur ed Din has been incarcerated. Yes, I'm sure. Fereshteh has been meeting with Moghaddam, no not that Moghaddam, the one who set a record by buying himself out for twenty millions. She has been meeting with your old friend from the Plan Organization, with the ex-Minister of Finance and a whole bunch of others who are giving her advice on how to get Nur ed Din out. I thought you should know."

Firouz put down the phone and after cursing a regime that would imprison Nur ed Din, wondered out loud, "If Ali Akbar had not happened to pass by Evin, would I never have been told that my best friend is in prison? Yassaman, please tell me, why do I have to hear about this from someone else. Why wouldn't Fereshteh call me?"

"Maybe it's because you are all the way over here in London and you haven't been back for the past ten years," I offered optimistically.

"But I still know a person or two, even in this regime," he countered.

"Then it's time to get on the phone," I responded, knowing that even after ten years of self-imposed exile, there were people he could call. He had often extended a helping hand and launched several brilliant careers, some of which had continued through the Revolution. And though Fereshteh may not have thought so, he still had a marker or two he could call in.

But it had been ten years. He had spent ten long years in self-imposed exile, ten years of walks in the park when the weather was good, backgammon and tea on Tuesday and Thursday afternoons rain or shine, an occasional dinner party here or there. Ten years sequestered with the Kensington library's sparse collection of travelogues searching for an answer he had still not found. Ten years with other exiles cursing their luck and blaming the Americans, the British, the Israelis or some other Cabala. Ten years of watching everyone else go about their purposeful lives.

After a sleepless night waiting for people in Tehran to be sipping their first glasses of sweet or bitter tea, he walked down High Street and purchased a phone card from the Pakistani vendor who sold magazines, chewing gum and lottery tickets, though never single cigarettes. Firouz came home, dialled the access number, input the security code, and began calling those who still might be able to do him a favour or two. Not knowing anyone in the prison system, he called the ones who did—the ones in the Plan Organization and the Ministry of Finance, the one in the Prime Minister's office.

He was surprised to learn that his cook's cousin was now the gatekeeper for the Revolutionary Court. That the neighbour he played soccer with as a boy had been in Khomeini's entourage and had trained the Hezbollah in Beirut before returning to work obscurely in the Ministry of the Holy War for Constructiveness. That the rascal of a police officer who used to wave the silver Benz through the red light could fix anything for a price. After ten years of exile, ten years of not calling and not caring, when he finally picked up the phone, input the access code and dialled the numbers that began oo 98 21, he learned the twists and turns their lives had taken. But after two days of telephone calls, two days of strained conversations, prolonged silences, and bad connections, he found himself empty-handed. At which point he rapidly calculated how much money he needed to live out his actuarial life in relative comfort and briefly considered paying off that rascal of a police officer.

And then he received a telephone call that began, "Firouz Khan, I understand you are looking to help your friend Nur ed Din. It really is no secret, you seem to have called half the people in the current administration, and at least as many from past ones. I do not think you remember me, but I know of you. You see, I am Agha Reza's son."

Though he had no recollection of the son, Firouz remembered the father. Agha Reza spent his days at the airport lounge waiting for a familiar face, someone not met by family or friends, someone who might need a ride. On more than one occasion, Firouz had asked his chauffeur not to show up so that Agha Reza might drive him home in the car with the blue beads.

It was a curious thing to do, but his is also a curious story. Agha Reza had worked for Firouz's family from an early age. As a boy, Agha Reza could think of nothing better than to be a truck driver, a taxi driver or a chauffeur. He lived for the days when he might wash the family car, caringly wax and polish it. When he might sit behind the wheel, adjust the mirrors, engage the hand brake, make sure the car was in neutral, press down on the clutch, pump the gas pedal twice and turn the key in the ignition. Agha Reza lived for the day when he would actually drive a car.

But Agha Reza's hands were twisted and deformed. He could hardly hold a pencil, let alone a steering wheel. Every time he went to take the test, the examiners laughed at him and sent him away. They never considered the fact that there were hydraulic steering wheels that even people born with broken hands might be able to drive. And if it was pointed it out to them, if they were told, "You can drive a Buick with one finger, haven't you seen the advertisement?" They would say, "This poor bastard will never have enough money to buy a Buick. In any case, I cannot issue a license restricted to Buicks or Cadillacs, I have the public good to consider. Is there anything I can help you with?"

Though Agha Reza could recite the entire traffic code

by heart, though he knew more about the internal combustion engine and the merits of the 1953 Bel Air than anyone ever should, he was turned away, ridiculed for even thinking he could ever drive a car with those crooked hands. When he walked into their offices, they laughed and said out loud, "Mario Andretti is back again. What am I to do with him? I've told him a thousand times not to bother me, but here he is. What do I need to do to make him understand? With hands like that, he should be a politician."

So strong was Agha Reza's desire that he persisted. So strong was his need that he suffered through their abuses. And then one day Firouz's uncle Hamed interceded. He knew about desire and he knew about need and, parenthetically, how to obtain the full value from a five rial hair cut. He made precisely three telephone calls, and that same day Agha Reza found himself with a driver's license and an eternal debt to Firouz's family.

It was his son who called out of the blue to say, "Firouz Khan, I am not sure if you remember me, I am Abol, Agha Reza's son. I understand you have been looking for someone to help get Nur ed Din out of Evin. I really don't know anyone in this regime. I'm not much for the kingdom of God on earth, I think God has enough problems as it is without trying to run Iran, but I do know the person who works the computers at Evin prison. You see, we fought side by side in the Fav campaign, but I will not bother you with the details. He is as tired of this charade of Islamic Republic as the rest of us. I asked if just this once he could do something for someone whose only crime was to grow roses.

"'It is impossible to get anyone out of Evin without an official decree from the Revolutionary Court,' my friend said. But he is the one who inputs the decrees and updates the records. He knows the passwords and the codes. He has figured out a way to alter the records so that Nur ed Din can be released and it will look like it was done by authority of the Revolutionary Court. He can get your friend Nur ed Din discharged. Say the word and he will be out tomorrow."

At a loss for words, Firouz said, "Abol jan, how can I repay you?"

To which Agha Reza's son responded, "It is nothing, just a word or two of code. Five minutes of typing. Forget about it. But sometimes, when you are not too busy, take a moment to remember my father. He always spoke well of you and your uncle Hamed."

There is one version of the story that says Firouz was responsible for Nur ed Din's release, and that it was Agha Reza's son who interceded through a data entry specialist in Evin prison. Though Bolbolouieh is not that far from Rafsanjan for crows to fly, it is the version I believe.

77

Having rescued his friend from an unjust prison, having opened unseen doors to a world he had left behind, Firouz went back to his rituals. I was amazed that he could return to a life punctuated by the morning paper, walks around the usual circuit in the park, afternoon tea in slim-waisted glasses, whiskey-sodas during happy hour, the occasional dinner party. Backgammon twice a week which he attempted to enliven with the time-worn lines "Play fast and bad," or "If you want to think so much about your moves I suggest we play chess." Upon winning, which he did quite often, he crowed, "I hear there's a fakir on a mountaintop in Nepal who might be a worthy adversary."

Sitting on the AstroTurf balcony of a Knightsbridge flat, all that was left of the splendid orchards of quince and pear trees, the fragrant gardens of tulips and oleander, if in a particularly good mood he might light a cigarette, turn to Babak to ask again with a wry smile, "Who waters this lawn?"

He went back to a life in which he knew fear in far less than a handful of dust. Catatonic as a group, they diagnosed each other in states of clinical depression as they watched everyone else go purposefully about their lives. They, in turn put on pin-stripe suits to go for walks in Hyde Park, to cash checks in Coutts, to buy twenty cigarettes.

They met in London cafés on Tuesday mornings to assert, "Blood was not getting to the Shah's brain," or to share, "I have it on good authority from a well-placed friend that the situation in Iran will soon be addressed. No, you don't know him, but he was in Reagan's office just last week. He saw the file on the President's desk, just under the one marked Nicaragua."

On these occasions Firouz reminded them, "Be that as it may. Just remember that the White Russian counts and countesses who took suites in the Ritz and the Georges V and drank every night to the imminent downfall of the Bolsheviks ended up elevator operators and concierges at those very hotels." Firouz's friends enjoyed the poignancy of the picture he was painting, but the message was lost on them— after all they had the resources to modestly toast the death of the Islamic Republic until the end of their years.

They missed the point. It was not a question of making it to the end of the month financially. It was a question of making it to the end of the day. Not just making day become night and night become day. Like World War I fighter pilots after the Armistice, nothing even remotely interested them. For years they had devoted themselves to one adrenaline-filled purpose, and there was nothing that could match the pure rush of dogfights in German skies. In exile they might as well have measured their lives in the proscribed trajectory of the same six by ten Dorchester cage.

Instead they used coffee spoons and rolls of the dice as café colonels lamented laconically, "Two thousand five hundred years of monarchy and I got stuck with the Islamic revolution." On the rare occasions when they did perform, they were whirling dervishes in auditoriums, pianists in convention centres, elephants in circuses.

78

Firouz went back to his rituals, and so did I, until the day I got a call from my cousin, Kiumars. "Just walk out of the office, princess. Say you're going down to the corner to buy a pack of cigarettes, and keep on walking," he instructed me with a laugh in his voice. "Hail the first cab you see, go straight to the airport and get on the next available British Airways flight to Tehran. I'll meet you tomorrow morning at the International Arrivals Terminal. The ticket is paid for, I've taken care of everything. I'll personally walk you through immigration and customs and we'll drive straight to my mother's for lunch." It was not exactly what happened. But one day, without making telephone calls or cancelling appointments, without consulting friends who would try their best to dissuade me, I got on the next available jumbo jet and flew business class courtesy of cousin Kiu to Tehran.

He was right, there was nothing to keep me living in a strange land. The war forced upon us was over, the revolution had won hands down and the only buildings I was interested in designing never could fit in London and Vancouver. "The spell is broken," Kiumars said, as if the white witch had prevailed. All he really meant was that the war with Saddam Hussein was over, the airport was open, and after ten years of the Islamic Republic solidly in power, no one even bothered to think about the pre-revolutionary days.

One day I picked out a number of appropriately sombre outfits and got on a plane. Firouz should have done the same. They all should have, there was nothing to keep them where they were. But they didn't. They kept on living their reasonable lives in exile.

When I was very young, I must not have been more than four or five, I remember paying my respects to the dead, and to a cousin whose mother had passed away. A cousin who did not stand composed in a dark suit and dark glasses solemnly

accepting condolences. Who did not throw in the first handful of earth and watch it scatter as even I knew he should. I
watched as he threw himself into the grave-pit, as he covered
his face and hair with dirt. As he tore at his clothes, tore at
his flesh, scratched his eyes, his cheeks, struck himself over
and over. I tried to look away as he begged from within his
mother's grave, "In the name of whoever you love, keep on
shovelling. Just do your jobs," he implored. "In the name of
whatever you hold sacred, just do your jobs."

Firouz and his friends did not scream and yell. They did
not pull out their hair and insist on being immolated, beg to
be buried alive. They did not weep, grind their teeth, long for
that moment when they would gasp for breath and couldn't,
long to be surrounded by blackness.

They went into exile instead. Reading their papers, taking their constitutional walks, impassively watching the news
at 6:00, the movie at 9:00, and holding forth as to why it had
all gone wrong. Had anyone bothered to listen, they would
have heard stories from the people who had run a country,
who had built a nation. Fantastical stories of the people who
in recompense had been dismissed, disowned and banished.
Stories of that vital meeting when the generals had urged,
"Give us the command to shoot," but the Shah had refrained.

"Guns and bayonets, guns and bayonets, you cannot solve
all the problems with guns and bayonets," someone had heard
him mutter. "Do it yourself, not strangers," another swore
were the words that left the Shah's lips.

But no one was interested in stories that explained how
one general was unable to issue the command to shoot while
the other with troops who revered him and were willing to
fight to the last drop of blood had walked away. How the
Ayatollah who had supported a king over a kingdom of God
on earth was removed from the equation. How a prominent
courtier managed to stay on long after the Shah had left and
lesser members of court had been executed. How a bomb
eliminated half of the Islamic Republic's parliament when a
prominent Ayatollah was conspicuously absent. An Ayatollah

who later consolidated power.

No one was interested. There had been a brief moment when Iran had been interesting. Overnight the cultured and intriguing olive-complected Iranians had been forgotten. When Iranians did re-capture the world's attention it was as a bunch of veiled or unshaven radicals who held America hostage for 444 days.

Not the Iranians courted by Carter and Kissinger, Rothschilds and Rockefellers. Those Iranians might as well have flown with the on-his-deathbed Shah from the Bahamas to America, from America to Panama, from Panama to Mexico, to be turned away at every port, fleeced by every immigration and customs agent.

Idi Amin who ate the flesh of his people moved to an undisclosed location in the South of France. Baby Doc who drank the blood of his people moved to Cap d'Antibes. But on his deathbed the Shah was turned away by ally after apologetic ally, to finally find a resting place in Egypt through the good graces of Anwar Sadat. Anwar Sadat whose assassin's name decorates the streets of Tehran. "Khaled al Islamboli Avenue" the streetsign reads. It used to be Park Avenue.

We were forgotten. Our country was forgotten, our lives were forgotten, our stories were forgotten. The gypsies had packed up their red and white tents and headed out in the middle of the night. The Carnival was in Indonesia, in Spain, in Brazil, somewhere else. No one was interested in Iran or Iranians. No one was interested in what we might have to say.

We were a generation of Iranians whose children would never know each other. Iranians who could have lived in Hollywood and worked for Lautner. But we spent the best years of our lives working for Iran. It was all we knew. When we finally did have time on our hands, when in exile we could figure it all out, sort out what had transpired, no one was interested. But we could not extricate ourselves. In our spare time, we read the Times, listened to the BBC, watched the CNN.

"Can you believe it? The Prime Minister of Italy accused and convicted of bribery, extortion and corruption. I know it's just Italy, but it's the first world just the same. And mind you, this year Italy's GNP exceeded that of Great Britain. Fancy that."

"Last month there were picketers in front of the World Bank who asserted, pretty convincingly I might add, that the Bank is approving dams whose sole benefit is to the contractors who build them. Remember, this is the same World Bank run by McNamara in its heyday."

"Come on, open your eyes, political offices in the United States are being bought by the ones who throw the most money at them. Just look at the mayor of New York."

"We were always so damn naïve. We saw Watergate as an amazing moment when democracy prevailed, and a president was brought to justice. We were so impressed by the impeachment that we missed the real lesson: Even the leaders of the free world abuse the trust of a people."

Late in life we put two and two together to realize the regime we had marched against, when it came right down to it, was no different from the JFK government we had so naïvely admired in our youthful idealism. For Camelot had its Mordreds and its Morgan Le Fays, its Guineveres, its Lancelots and perhaps a Parcifal pure-of-heart or two on a quest for something holy. It had its clandestine love affairs and the ill-begotten fruit of unspoken liaisons. Unequal jousts and unfair pitches. Misbegotten offspring, misplaced ideals, and a J. Edgar Hoover administrator or two. Not quite round tables. And the shining white knights, the maidens in star-covered caps and flowing Rapunzel locks.

Years later it came to us that we too had lived in a Camelot. A Camelot, however flawed, that had been devoted to the advancement of a nation.

79

"It has been fifteen years since I last saw Nur ed Din. Tell me, how does he look?" Firouz inquired on one of my visits to London. "Was he terribly broken in prison?"

I told him again of the last time I had seen Nur ed Din and Fereshteh. Said they were in good health and spirits, that they remembered him frequently. I encouragingly observed that the years had not been too harsh.

"I remember the day we met at the American School," Firouz started, playing with the ashtray. "I remember Nur ed Din in Beirut. I distinctly remember Nur ed Din at my apartment, at his uncle Mustafa's house and on the trips we took to the Caspian. But," he confided, "when I think of Nur ed Din, he's always in the same white button-down, the same blue polo shirt." Taking a deep breath, he continued, "Yassaman, it breaks my heart to say it, but when I try to remember Nur ed Din, all I remember are photographs of Nur ed Din."

Firouz was devastated that he could not remember the smile breaking across Nur ed Din's face, his gestures, the way he walked, or even accurately recall the colour of his eyes.

"It must be hard, Firouz. But you could go back and see him, you really should. There is nothing to prevent you from going to Iran. I have well-placed friends who have discreetly asked on your behalf, and they tell me you have no difficulties," I ventured, knowing full well the response. We had had this conversation before.

"Do you hear what are you saying? They imprisoned Nur ed Din whose only crime was growing roses. And you expect *me* to go back?" Firouz countered with his irrefutable logic.

"You know as well as I do that they only imprisoned Nur ed Din because they wanted Bolbolouieh. As for you, they have already appropriated everything you own," I argued. "Everyone knows if you don't try to reclaim your property, you won't have any problems."

"I refuse to go back to a country where they can imprison a man like Nur ed Din just to confiscate his property," Firouz countered, closing the book on that particular discussion.

It pained me to think that Firouz had simply spent too many years in exile, too many days and weeks away from home with those who maintained Iran was no longer a place to live, no longer a place they would even want to visit. With those who, if they had ever loved her, had since inhaled the sweet scent of the blue flower of forgetfulness.

On my trips to London I told Firouz the stories of the streets we had walked together, but he was not interested. He did not want to know what had become of his uncle's house or how the villa in Dezashib where we had spent a stolen afternoon had been confiscated and transformed into a centre for calligraphers. How I had found the stone bench with moustachioed lions on which we had reclined in a memorable photograph. How the Armenian café still served bon chic pastry, how the Marie Antoinette palace on Jordan Avenue had been transformed into a home for wayward women.

He listened politely, but it was clear he did not want to hear how when I went to release a friend imprisoned by the Revolutionary Guard, I found myself staring at the portrait of a forgotten friend in the confiscated parlour of a confiscated house where Firouz and I had spent many a pleasant evening. Though I told Firouz stories of the places he loved, he would not listen.

80

So I went back and from half a world away watched Firouz search through old travelogues four at a time. From that barren Thief of Baghdad mountainside I watched him read other people's descriptions of the one he loved. It must have been terribly painful to have someone else describe the way the colour of her eyes changed when she was angry, the way her hair fell on her shoulders when she slept, failing to note the way she turned and smiled sleepily when kissed on the shoulder. Other people not capturing the huskiness in her voice when she was bored or tired, the lilt in her voice when she had wine at lunch and was trying charmingly to hide it. Other people trying to describe the one he loved and failing the Rorschach test of her birthmark. Other people not getting it right at all. How could he submit himself to that kind of torture? How could he suffer through someone else's misdirected, misguided, mistaken insights into the one he loved?

But he always had a remarkably high tolerance for pain and was willing to suffer through their two hundred and fifty pages in the hope that somehow one of these authors might have noticed a clue he had missed, that he had taken for granted, that he had overlooked. Just to see if they had happened to be there at a moment when she let her defences down. Like the time, that tall, turbaned Indian parking lot attendant mimicked the steps and seductive glances of Bollywood blockbuster stars in his six by ten booth, his eyes glued to the television.

"There is always a casual passer-by who catches a glimpse into your loved one that you miss when you look away for a moment," I had said, knowing it was what he wanted to hear.

As I watched from half a world away, he read the books and jotted down their painful notes. "The normal state of affairs in Khorassan is war. Petty plunderings, murders, brigandage, small insurrections, executions of five, ten or twenty robbers take place weekly, and cavalry engagements, sieges of fortresses or towns annually, with a considerable war every five or ten years," he wrote in his flowing hand.

He reflected that it was no different with the rest of the nation. In Iran, it seemed there was a major upheaval every twenty years, and it was a well-documented fact that no reigning king save one had died a natural death on the throne for centuries. We needed no ghost come back from the grave to tell us that. "What the hell was I thinking? Who was I kidding?" he asked though no one else was in the room. "How could I have not done the simple addition to realize that the roughly twenty years of relative stability would be up during my own actuarial lifetime? How could I have believed that this time it would be any different?"

He noted the quotes that spoke to his predicament, and the quotes by a Frenchman who advocated that one needed to remove a sense of time, a rigour in arithmetic and in precision in order to survive Iran. These Firouz noted, but they did not give him satisfaction. The concept that one needed to accept imprecision to be able to survive in Iran did not strike Firouz as witty or poetic, it only served to bolster the theme of futility.

But it was a theme expressed in text after text, in history after history. The futility of human endeavour was the one thread that ran through every story, flavoured every discussion. The landscape was littered with the evidence. The glorious ruins of decaying palaces were just the most Ozymandius-obvious. The valiant efforts to build, to create, to make, were met at each turn with the Arsalan invitation, "Come to Merv to see how lowly in the dust I lie."

If Firouz did not believe the stories, if the histories did not ring true, if the political instability and the upheavals were not indication enough of how impossible it was to have any lasting effect, if he still believed things could be done, all he needed to do was remember the landscape that was Iran.

"It is like so much of Persia, a superworld of space and light, where Nature's work seems only half finished, a place for clouds and storms and sunlight, but not for the trivialities and meanness of men. Where distances have no end and men seem but accidents, where silence and remoteness are your companions, and eternity your destination," was Copley Amory's observation in 1954.

Christopher Sykes, who must have had more time on his hands, expressed it in more succinct terms: "Persia is an overwhelming and terrible memorial to the transitoriness of earthly things."

Firouz registered the quotes in his apartment overlooking

the park in London. Examining his own life, he recognized the abundant futility of it all. But he could not live life like that. So he sought in old travelogues answers other than the obvious. He could have taken comfort in the arms of one who understood him better than he understood himself, who knew where it hurt and how to make it go away. The soothing touch, the soft skin, the sweet perfume, the understanding embrace, the knowing eyes, that oh so brief moment when all would be forgotten. But he chose to read instead.

81

From that mountainside half a world away, I watched and wondered how deeply Firouz had inhaled the scent of the enchanted flower, wondered if he would even recognize the imprint of his lover's footsteps. One morning in early November he surprised me by waking up to remark, "It must be walnut season in Tehran." He surprised himself by remembering that the walnut vendors would be sitting by the side of the road with pyramidal piles, kerosene lamps and blackened fingers.

He hadn't had fresh walnuts in ages. He hadn't thought of fresh walnuts for years. But then again he hadn't had baby green almonds, the kind you dip in salt and that parents never let their children buy on the side of the road, which is where they taste best. He had forgotten the taste of white mulberries that are sweetest when they are overripe and bruised.

Once, on a drive to the Caspian, he had bought white mulberries from a couple of kids along the high road. Except the scoundrels had filled only the upper portion of the jug with berries. The rest was twigs, leaves, and the Incidents section of the Keyhan International. He had not found out until he was miles away. While showering, Firouz barely managed to restrain himself from chuckling out loud at the memory. And then he thought of the drive to the Caspian. The restaurant in Gachsar guarded by the spray-paint-silver lions with bright red tongues. The store where Mamdal always stopped to buy thick strained yoghurt. Firouz had been there to see Mamdal strike up an instant friendship with the shopowner, the only other person who limped as he did, suffering, presumably, from a shattered left hip. Mamdal had immediately recognized the limp, and later learned to recognize the overbuilt arms and chest, the heavy upper body. There was a complicity between them, as if each had found the only other person in the world who could understand. The village children caught on and whenever Mamdal came to the shop, they would make a point of addressing him by the shopkeeper's name, as if by mistake. "Mr. Hosseini, could I get a pound and a half of cheese. Oh, I'm sorry, I took you for the wrong person," they would say. And Mamdal loved it.

Standing in front of the mirror, Firouz remembered the yoghurt seller and the precarious café that had subsisted under the shadow of a precarious rock every day since he could remember. Defying sense, shaking their fists at gravity, the owners had made a business of their bravado. And if they were brave or stupid enough to live every day under the shadow of the impetuous rock, then how much of a risk could it be for their customers to spend an hour or two on a drive back from their seaside vacations?

Firouz only stopped when with Maryam, who insisted, "If I have to stop for you to overpay the man with the limp, then you might do me the courtesy of stopping at the *kafeh* under the rock. You must admit they have the best kabab and the most scenic setting. And if the rock is to fall over during our lunch, who is to say that it was not meant to be?"

With the way things had played out in his short life, Firouz would not have been surprised if the *kafeh* still stood while islands of stability had been destroyed. Mehdi, our friend who felt the player should change, used to say, "There's no rhyme or reason in this world. I might fall and you may die." But Mehdi had not fallen, and Firouz had not died—yet. Though many *had* fallen, and many had died.

82

S tanding in front of the mirror, Firouz reflected on his zig zag life, the snow and the distant tree. He acknowledged that his moment had passed, that he would never arrive at the destination he had aspired to every day of his Gary Cooper-Prince Charming life. He would never awaken a slumbering nation with his kiss.

The moment when the nation could be awakened had already passed and would not return for another one thousand and one years. Not until the stars were aligned again, the elements in place, and some other hero blew on the device representing wind, lit a match by the one for fire, poured sand in the one for earth, poured his sweat into the one for water, evoked the fifth element, and saved the universe.

To my surprise, Firouz sighed a sigh of relief knowing he no longer needed to play that particular hero.

With somewhat less relief, he realized that he no longer needed to play Henry Higgins to Eliza's Fair Lady. He no longer needed to assure himself that she spoke with the right accent, that she wore the right clothes for the ball or for later that night. He no longer needed to engage in that absurd song with Pickering about why a woman couldn't be more like a man. He could forget it all and play the idiot who was thrilled just to be on the street where she lived. And he reflected that even if he did walk the stage set singing sincerely, "I have often walked down this street before," there was no reason for her to love him back.

He was old and tired, a shadow of his former self. Thinking of how he had aged, how the best years of his life were already behind him, realizing how exhausted he felt, Firouz recalled a story my father once told me. It was not a story he ever encountered in his numerous travelogues, not a story western travellers had ever cared to repeat. Though Joseph is well known in western literature, it is as an interpreter of grapes and loaves, sheaves of grain. For his seven lean and seven fat years. For his brothers, the sun and eleven stars. Joseph is well known in the west, but not as a lover.

Yet, Yousef is the quintessential lover. A man of such beauty that when he entered the room, those of Zoleikha's handmaids peeling oranges placidly cut their hands. But there is more to that story than Yousef's beauty. It is also a story of Zoleikha's innocence. If she tore his shirt when he refused her advances, it was because she could not help herself. The anecdote of the blood oranges, western writers related and Persian painters rendered in coffee-house paintings. Fereshteh collected them. But there was more to the story than the often repeated scene. What travellers did not relate and what I told Firouz one autumn day, while walking under arching and entwining plane trees tinged here and there with a blush of colour, was the love story of Yousef and Zoleikha.

Long before they met, Yousef would visit Zoleikha in her dreams. Her handmaids could not understand why she slept so much, why she sought out sleeping balms and soporifics. Why she spent more hours asleep than awake. When Potiphar asked for her hand in marriage from distant Egypt, she agreed, so sure was she that he would be the one who visited her nightly. Disillusioned with a life where you dream of one man and end up with another, she married Potiphar anyway.

When she did finally find the man of her dreams, she sought to make him love her. But Yousef had devoted his heart to one love only. For years Zoleikha tried to have him open a place in his heart to something other than the divine, to allow some space in his heart for the ones who tossed and turned in wrinkled sheets. For years she tried to make him see her, but she failed. She did not succeed in changing him from his chosen path, from his one chosen love. Her love remained unrequited for years.

After he had refused every one of her advances, in an act of desperation, she sent the most beautiful women in the kingdom to seduce Yousef, in the hope that one would capture his heart, would convince him to love a woman rather than devote a lifetime to the divine.

She selected the ones with the qualities she lacked. The ones with blue eyes and the ones with green eyes, the ones as fair as the moon, and the ones with the darkest of complexions. The ones who wept when they made love, the ones who broke walnuts between their thighs. She sought them out and enlisted them in her mission, intending, once one succeeded, to slip into his tent on the wedding night. But Yousef resisted the laughter in every walk, the suggestion in every raised eyebrow, the desire in every bitten lip. He remained constant in his love, in his devotion to his God. He continued to devote his breathtaking, orange-slicing beauty to a lifetime of communion with the eternal.

Then one day, when she was old and grey, though he remained as young and beautiful as the day she met him, the Angel Gabriel intervened. Gabriel could not help it. Though he could tolerate a year or two of unrequited love, he could not accept it for a lifetime.

Convinced of Yousef's love for the Divine, convinced it had endured decades of hardship, convinced that Yousef's love had survived every temptation known to man, Gabriel finally intervened. Or perhaps Gabriel decided, after all the tests, that Zoleikha's love of God was pure. She had forgotten herself, she had destroyed herself in the love of Beauty. She had not tired and she had not faltered. She had devoted herself to Beauty, which, along with Tenderness, is an attribute of the Divine. Knowing this, Gabriel of the Splendid Beauty intervened. The angel finally relented. He united Yousef and Zoleikha.

But years had passed and Zoleikha was old and wizened. So Gabriel gave a tired Zoleikha the youth that Yousef never lost. In the process he also gave them what is so rare in Iranian love stories—a Hollywood ending.

83

Removing an old Gillette razor from a faded crocodile case, Firouz reflected that though he never expected to be saved by an angel, his devotion was no less than Zoleikha's. He reflected that he had been no less fervent in his love for his country, no less single-minded in his pursuit. He too had remained constant despite the temptations. He too had devoted his better-than-Perry-Como good looks to the one he had always loved. He had passed every test.

And though his devotion was not to a God, though it had never been a God, though it had always been to a country and a principle, he had still sacrificed his youth, his ardour and enthusiasm. He too had taken the hard road. He was still tired, spent and old beyond his years. He was still empty-handed. And though he never believed an angel would intervene, he had spent it willingly. He could live with the loss of youth; it was the natural course of things. He could accept that he no longer turned heads as he once had. That was bound to happen.

"In any case, it really doesn't matter. When it comes to the seduction of Iran, youth and beauty are obviously not the determining factors," he thought to himself. It was abundantly clear from the white-bearded-one's homecoming that Firouz needed no angel to restore his beauty. He was just too young and handsome. "Maybe I should grow a white beard and wait a decade or two before returning from my self-imposed exile," he laughed acerbically to himself.

Thinking of angels, Firouz remembered that in the Islamic tradition man is "a little less than angels," and noted that Fereshteh was more than one. He remarked that though Nur ed Din had never received a sign, he had been sent a messenger. He remarked that Gabriel, who gave Zoleikha her youth, was also the one who announced the incarnation to Mary. The one who brought the Glorious Quran to Muhammad in the cave.

"Read," said Gabriel.

"I cannot read," came Muhammad's reply.

Firouz remembered the Oscar Wilde angel who brought God the two most precious things in this world—a cracked lead heart and a frozen-to-death swallow that forsook the Nile for a statue that shed tears. He wondered what in the world an angel would bring back from the streets of Tehran.

He remembered the Angel Azrael who needs no permission to enter any home. Who forever writes names in one book and forever erases them in another. He remembered the Blue Angel and twisted, tragic, unrequited love. He quickly thought of the City of Angels that he had briefly inhabited. He remarked that in America there was a city named after angels, and in Iran there was a street named Fereshteh. He wondered if they might have renamed it, like practically every street in Tehran, to honour a martyr.

And then suddenly, as I watched from afar, Firouz removed a bag from on top of his wardrobe, packed it in five short minutes, strapped the straps and changed the combination by one digit so it no longer revealed the month and day of his birth. He put on his favourite double breasted suit and selected a paisley tie. Humming a tune he had sung in the shower, he locked the door to his flat and hailed a cab. "Heathrow," was the magical word he said. "Terminal 2." As I looked on through crystal, he exited the taxi and paused to remember Cyrus' euphemistic remark, "I've packed my bags, checked them in, gone through security and passport control, and I'm sitting in the departure lounge waiting for my flight to be announced."

But Firouz was not waiting for that flight to be called quite yet. Before the black and white letters flipped through Abidjan, Bangkok and Calcutta, Gothenburg and Jakarta, Menaus, Paris and Zagreb to announce the flight that we are all ultimately booked to board, he waited for them to reveal flight 741 to Tehran.

Flashing his most knowing smile, he purchased a one-way ticket, checked in his luggage, and went through passport control. He extracted all metal objects from his pockets, the fountain pen clipped to his shirtfront, the silver bracelet from his wrist and went through security. I watched as he skipped the last plate of bangers and beans that he would have in a long while.

In the departure lounge, across from Boots pharmacy he wondered why he had not done this sooner. And then he paused to think, "Will she recognize me? Will she casually cross the room, look at her watch, smile and ask, 'What has taken you so long?' Will she finally show me the tenderness I have known only in deserted streets, or when we assumed false names?" And then he asked himself, "After all these years, will I recognize her?"

"There is no question about that," he replied. "No matter how large the crowd, no matter how big the city. After all, she is the only one I ever loved."

As I watched with bated breath, he walked to the gate to board flight 741 by section, to politely but not attentively listen to the stewardess demonstrate how to buckle the seat belt and strap the oxygen mask. To take the hot towel and refuse the peppermint candy. To sit through another average film and eat one more less-than-average meal. As I reached for my father's hand and promised to keep my promise, Firouz boarded the British Airways flying carpet that would bring him back to Iran.